LORDS OF THE LEVELS

LORDS OF THE LEVELS

A Novel of the Paranormal

MICHAEL BENTINE

GRAFTON BOOKS

A Division of the Collins Publishing Group

LONDON GLASGOW
TORONTO SYDNEY AUCKLAND

Grafton Books
A Division of the Collins Publishing Group
8 Grafton Street, London W1X 3LA

Published by Grafton Books 1986

British Library Cataloguing in Publication Data

Bentine, Michael
Lords of the levels.
I. Title
823'.914[F]   PR6052.E54/

ISBN 0-246-12698-1

Typeset by Columns of Reading
Printed in Great Britain by
Billings, Worcester

For my son Richard,
who looks more deeply into things and
therefore sees more than most

with love

CONTENTS

AUTHOR'S NOTE

All the events and characters in this novel are purely fictional – products of my imagination. However, I have been pondering for many years on my own encounters with the forces of evil during war and peace, and have transmuted the essence of my experience into the fiction of this book. Writing it has been an exorcism for me, but unfortunately newspaper headlines about drug smuggling, satanism and corruption in high places show daily that the kind of events described here are all too probable.

As to the paranormal content of the book – remote-viewing, psychometry and dowsing – I can only tell you that I have seen remarkable demonstrations and conclusive evidence of these strange powers of the mind during my researches over the past forty-five years. These psychic abilities are often absolutely genuine and, amazingly, many people use them.

MB

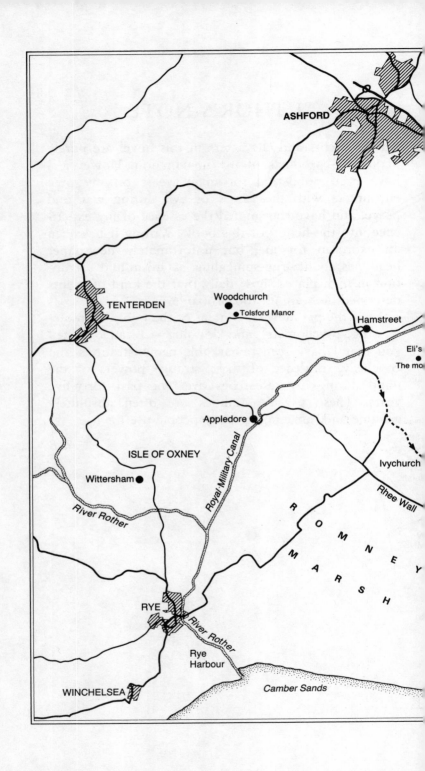

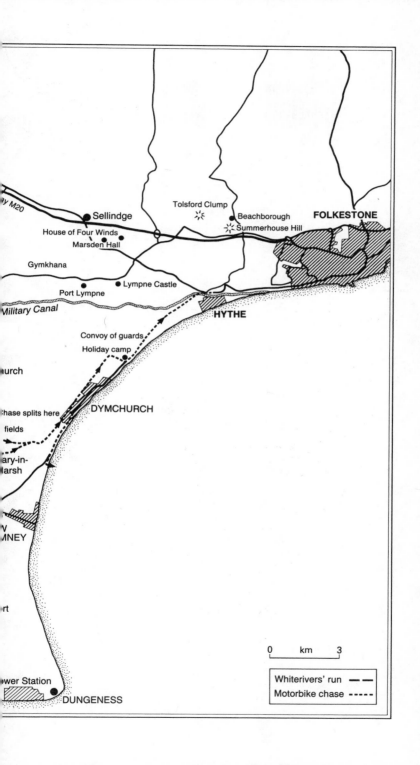

Sellindge

Tolsford Clump

Beachborough

FOLKESTONE

Summerhouse Hill

House of Four Winds

Marsden Hall

Gymkhana

Port Lympne

Lympne Castle

Military Canal

HYTHE

Convoy of guards

Holiday camp

urch

Chase splits here

DYMCHURCH

fields

ary-in-
arsh

NEY

rt

wer Station

DUNGENESS

0   km   3

Whiterivers' run — —

Motorbike chase - - - - -

CHAPTER 1

Shadows in a Dream

Darkness mantles flat marshland with its maze of deep dykes. Teeming rain pelts down. From the black bulk of flanking hills a single light appears — the headlamp of a powerful motorbike moving fast on the icy, twisting road. The racing machine carries two riders, hunched figures in rain-glistening leathers, helmeted heads held close, their bodies pressed together. The passenger — a girl — glances back. She clutches the rider tighter. Lights appear behind, headlamps of pursuers. Terrified, the hunted pair race through the streaming rain. The bike skids round a vicious corner. The glaring head-lamp lights a road covered by a moving mass of giant frogs. The girl screams; the rider grips the brakes, desperate to control the shrieking tyres. The bike smashes into the mass of squelching frogs, scattering them like fragments of amphibian bombs.

The machine rears up, hurtles across the deep dyke and crashes against the opposite bank, trapping the broken riders beneath its twisted frame. The tank explodes. The mass of red-hot metal, scorching plastic, burning rubber and melting bodies slides down the bank and disappears, hissing, below the surface slime.

The only sign of tragedy is the array of squashed amphibians splayed across the icy road.

The rain drips to a stop.

A cock crows.

I awoke, sweating, from this nightmare on three consecutive nights — the 11th, 12th, and 13th March 1984. On each occasion I noted the time as being 3 a.m.

The nightmares marked the beginning of the most

extraordinary sequence of events I have ever experienced — and my life has had more than a fair share of strange happenings. The dreams turned out to be predictive: events were casting their shadows before them.

I, Daniel Fortune, am Professor of Parapsychology at Wessex University, a no-nonsense assembly line for the absorption of modern technology. Set in Dorset, it consists of a group of hideous concrete barracks. Its busy campus is alive with purposeful students, hurrying from tutorial to lecture and from laboratory to library in their pursuit of those all-important grades which will give them the chance of a job.

Therefore it comes as a shock to find, among all this technological cost-effectiveness, a brick-built bunker which houses the brand new Department of Parapsychology and Paranormal Science. This seems an unlikely choice as a secure, pensionable career for the young hopefuls who have studied so hard to win a place at the university.

The academic faculty was unanimously against the founding of this chair of contentious heresy, and still thinks of it as a waste of money and laboratory space. However, the university was offered one million pounds to be used solely to establish a department for research into the shadowy world of the paranormal. If they didn't accept it, the money would go elsewhere. The Dean and faculty swallowed their pride and accepted the cash, together with the indigestible terms of the gift, but cut every corner to provide the cheapest possible construction to house the department.

It stands in a remote corner of the university grounds, directly behind the boiler house. This makes it tolerably warm in winter and totally untenable in summer, when our paranormal research has to be

16

conducted outside, as an alternative to mass heatstroke in our lecture hall cum sauna. Though this Department of Parapsychology and Paranormal Science is unloved, unhonoured, and unwanted by the faculty, it is over-subscribed, with a long queue of would-be students. I am unashamedly proud of it and of my small team of assistants; it has become the focus of my life.

Let me give you a brief personal history. I was in the Navy during the war but was wounded in the leg, which resulted in my being trained for Intelligence duties, and as soon as I was fit enough I was transferred to MI9, Colonel Airey Neave's Department of Evasion and Escape. Our job was to smuggle downed Allied aircrew and others out of Europe, via Spain, Sweden or Switzerland.

After the war I felt totally disillusioned and disgusted at the number of Nazi murderers who avoided the consequences of their crimes, so I resigned from the post-war Navy, on the grounds of ill-health, took my small pension and a student grant and went to read medicine at Oxford. I then won a scholarship to the University of California at Los Angeles, where I read psychology. I went on to do research at Stanford and returned to Britain with a doctorate in parapsychology. In London I met and married a wonderful girl whose father was a neurologist. As a wedding present, he invited me to join his practice in Wimpole Street. My happiness was complete when my wife Patricia gave birth to a fine son. Life had never been so good.

Three years later I buried them both, after their mind-stunning death in an unforgivable accident caused by a young pop-musician on a mescaline trip. Had he not died in the resulting explosion, I would have killed him myself. I never knew such mental pain could exist.

17

To atone for my outburst of hysterical hatred, I devoted myself to my work. I remained in the Wimpole Streeet practice where I developed some unorthodox methods of treatment: hypnotherapy and certain parapsychological techniques to deal with the ghastly effects of drug-addiction in the young. Among others, I cured the eldest son of a multi-millionaire who, in gratitude, donated a million pounds to the boy's university, provided that the faculty founded a chair of parapsychology and that I became the incumbent professor.

The foundation grant was generous enough to provide my department with adequate funds to pay for the salaries of two assistant lecturers in parapsychology, and I thank the gods that I chose them wisely. We are referred to by the rest of the university as 'the fruit and nut cases'.

Robert Whiterivers is the offspring of the marriage of Frank Whiterivers, a Navajo Indian who became a captain in the US Marines, and Siobhan O'Hanrahan, who at the time – 1952 – was on assignment from the *Dublin Times* as a photographic journalist and war correspondent in Korea.

Captain Whiterivers gained a Congressional Medal of Honor for bravery in Korea at the battle for the Yalu River, where he lost a leg. He, Siobhan and baby Robert settled in Sante Fe, where they lived on the Captain's pension and on what Siobhan could earn as a photographer. Young Robert was raised as much by Navajo medicine men, as a sorcerer's apprentice, as by his parents, the disabled Frank Whiterivers having taken refuge in alcohol.

Robert is a born athlete. His broad, arrow-headed frame stands well over six foot, a little taller than me. He is also as bright as an Arizona sunrise. Thus equipped, mentally and physically, he won his way to Stanford University, where his track record as an athlete became legendary and his academic career, in physics, exemplary. When he graduated, *summa cum laude*, Stanford accepted him on a research foundation, as much for his being an all-round athlete as for his academic attainments.

While working on his doctorate Robert's paranormal abilities became widely known and he was much in demand as a demonstrator of dowsing. By using his ability to 'search-and-find' through the ultra-senses of his mind, he can locate practically anything with great accuracy. By his remarkable powers as a psychometrist Robert can also pick up the past history and associations of any object – from a letter to a lump of rock. He can sense the whole sequential story attached to a piece of jewellery or to any other article worn by a person for some length of time.

I first met Robert at Stanford during a series of extraordinary experiments. When I met him again in London in 1983, I asked him to join me in my new department at Wessex University. It is my good fortune that he agreed to do so.

My other associate is Dr Romola Kobrak, an attractive Hungarian-Jewish psychologist who, as a small child, was a refugee from the unforgivable Russian invasion of her country in 1956. Not that she remembers that event, because she was only two when her aunt, Nadia Feiffer the concert violinist, crossed into freedom with baby Romola in her arms.

That dreadful time also orphaned the child, when both her mother, Nadia's twin sister Katia, and her father, Paul Kobrak, died while helping to succour wounded students from the conservatoire where they were teaching music.

Her Aunt Nadia made a successful transition to British concert platforms and eventually enabled Romola to read psychology at London University, where she threw herself into an over-challenging programme of intensive study while at the same time developing her own talent as a musician.

At the age of twenty-three, on the verge of gaining a first in psychology, Romola suffered a nervous breakdown. During two years in analysis, she developed an amazing ability to view events and places *remotely* irrespective of time and space, anywhere in the world. She later went on to complete her studies and gain her doctorate.

Romola is everything that I could ask for in a colleague, in a friend and in a woman. The gentleness of her nature is a part of her beauty, and warmth radiates from her as a visible aura. She is a true daughter of Gaia, the Earth Mother. I am fortunate to be her friend and confidant.

This then is my 'Psi' squad. Both of them are dark-haired, Robert's being cut very short and Romola's a waist-length cascade. He, surprisingly, has blue eyes, from the Irish side of his family, whereas hers are Vandyke brown. Both of them are tribally orientated, Robert with a passionate awareness of his Navajo heritage and Romola with her devotion to her Jewish background. They are in complete contrast physically and enjoy a close mutual attachment, mentally and spiritually, yet, oddly enough, neither is sexually attracted to the other.

I respect and admire them both as my colleagues, and feel fortunate that they have also become my surrogate family.

In the story which follows I will try and tell, as factually as possible, how we fought against a great evil and, in doing so, nearly lost our lives. Had we not used our ultra-senses, none of us would have survived.

CHAPTER 2

The Companions of Chaos

We were approaching the end of the Easter term and were congratulating ourselves on how smoothly it had all gone and how enthusiastic our fifty students had been over the surprising results that we had achieved in those magical weeks.

Robert Whiterivers was an odds-on favourite with the girl students, who made up over half our class, and his athletic prowess had made him *persona grata* with the rest of the university. However, it was his exceptional psychometric powers that captivated our students.

He had started off on an original note: 'I'm Robert Whiterivers. For your information, I am half-Navajo and half-Irish, so let's get all the Indian "white-man speak with forked tongue" and the "Paddy is an idiot" jokes out of our systems right now. I am also a black belt in karate and have a short fuse! I am here to show you how effective psychometry and dowsing can be. Let us take psychometry first.'

Robert indicated a tall youngster in the front row. 'Lend me your watch.'

The young man handed it to Robert, who held it against his forehead.

'You are Michael Sanderson, aged twenty. You come from Rotherham and you won a scholarship to this university. Your father's name is James and your mother's name is Mary.'

The student gasped: 'How did you know that?'

The atmosphere was electric.

'It's all here, in front of me, on the form you filled out.'

Robert grinned as the students guffawed.

He continued: 'Your grandmother's name was Eloise, or Heloise. She gave you this watch for your seventeenth birthday. You treasure it because you loved her very much and you miss her since she died last year of cancer.'

The student protested, 'That shouldn't be on the form; that's private.'

Robert smiled, 'So it is, and it's not on the form. That information is part of the watch.'

Our students come from a broad spectrum of British society, ranging from the sons and daughter of miners, bus-drivers, bookmakers, and fishermen to those whose parents are scientists, musicians, police officers, social workers and industrialists. I am happy to say that they are as bright a bunch of youngsters as you will find anywhere in the world. Their diffuse ethnic, social and religious backgrounds are no hindrance to their comradeship and they all have an absorbed interest in our mutual journey of discovery, so we get along well.

As a major part of the experimentation, we demonstrate dowsing, an art at which I am competent, Romola is excellent, and of which Robert is a master. This ability to search-and-find fascinated our undergraduates, who became, eventually, proficient in its practice.

On field trials, Robert dowsed and located five deep wells. He also accurately predicated their rate of flow per hour to within a few gallons, the purity of the water and its exact mineral content.

Romola was adept at finding lost articles; using two bent wire rods as the focus for her dowsing ability, her results were well above the mathematical laws of chance. She located lost rings, a missing gold watch, a mislaid corneal lens hidden in the grass of the football pitch and, best of all, a stray kitten which Romola pinpointed by using a pendulum suspended over a large-scale map of the district. To the students it was uncanny.

I confined myself to finding underground electric cables, buried gas-pipes and other simple demonstrations of dowsing which, years before, I had decided is latent in most of us, as children, and was one of our survival senses inherited from remote ancestors but now dulled.

Several of our students showed an unexpected ability for 'remote-viewing', but none of them equalled Romola's extraordinary powers of mind-projection to any distance and through time as well.

The strange worlds of the unconscious mind are infinite and how far you reach into these hidden depths is only limited by the horizons of your imagination. As Robert points out to his students: 'Instinct is more reliable than reason but logic is an excellent filter and prevents the researcher going overboard on a "trip" launched by wishful thinking. It also helps to preserve your sanity, which can become threatened if you allow obsession to take over.

'Learn to recognize and to trust your instincts, as women do. They are far better than men at intuitive thinking because they live more natural lives, governed by their lunar menstrual cycles. Of course, women use logic as well, but there is no doubt that their intuition is seldom far off the mark.'

This last statement is always greeted with cheers from the girl students and is now met with fewer and fewer cat-calls from the lads. In fact, there is much proof of female superiority in clairvoyance and other forms of mediumship.

One of Romola's triumphs was her 'remote-viewing'

of a student's home in Scotland. While Romola lay on the examination couch at Wessex University, her mind soared out of her body and, using the contact of her student's right hand on her forehead, she 'viewed' the girl's home and described in detail the youngster's bedroom. This was in the wing of an old castle which her parents operated as a hotel in the Scottish Highlands.

Romola described the girl's dressing-table and the objects on top of it which, strangely enough, differed from the usual layout of the room and were unfamiliar to the girl. However, by making a telephone call to her parents the student then established, to her own amazement and Romola's delight, that Romola had been a hundred per cent correct. A new dressing-table had been installed as a surprise for her home-coming at Easter, and on top of its glass cover was a complete antique-silver toilet set which was intended as a present for the girl's twenty-first birthday.

The term drew rapidly to a close, the fascination of its unusual curriculum speeding up the passing of the days and nights, but just before we broke for the Easter vacation I received a letter from Sir Edward Tolsford, whom I had known since childhood.

Edward is the last of the Tolsford line of distinguished country squires who, for centuries, have held sway over Tolsford Manor and the lands overlooking Romney Marsh. This is the strange dyke-cut area of Kentish flatlands which were first drained by the Romans. It is kept from total inundation only by the long seawall that fronts the marshes and holds back the voracious English Channel. That is about all that the rest of the world, including Britain, knows about the 'Levels', as they are called, except that a particularly fine breed of sheep comes from Romney Marsh. For the people who find their way to these flatlands, they can become an enchantment. To the Tolsfords, for centuries, they have been a way of life. Romney Marsh folk, whether squire, farmer, innkeeper, artisan or fisherman, are a race apart. In their own words, they are 'Levellers'.

I was so disturbed by the tone of Edward's letter, which begged me to see him as soon as possible, that I asked Robert to psychometrize it.

The moment he took hold of the letter, he said: 'This reeks of anxiety. The writer is deeply troubled about something.'

'That hardly sounds like Sir Edward Tolsford. He's an old shipmate of mine and has strong nerves. He survived four years in German prison camps and yet never lost his sense of humour. But a man that Colditz Castle couldn't beat could be suffering from some serious degenerative disease. That might explain his nervous state.'

Robert continued: 'This friend of yours, Daniel, seems to think of you as his last means of escaping from whatever is driving him half mad. I tell you, Prof, this letter casts a long shadow.'

I was worried and the same afternoon I wrote an express letter to Edward inviting him to come and see me at the weekend. Therefore I was taken aback when my old friend turned up after lunch on Thursday.

When I saw Edward, I was shocked at how much he had changed. He was many pounds lighter than his tall frame warranted and his face was strained. He was shaking and I noticed that he was holding an aerosol inhaler, indicating that he suffered from asthma. It had been over five years since I had visited Edward at his lovely manor house set high above the Marsh and I now hardly recognized him.

I took my friend back to my house which lies just under the Cerne Abbas giant, that ancient figure of a titan cut out of the chalk-lined turf of the Downs. It is carrying a huge club. I believe it represents Hercules.

The Dorset farmhouse, with its clay-tile roof and cladding of tar-soaked ships' timbers and white plaster, is the home I share with Robert. It is full of peace and I hoped that it would have a soothing effect on my guest; but Edward's nerves were in a bad state. Even the short walk up the garden slope had caught him by the throat and he was forced to use the inhaler to restore his natural breathing. Obviously he was in need of help and it wasn't long before he asked for it.

'Daniel, I swear to you that I'm not suffering from paranoia but I sincerely believe that my home and the whole of Romney Marsh is under some kind of spell. Do you believe in witchcraft?'

Quite an opening gambit!

'I do,' I replied, to my friend's evident relief, 'if by witchcraft you mean using the latent power of the human mind to bring about changes which would not normally happen. I've seen far too many effective earth-magic rituals to believe otherwise.'

Edward relaxed, his breathing returning to normal. He continued, 'Then you'll know that I'm not crazy when I say that the Romney Marshes have been *hexed* – as though some awful curse has been put upon them.'

I wasn't certain how to react to his obvious sincerity. I kept my tone of voice as conversational as possible while I carefully watched his reactions. 'That may be so, Edward, but what makes you so certain?'

'There are many reasons. As you know, the Marsh is an eerie place which can change from the bright sunshine of summer into a chilling sea-mist and from that whip up a gale-force storm in twenty minutes.

You've known it and roamed over most of it with me since we were children, but in all my years of love and respect for that land and its ugly moods, I have never known it like this. I tell you, Daniel, today there's something very wrong with the Marsh. I suppose it is more or less the same as it has been, in appearance, for the last fifty years, apart from a few more retirement bungalows on its fringes. Only the atmosphere has changed in a very disturbing way. . . . I've even begun to wonder if it's affecting my reason. Perhaps I'm going mad.'

I leaned close to him, taking in his craggy pallor so different from his usual healthy outdoor complexion. Only the characteristic barrel-chest of the asthmatic filled out the top half of his gaunt body. He was shivering again, although we sat before a cheerful springtime fire of crackling logs.

'No, Edward,' I said slowly and with as much conviction as I could muster. 'You are not mad. Deeply disturbed, yes, but definitely not mad. In fact, old friend, you are one of the sanest men I know.'

Edward let out his breath in a long sigh, his hands shaking as he clutched the blue inhaler.

'By the way, you're using that inhaler far too much,' I warned him.

He shook his head. 'Thank God for that asthma pump! It has stood by me well and sometimes I think it saves my life.'

'Possibly, but it can become addictive. Your own doctor must have told you of the danger.'

'Of course, but it's not just the inhaler that's been giving me the shakes.' His face again became tense. 'That Marsh is haunted!'

To try to lighten the atmosphere I said, 'Haven't we always said that? Remember when we were kids how we nearly came to grief in that snowstorm? Your father was furious that we had gone out with such a threatening sky, but it all happened too quickly, even for you, and you know the marshes from Hythe to Appledore, dyke by dyke. Remember? In that sudden white-out even you got lost, but you saved both our lives. I panicked; you kept your head!'

He smiled and quoted Kipling:

'If you can keep your head when all about you
Are losing theirs and blaming it on you. . .'

We are both fans. 'Kipling loved the Marsh as much as you do, Edward,' I said. 'That story of his about the marsh-witches, what is it called?'

' "Dymchurch Flit",' he replied enthusiastically. 'It's a masterpiece! Even Kipling liked it and he was hypercritical of his own work. My father knew him well and used to dine at Bateman's with him. Kipling loved that old manor house. His children had given him so much joy there and when his son was killed in the First World War he clung to Bateman's. He hugged it to him as though his son was still there, as a child.' Edward paused awkwardly. 'I'm sorry, Daniel, that was stupid of me. Your own loss must still hurt.'

I had felt the pain jolt through me but firmly rejected it. 'I don't feel that either of them has gone. Once that awful stunning shock is over, how you feel about your dead is entirely up to you. You can mourn them forever, or be sensible and get on with living. I hold my family close in my memories of all the joy they gave me.'

'Well done, Daniel.' Edward looked relieved. 'I forgot about my own terrors for a moment when we talked of Kipling. He really understood the Marsh and all its changing moods. I wonder what he would have made of it today? It has all gone so dreadfully wrong.'

'Start at the beginning,' I said. 'Nothing is insoluble. Don't worry about your mind. You're quite sane, but I would like you to see a specialist about your asthma. I'll give you the name of a good allergist.'

'The hell with the wheezing, Daniel. I've got more important things on my mind.' His petulance surprised me. 'This whole bloody mess started some time ago, almost to the day when they finished building the nuclear power-station at Dungeness.'

My professional interest quickened. 'Do you think that there is a connection between the power-station and your feeling that the Marsh is haunted?'

'I did think that the reactor might be affecting the marshes. God knows, it's not the best-looking building and I wish it didn't perch there so blatantly on Dungeness, but the fact that it's ugly doesn't make it a threat to the health of the Marsh. It's been built too well and too carefully for a radical fault to develop. I don't think we need worry about any nuclear leakage and radiation poisoning.'

Our conversation, from its strange beginning, had become easier, more rational and relaxed. I felt I was winning and getting through to Edward's normally well-balanced mind and his habitually moderate point of view. I tried another tack. 'Obviously there are big power pylons crossing the Marsh, carrying the current over the countryside. You may not have heard of it, but there is a strange phenomenon connected with power leakage from overhead lines. Perhaps this has caused a tense, depressed feeling among the Marsh folk. It is an accepted scientific fact and it is certainly a point for you to consider.'

'That's interesting, Daniel,' Edward briefly pondered on it, 'but that's not what I've been talking about.' He smiled sadly, paused to fish out his pipe, then, seeing my look of disapproval, put it away, shamefacedly. 'Stupid of me, I know, but I still like to suck on my pipe.' He grinned like a schoolboy caught smoking behind the bicycle shed. 'I don't light it. I suppose it's like having a briar thumb in my mouth.' His tone again became serious. 'There's been a deliberate attempt to scare the daylights out of the Marsh folk. In one night, in 1976, all the stone crosses in the graveyards of five of the famous old Marsh churches were smashed. Big, heavy granite and marble crosses were deliberately desecrated with sledgehammers. Why?'

I whistled. 'You mean to say that no one interfered or called the police?'

'It has hardly been mentioned, yet every graveyard from St Mary's-in-the-Marsh to the Isle of Oxney was desecrated that night. I know the Marsh folk are superstitious and it's often a case of Christianity by day and the old pagan religions by night, but there's a vast difference between that and the sort of sacrilegious mayhem of that evil night.'

'Who in hell would do a thing like that?' I asked.

'Quite so! Who in *hell*? That night, the Marsh folk were too bloody terrified to have anything to do with such things. Whoever did it came from some other part of the country. In any case, our people are too fond of their fine old churches to lift a finger against them. No, Daniel, it was black magic, a deliberate act to scare the local people and keep them tightly shut up in their homes at night. Do you follow me?'

Light dawned. 'You mean smuggling is back on the Marsh?'

He laughed harshly and again quoted Kipling:

'Five and twenty ponies

34

Trotting through the dark —
Brandy for the Parson
'Baccy for the Clerk;
Laces for a lady, letters for a spy,
Watch the wall, my darling, while the
    Gentlemen go by!

'Rudyard said it all, but those were the old days. Today it's heroin or cocaine, mescaline, marijuana, amphetamines — you name it. There's millions involved — so what is more natural than an attempt to scare the pants off the Marsh folk and keep them out of it? That way, there's a free run for the contraband.'

'But surely the Marsh men are traditionally smugglers. We even saw a run one moonlit night before the war. I remember how frightened I was. Your father was furious with us because we had sneaked out that night. I also remember him tanning your hide.'

Edward smiled. 'Father was only scared because we'd done such a risky thing.' He paused. 'But he also said something strange, Daniel. I can still remember his words across all those years: "It's none of our concern, Edward. Smuggling is Marsh business. *Ours* is to keep the Marshes safe. We're the Lords of the Levels and our motto is 'Love God, honour the King but first maintain the wall'." Daniel, you know as well as I do that without the great seawall the Marsh would be drowned, like Lyonesse. My family have been Lords of the Levels for centuries. I was a "Bailiff" until these old offices were done away with, along with so many of our cherished old traditions. Nowadays the governance of the Marsh is in the hands of the County Council. The Lords of the Levels are redundant.'

Edward's eyes had a misty look in them, as though he were scanning a far horizon. 'Marshmen still "run"

35

their traditional cargoes of contraband — tobacco, and spirits, mainly brandy and rum. Nowadays they've added illegal immigrants and even, unwisely, dogs belonging to rich women who want to dodge the severe quarantine laws. But drugs? No, I don't think so. That's not their way. Anyway, the stuff is coming in by air, so the rumours tell us.'

'How?' I asked.

'Dropped by night, from light aeroplanes, then someone, somehow, locates the packages and high-tails them off the Marsh to some central distribution point. Probably in London.'

'Surely, Edward, the Customs and Excise people are on to this sort of operation?'

My friend laughed. 'They're only a fraction of the number that they need to patrol the Marsh. Remember how difficult the marshes were to defend during the last war? Even the Duke of Wellington found that out. That's why the Martello Towers along the seawall and the Military Canal were built. In the last war, planners had nightmares trying to set up enough blockhouses and pillboxes to defend our intricate maze of dykes and fields. You would need an *army* of Customs men to cover the whole Marsh. It's hard enough to find one small fishing boat at night, especially among so many local fishermen, all landing their catches at the same time. To pinpoint a small package, air-dropped at night, you'd need literally hundreds of trained men. No way, Daniel. And I'm sure dope smuggling is the key to the whole filthy business.'

I was forced to agree with him and the further my friend proceeded with his story, the more his logic impressed me.

'You mean to say that the churchyard desecrations were carried out just to keep the Marshland people in their homes, behind locked doors? Is that your spell, Edward?'

'No, that isn't all. Drugs are dreadful enough in themselves and evil men are obviously behind it all, but there is such an atmosphere of terror on my marshes. A sort of brooding unease lies like a mist over Romney Marsh by day and fear seems to stalk the Levels at night. For God's sake, Daniel,' he said, 'help me to –' he sought for the right word – 'to *exorcize* this terrible evil that holds the Marsh and my people in its grip!'

I smiled reassuringly, in spite of my own reservations. 'Don't worry, shipmate, we'll smash this thing together.'

'Then you'll come down to the Marsh soon?'

'Yes, and what's more I'll bring two of the best friends I have. My colleagues will help me deal with any mumbo-jumbo that's going on.'

Sensing the moment as ripe to change the subject, I asked casually, 'By the way, how is my goddaughter?'

A surprising reaction came from Edward, who started up in alarm. 'For God's sake don't tell Deborah that I came to see you. She wouldn't approve of it. Promise you won't tell her!'

'Don't be ridiculous,' I protested gently. 'I've known Deborah since she was born. I know I'm not much good as a godfather but why on earth would she adopt an attitude like that to me of all people?'

Edward was worried. 'I don't seem to know her any more. My own daughter is like a stranger.'

'Don't worry about that. It's probably just the generation gap. How old is she now? Twenty-five? Isn't she engaged?'

'She's nearly thirty; you've missed a few years. No, she's not engaged,' his voice lowered, 'and she doesn't have a boyfriend. Since Mary died it's been lonely for both of us. Deborah, as you know, is a fine horsewoman. She was all set for this year's Olympics, but when her mother died she gave up her show-jumping ambitions to look after me. Maybe she resents being tied to an old asthmatic father. I just don't know.'

'Nonsense, Edward. She adores you.'

My friend smiled wanly. 'We used to get on so well together.'

'Are you sure you're not imagining this?' I asked gently.

His reaction was instantaneous. 'I think she might be one of *them*. What shall I do?'

I put a comforting arm around his shoulders as my friend unexpectedly burst into tears.

'Come on, Edward. This whole thing has really got you down.' I paused, then asked, him, 'What do you mean by *one of them*?'

My distraught friend looked up. The room suddenly seemed filled with shadows. His voice was a whisper. 'They are the Companions of Chaos. They are behind all this horror. I'm terrified that, somehow, they've got a hold on Deborah.'

I got us both a brandy while my memory riffled through its subconscious files. Then I remembered. 'These *Companions of Chaos*, as you call them, would they be the revival of a traditional smuggling gang? Are you sure this isn't a case of some Marsh legend being revived to keep the inquisitive out of the way?'

Edward brushed my suggestion aside. 'No! These shadowy figures are more than rumour and something less than substance. The police don't seem to have a clue as to who they are. They're not known criminals and there is no previous record of their existence. Yet they spread terror over the whole area. They use motorcycle gangs – Hell's Angels type of thugs – to cause chaos when the locals don't fall into line. Of course, the Marsh is full of motorbikes because it's the cheapest form of transport and most farm-workers use them. The Marsh roads are still as winding and treacherous as ever and these nippy machines are ideal for both road and off-track use.

'But the gang-bikers ride great, powerful machines capable of high speeds. These gangs, or ones like them, have been run out of Folkestone and Dover because the local police there have a large enough force to contain them. But around Tolsford Manor, on the fringes of the Marsh, although they leave Rye and Winchelsea alone, the gangs seem to come and go as they please and our local police force can't do a thing about it. The Marsh police are too few and are not equipped to deal with gang violence, and by the time they've called in the county police, the gang has gone.'

At this point my subconscious mind came up with a detailed reference. 'Edward,' I said, 'the "Companions of Chaos" was the description given by a scholar of the occult, William Gray, to people who practise black magic as opposed to the "Companions of Cosmos" who practise the ancient seasonal rituals and earth-magic of our ancestors, in other words, the white magicians. Your Companions of Chaos are satanists, but I can't imagine aberrated people like that, who must have a reasonable standard of classical scholar-ship, racing around on high-powered motorbikes. It doesn't make sense.'

'No, Daniel, this gang of thugs is just one of the paid instruments of terror that keep the marshes in a grip of fear. They were probably responsible for those savage sledgehammer desecrations of the graveyards.'

'Just *one* of the instruments of terror? You mean that

there are *other* forms of terror being used on the Marsh?'

My friend's eyes were fever-bright. 'We have recently had a widespread outbreak of *animal mutilations*. Sheep and even dogs and cats have been found *disembowelled*. The poor creatures must have suffered agony. And their remains were staked out in some revolting form of ritual pattern. But worst of all –' Edward was almost unable to speak – 'I have an appalling fear that there has been some *child* sacrifice on the Marsh as well. I have no firm evidence, of course. . .'

I felt sick. 'That can't be the work of Hell's Angels. They're just groups of tearaways that started in the fifties and sixties when youngsters began to earn enough money to pay for their powerful motorbikes. They're hell-raisers all right, but most of their violence is associated with rival motorcycle gang-warfare. Ritual animal-mutilation and particularly child sacrifice would require a sadistic dedication to evil and a considerable knowledge of black magical practices.'

'Of course you're right, Daniel, but the devil alone knows why they should do such terrible things.'

'Satanism and devil-worship are far more widespread than you'd imagine, even in your worst nightmares,' I said, 'and in recent years the temporal power of the "Lord of This World" has increased exponentially. The vicious group activities of a black magical coven which is intent on practising every sexual aberration known to man in order to raise power for some application of the dark force against an enemy they wish to destroy or a community they wish to control can be a very real menace. If you combine that sort of twisted ambition with knowledge of ritual incantations and mind-manipulative techniques *and* extensive drug abuse, you've got the sort of situation whereby your Companions of Chaos can terrorize a whole county. Tell me, do these bikers carry pillion-riders?'

'No, they don't and that's odd. They ride in groups, but I've never seen them with a girl on the pillion.'

'There must be a strong discipline behind them. The Hell's Angels gangs are mainly sex-orientated, fairly aberrated as well and deeply into the drug scene, probably more marijuana and speed than heroin or cocaine, which until recently have been much more expensive. It has never seemed to me that Hell's Angels are flush with money. Your bike-gangs sound more like shock troops than conventional leather boys. I've got good friends in Special Branch. I'll ask them if they've any information. These gangs are the province of the conventional constabularies, but you never know. Branch are up to their eyes in combatting terrorism, protecting foreign diplomats and generally keeping "undesirables" out of Britain, but they might have something on your bikers.'

My old shipmate smiled. 'You're not still at that game? Intelligence, I mean?'

'Lord, no! I gave that up years ago, when I was demobilized and signed the Official Secrets Act. But from time to time I assist the police, especially Special Branch, as a so-called expert medical witness. But to come back to the point: I believe the whole of your story and I'm certainly going to come down to the Marsh as soon as this term is over. I'll discuss your problems with my colleagues. I'm sure they'll want to help in any way they can.'

My friend shifted uncomfortably in the chair. 'I'd rather you didn't stay at the Manor, Daniel. I know that seems dreadfully inhospitable when you have been such a kind and generous friend, but I think it would be too obvious to Deborah and I *am* afraid she's become involved with these ghastly people, whoever they are.'

'Think nothing of it. I've got a large motor-home, from which I do all my field research. I visit haunted houses and remote places where unusual phenomena have occurred, that sort of thing. It's my greatest extravagance. I've had my Winnebago motor-caravan equipped as a laboratory. It has video-cameras and recording machines and I can handle almost anything from medical problems or electronics to general chemical analysis and photographic processing. The Winnebago is also equipped with a radio-telephone. Find me a good, quiet spot on a Marsh farm where I can get local dairy supplies and plug into the farmer's electricity and water. We'll operate from there. My colleagues have shared it with me before and it works out very well.'

I dropped Edward at the station in the late afternoon. He wanted to get back to the Marsh as soon as possible. Deborah would certainly be waiting for his return from his supposed visit to a London specialist.

Edward's attitude was that of a guilty husband playing truant from a domineering wife, but at least I had given him hope. I just wished that I had as much confidence as he had in my ability to handle this horrific affair, which seemed to have baffled the local police as well as Customs and Excise. I resolved to tell Robert and Romola as much as I knew and what I had guessed, and then take Robert down with me to the Marsh, leaving Romola to act as liaison with the various sources of information that I might need. This was really an excuse to keep my gentle Hungarian assistant out of the danger area, because I already had a strong sense of the very real perils that we might encounter.

CHAPTER 3

The Dark Side of the Marsh

Because of the stringent laws of the land, we couldn't arm ourselves conventionally with guns, and since both Robert and myself are not into blood sports even sporting shotguns were out. However, my Navajo friend can do amazing things with a sling-shot and I am a keen archer, having taught the bow to paraplegics over many years as part of their therapy. Archery is a great discipline psychologically, helping to rebuild a life shattered by accident or a stroke. Therefore I became skilled at it and I assure you that a blunted arrow can do a lot of damage, while a 'broad-head' hunting-shaft or even a sharp target arrow can kill at well over a hundred metres. I felt confident that Robert and I could deal with any motorbike thugs of the leather-clad 'chopper brigade'. However, speaking *esoterically*, we might find ourselves hardpressed to hold our own against the sort of powerful dark forces which I now strongly suspected were behind this dreadful business. But above all, any counter-operation against the forces of evil would be a real blow against the appalling widespread use of hard drugs among the young. I explained all this to my colleagues, who responded in the way I had expected.

Robert was angry. 'Jesus! I'd like to get my hands on those bastards. From what you tell me of the Romney Marsh, it sounds like a marvellous place and I hate people who louse up the natural balance of the earth. For that reason alone these sons of bitches are worth fighting. I'm sure sorry I missed Sir Edward. He sounds like a great guy. I'm with you, Daniel. Esoterically and exoterically, let's terminate these creeps with extreme prejudice, as the CIA likes to call it.'

I hoped he was joking but I didn't doubt his sincerity.

Romola, in her own shy way, was equally determined to back me up, but she was resentful at not being included in the field trip. 'Daniel, I see your point about my staying here as your main contact, and I realize that there will be plenty for me to do to help you with any information or background research that you may need, but I am a psychic. I sense that you're alarmed and that worries me. You're not a man who easily succumbs to fear but you are a sensitive and you feel badly about this whole thing. Robert feels the same way, but then he revels in a challenge. You, Daniel, at your age, have already had too many challenges. I sense that there will be danger. I want to be with you. Please let me come to the Marsh – if not right away, then as soon as possible. I'll stay here to get things going, but with your radio-telephone you can contact anyone you need. Please let me be with you.'

I find saying No to Romola very difficult, especially when she has that misty glow in those startling eyes. There is something so disturbingly appealing about her that, were she not half my age and my valued academic colleague, I know that I would throw my hat over the moon and try my chances with her in bed. But Romola Kobrak is the sort of woman you marry not just enjoy as a casual sexual partner.

When my wife and baby son Ian were killed I never expected to remarry. I believed that you don't find perfection twice in a lifetime. I know that Romola Kobrak feels a great deal of affection for me but the difference in our ages is too great for me to hope for more. I have seen a number of marriages between spring and autumn come to bitter grief when spring has

46

turned into summer while autumn has degenerated into shivering winter. It is not a sensible arrangement, at best. The joint suicides of my friend and colleague, Arthur Koestler and his much younger and equally splendid wife, have done nothing to alter my opinion of age-divided marriages. I love Romola too much and too tenderly to want to see her hurt. I am now sixty-two years old and I have lived a tough and demanding life which has taken its toll over the years. I have enjoyed a number of most rewarding relationships with attractive women who, I hope, also shared my pleasure and satisfaction. But Romola Kobrak is something quite different from a modern, liberated, pleasure-seeking woman. She makes me glow inside, just by being with her, and I would be happy, if somewhat jealous, to see her mated to a suitable man worthy of all her gifts and graces.

As Alan Shepard, the first American astronaut, said just before his historic lift-off: 'Dear Lord, please don't let me screw up!' This especially applies to my relationship with my much-admired colleague.

About Edward's problems I found myself asking my conscience: Why get involved with something like this when the whole thing could be a straightforward series of criminal acts by the Mafia, or some such organization, who are using these terror methods to make their operations more effective? Why put your team and yourself at risk without any official authorization or back-up, except under the 'turn a blind eye' and the 'old pals' acts, and take on a job for which you are ill-equipped, hopelessly outnumbered and untrained in anti-narcotics operations? Are you being carried away by Edward's pitiful plight and going along with his wild stories because you've known him as a good friend almost all your life, or is there really a paranormal side to this whole fantastic affair? Why start thinking about using bows and arrows – of all things – against a gang of motorbike thugs and drag Robert along, with that deadly sling of David of his? Above all, why allow Romola to be put at risk?

All these reasonable questions and objections spun through my mind during a sleepless night. When the rising sun finally shone through the spring drizzle, I knew that I had to go. I also knew that every trick and scrap of knowledge I had picked up during years of experience of the paranormal would be used and, more than that, would be vitally important in the coming struggle. The material side I could handle with the help of one or two good friends in the security forces, together with my few remaining contemporaries from wartime Allied Intelligence. The *esoteric* aspects of the struggle I believed I could contain with the help of my two trusted friends, together with the help of God.

The final argument that persuaded me was the grim result of wide-spread hard-drug smuggling. The shattered lives of the young, the wrecked hopes, the misery and despair of the families involved, were reasons enough to fight these evils. As Robert said, later: 'If that isn't worth getting up off your ass to fight, then, as a race of beings on this planet we've had it! Humanity would be better off if we just dropped the bombs and nature started all over again.'

Having wrestled with the demons of doubt, I ate a hearty breakfast and gave myself a bad case of indigestion.

Ten days later, Robert and I kissed Romola goodbye and drove the heavily-laden Winnebago towards Rye. Spring in these lovely islands of ours has inspired great writers from Chaucer to T.S. Eliot. Quoting these poets on the subject of the British spring and telling my companion about the long cloak of history that mantles the downland of Southern England was a happy way of passing the journey. The first apple and cherry blossoms were already emerging into the sunshine, which alternated with the short April showers. The hedgerows were green with buds and thick with thrusting young sap-filled branches, alive with tiny creatures emerging from their long winter hibernation. I felt the stirring of the earth and caught the breeze-borne scent of bursting blossom. Robert was full of wonder at the sight of that beautiful rolling countryside turning in its sleep as April heralded the return of spring.

Both of us became so absorbed with the fascination of the passing scene that I found myself turning our motor-home in the direction of the village of Burwash. I felt strongly that I must take Robert to see Bateman's, Kipling's home. Like most Americans, my colleague was delighted to visit such a famous old building.

We spent a couple of memorable hours wandering around the house and its peaceful grounds, which are now safely in the capable hands of the National Trust. We paced over the adjacent fields, where much of *Puck of Pook's Hill* was set, and visited Hobden's Mill, now restored and once again operational, producing fine local flour. It was, however, in the formal, willow-shaded gardens and particularly in that beautiful old manor house, that we both found our contact with Kipling at its strongest. His gentle spirit seemed to be everywhere. It was only when we were in the small shop, which is neatly incorporated into the restored oast-house, that we both returned to reality. Suddenly Robert said: 'We're being watched! Don't turn around, but we've been under surveillance for some time by a man in grey. Damn it, he just left.'

My colleague quietly slipped outside with that deceptively easy lope of his, which covers the ground as fast as most men run. I followed and only caught up with him as he turned towards me by the gate.

'He's a chauffeur and he just drove off in a Rolls-Royce. I couldn't catch the number. Why would a chauffeur watch us like that?'

'Your guess is as good as mine. Idle curiosity, perhaps? You're not exactly inconspicuous, my tall Navajo friend.'

Robert laughed, with that deep characteristic bark of his, and slapped me on the shoulder, catching me off balance on my weak leg, then neatly fielding me before I went over. Sometimes he forgets how strong he is.

'You know, Prof' (Robert calls me that when he wants to make a point of argument), 'I'd stake a few dollars that the chauffeur was expecting us. Maybe he even followed us here, and now he's gone to report back to his boss. I figure that these Companions of Chaos knew we were coming. I'm certain I'm right.'

'I'd trust your instinct any time. But how would *they*, whoever they are, know that we were here?'

'Could be Sir Edward let something slip to his daughter and she passed it on.'

'I shouldn't think so. Anyway, it doesn't matter too much. We've got a good cover story. As far as these people are concerned, we're just two nature-lovers visiting a great centre of bird-life and botanical beauty. There's plenty of those enthusiasts turning up on the Marsh for most of the year, especially in the spring-time.' I consulted my watch. 'We've spent more time here than I planned. We'll have to get a move on if we're going to make that farm before it gets dark. The Marsh is a tricky place at night and I'd prefer to find the farm before the light goes.'

As it happened we were lucky to make it alive to Tenterden.

A Winnebago is as well built as any motor-home can be, probably more so, with its powerful diesel engine and excellent power brakes. So I didn't expect the brakes to fail completely on that first steep hill which drops sharply from Burwash on the road to the Marsh. One moment we were picking up speed down the winding incline and the next few seconds saw me fighting hard to keep the heavy motor-home on the road, which was wet and slippery after the showers.

Thank God, there was no traffic about and we were saved from a bad wreck by the thick ash and thorn hedges that lined the road. Blessedly their springy solidity helped me to slow down the speeding vehicle. I aimed to hit them obliquely as we swayed from side to side of that twisting hill. Someone unseen must have been helping us, because the power steering didn't fail. Creaking and lurching, with our stout metal sides screeching against the speed-absorbing hedgerows, we gradually slowed down in over-revving low gear, to come to a breath-catching stop canted steeply up on the grassy bank at the foot of the hill.

'Shit!' breathed Robert, in a long sigh. 'Now I'm sure we're being watched. Somehow those bastards knew we were coming and they've guessed why we're here. That son of a bitch sure as hell fixed your brakes!'

'In broad daylight? At Bateman's? How?'

'That's easy, Daniel. For Chrissake, who notices a chauffeur fooling around with a monkey-wrench underneath the hood of an automobile?'

I contacted the local Automobile Association by radio-telephone and in twenty minutes a cheerful Kentish mechanic arrived and clucked in sympathy over our lucky escape. On examination, the mechanical failure was pinpointed in the brake cylinder and its connections, which had loosened and drained out all the hydraulic fluid.

'Can't think how that could have happened,' the puzzled mechanic sucked his lower lip in perplexity and gave a wry smile, ' 'less of course you done it yerself?'

He chuckled at his own wit and towed us into Tenterden. An hour later we were assured by the garage manager that the rest of the damage was confined to shallow dents and scratches where our tough, aluminium-shelled motor-home had scraped along those thrice-blessed hedgerows.

CHAPTER 4

A Paranormal Reconnaissance

At last we were on our way across the outlying saltings of the Romney Marsh. By the time we entered the winding maze of twisting roads that weave their way across the Levels, we had recovered from the shock of our near-fatal experience and were enjoying the last part of the drive. The late afternoon sun was dipping behind us, making a spectacular show of its setting, starkly silhouetting towering cumulus clouds against its westering glow.

'I asked a friend what he thought about the Romney Marshes and he described them as dull, flat and boring,' Robert remarked.

I chuckled, 'A lot of people can't grasp the elusive charm of the Marsh, or else they see it in poor weather. You've got to find it like this, in a spring sunset, or happen on it as dawn breaks over the ridgeback of the Folkstone Leas and floods the sweep of the bay with chrome-orange light. Then you feel the compulsive pull that will bring you back again and again.'

'You're quite a poet, Daniel!' Robert looked at me quizzically. 'You're full of surprises. I see your point. In spite of our aggravations with the "Winnie", we sure struck lucky with the Marsh at sunset! It has got a lot going for it.'

After consulting a large-scale map, we finally located the farm and met its genial owner, Elias Whitgift.

'Sir Edward told me to expect you earlier.' He scanned the bodywork of our motor-home. 'Had a little accident then?' His tone was cheerfully solicitous.

Here was a man who noticed things. Edward had picked our landlord with that astute eye for character which had made him a good Naval officer and a well-respected squire.

Eli Whitgift's ancestry was reflected in the solid compactness of his stocky Marshman's build. His name indicated his Romney heritage. Eli was descended from a long line of Levellers. His swarthy complexion also proudly proclaimed him to be part Romany.

We were soon snugly settled on a wide concrete and gravel hard-standing, sheltered from the easterly gales by a thick stand of trees and flanked by a deep dyke. Electricity and water were connected up and we were ready for business. The Whitgift farmhouse lay a hundred yards from us, down a narrow track. We were private enough for our needs, yet close enough to sufficient fresh milk, eggs and butter to supply even Robert's trencherman's appetite.

We felt good about the place, and our welcome from the farmer's apple-cheeked wife, with her gift of home-baked bread, further assured us that Edward had chosen well. The whole setting was exactly what we needed for our base.

The farmer promised to let the Squire know that we had arrived safely. I was sure that Edward had briefed him on some aspects of our presence on the Marsh.

Annoyingly I couldn't contact Tolsford Manor directly, because of my promise not to let Deborah know that I was on the Marsh. It was another aspect of the investigation that disturbed me. I felt badly about not taking Edward's daughter into our confidence. Robert's remark that she might have been the source of leaked information which had put the chauffeur on to our trail also worried me.

However, our job was to get on with our paranormal reconnaissance of the Marsh. Why paranormal? Because we were trying to assess the atmosphere – the *ethos* of the place, as the Greeks referred to the ambience of an environment. To do this properly, the best way that I know is to dowse it, to find the lie of the land or, as Robert and I thought of it, the 'leys' of the land and how they were laid out.

These contentious lines of force, the so-called 'ley-lines', are as real to dowsers, or diviners, as the parallels of latitude and longitude are to navigators. Both sets of lines are invisible and both of them are used to determine position and situation. Leys can cause an actual feeling of their presence, power and direction, and this affects the rods, hazel twigs, spiral-spring devices, pendulums or whatever indicator the dowser is using to detect them.

In China, for thousands of years, dowsing, or divining, was considered to be all-important in planning and setting out the landscape like a giant garden. This ancient Chinese art is called 'Feng-shui' and Kipling referred to it in his little book *Something of Myself*, describing Bateman's as having a 'Feng-shui' which the Kiplings found to be good. 'Feng-shui' is the art of divining the proper positioning and alignment of any new building, or other radical alteration to the landscape, in order to assess any effects that these might have on the immediate environment. Basically it is the whole aesthetic, i.e. 'spiritual', principle behind what has become known as Town and Country Planning.

In the case of Bateman's, like Blenheim Palace, Castle Howard, Woburn Abbey and many other fine country houses built during the 'golden age' of architecture in Britain, their correct positioning and alignments, as well as the fine proportions of these buildings, have generated a Feng-shui that is still felt by visitors and residents alike hundreds of years later.

The words themselves actually mean 'wind and water' and refer to the powers generated by the 'Lung-mei' – the 'dragon' lines of energy that flow in a great network over and under the earth. Many Chinese believe that these forces are both positive – *cha* – and negative – *chi* – and are the energy equivalents to Yin and Yang, the feminine and masculine principles in nature.

Dowsers believe that these 'subtle energies', as they call them, are generated by mineral masses such as quartz rocks, by underground streams, which can be either beneficial or harmful to persons living above them, and by springs, sources, geysers and other natural generators of energy which form the vascular and nervous systems of our living planet.

If these forces and their positioning and alignments are taken into account during the planning states of any construction project and the proper canon of proportions is then used to achieve the best possible architectural results, the outcome must be beneficial to the environment and to the people who will work or reside in the buildings. It is simply applied common sense when you analyse it, and common sense is a mixture of the instincts inherited from our ancestors and applied logic acquired by our own experience and learning. Technology alone, no matter how skilled, cannot achieve these results. *Art* is required just as much as science.

Ridiculous? I don't think so and neither do many architects, engineers and surveyors, whose life experience and intuition tell them how to set about their projects in the best possible way.

As to the existence of these lines of force, the leys, consider how radio-location and radio-direction-finding work, by affecting the needles of radio compasses or the appearance of cathode ray tubes with invisible wireless waves of electro-magnetism. By using Decca or Loran guidance systems installed in aircraft or ships, their positions can be pinpointed exactly on or above the earth. You can't see these forces, but they do exist and can be used and manipulated once their principles are understood. Millions of travellers put their trust in them to guide them safely to their destinations. For diviners it is the same with leys, and by using them some dowsers can find their way in bad visibility or even pick their path through a minefield, utilizing their inborn ability to search-and-find a way to safety. In the case of thick fog and especially minefields, the absolute faith that the dowser has in his abilities is the final test of that person's paranormal senses. I know of a number of cases in peace and war when dowsers found their way to safety in this way, most recently through the minefields of Vietnam.

The ley system seems to be generated partly by natural forces such as I have outlined and partly by man-made modifications to the environment, such as open-cast mining, extensive road-systems and artificial canals or any other radical alterations, including buildings, parks, stone-circles, monuments, tunnels, graveyards and other human artifacts. Subterranean sewers, gas-pipes and electrical cables also affect the ethos of the environment; diehards who say they don't can't be thinking logically.

When the nature of the ethos has been drastically modified by a large, ugly building, by the unsightly scars of an open-cast mine or by any other badly planned project, the whole atmosphere and balance of the environment will be affected over a large area of land; and it follows logically that this will also affect the state of the wildlife in the region as well as the lives of the people there. That is what ecology is all about. The preservation of the balance of nature. *Ethology* is its spiritual equivalent.

A half-day's general survey of the area by dowsing told us that Edward was right. There was something dreadfully wrong with the leys of the Marsh. Either somebody who understood how to manipulate these subtle forces had been at work, altering the lines of 'ley-power', possibly by ritual means – a statement wide open to ridicule and disbelief – or the radical alteration of the skyline by the construction of the nuclear power-station, with all the social mistrust of such things, could have caused the area's atmosphere of unease. Whatever the reason, the violence that had taken place had affected (psychometrically) the local atmosphere by a process of osmosis and association. Deliberately broken fences, smashed farm gates, fouled dykes and desecrated country churchyards can easily generate a psychological aura of fear and unease. Whatever had caused these violent disturbances in the normal tranquillity of the Marsh, a few moments' work with our angle-rods and pendulums told us that the leys criss-crossing Romney Marsh were in one hell of a mess.

Our method of travel was ideal for the local conditions. We both rode compact Honda trail-bikes and carried them slung across the back of the Winnebago in a double rack. This was a steel cage which could be lowered to ground level by means of an electric hoist.

Equipped with foul-weather gear, crash-helmets and riding boots, we could wander at will in nearly any weather. Riding these bikes, we were able to area-dowse the Marsh, even from apparently inaccessible places, and in spite of the disturbing results, Robert

60

was becoming enchanted with the whole place. 'It is so completely different from any landscape I know in the US. I could become addicted to these marshes. I just wish there wasn't this uneasy feeling overlaying the natural tranquillity of the Levels. The bird-life is so extensive and the botanical richness of the wild flowers is stunning.'

Edward was a botanical fanatic when we were boys and he had showed me many of the wildflowers with which the marshes abound. Lady's smock, the 'cuckoo flower', was just blooming, as the cuckoos returned to the flatlands. Snakeshead and early marsh-orchids were starting to emerge as we approached May Day, while marsh helleborine was evident growing among the bullrushes. As yet the main crop of meadow sweet, yellow flag irises, water-violets and guelder roses were a month away from appearing, to take the Marsh into summer; but the warm, wet spring had brought on enough of the wildflowers that grace the Levels to delight Robert's plant-hungry desert-bred eyes.

'I fell in love with it all when I was five years old,' I said. 'Edward's father was also a Royal Navy man and he and my father had served as midshipmen on HMS *Colossus* at the Battle of Jutland, the last great dreadnought battle in which big guns and torpedoes were the deciding factors. I used to come down here with my father and the two men would refight that bloody seafight over and over again, using fleets of tiny model battleships on the billiard table to illustrate the complex manoeuvres. Edward and I were allowed to move the dozens of little ships and even to this day we can both recite the whole progress of the battle. As cadets at Dartmouth, and later, when we were on leave from the Navy, we would often come down here and wander all over the Levels, sailing dinghies in summer out in the long bay between Folkestone and Dungeness and, in winter, exploring the ancient ruins of the Marsh, or lazily canoeing down the Military Canal. Neither of us was a keen shotgunner and we were more interested in preserving the wildlife than in destroying it, but we're both fishermen and you'll not believe how good the local fish can be.'

'You make it all sound wonderful, Daniel, but I guess our Californian mountain trout would come pretty close. I can see why you love these marshes, and why Sir Edward is so important to you as a friend. I can't wait to meet him. When will we go to see him?'

'Soon, I hope. I'm waiting to hear from Eli. He's acting as the go-between. The problem, as I told you, is Deborah. Do you still think she knows why we are here and when we came?'

'I don't see how else those Companions of Chaos could have gotten onto us so soon. Unless, of course, someone who is capable of such things was "remote-viewing" and "over-saw" Sir Edward's visit to you at Wessex. That's a possibility.'

'Why not? I just hadn't considered it. If these people, whoever they are, will go so far as to try to kill us, then they may well be satanists and it's possible that they could be using a psychic in their coven as a remote-viewer, using a crystal perhaps?'

'It figures, Prof, or, of course, it might be that Sir Edward's daughter is under their influence and that she's the culprit. I'd sure like to meet that young lady.' My friend sounded intrigued.

'She's a stunner, Robert. Slim, blonde and a fine athlete, but unlike most of the horsy set Deborah has a good sense of humour, just like her mother, with whom, between you and me, Robert, I fell deeply in love, but Mary wisely chose Edward and married him

62

just before he was shot down and taken prisoner. She waited for him for four long years and when he came back she tried to have a baby right away, but it was six years before they finally had Deborah. Mary, Edward and I knew each other as children, so the link between us was very strong.

'Later, when I met Patricia, I knew I had found someone like Mary, only Patricia was brown-eyed and had long dark hair just like Romola's, whereas Mary's was fair and cut short. I am sure you'll like Deborah. I do, very much. I just can't make out what all these Tolsford family troubles are about. Deborah is not the type of girl to resent looking after her sick father, whom she adores. It's got to be something else.'

'I hope to God it isn't drugs,' I silently added to myself.

For three days we quartered and requartered the Levels until Robert had absorbed a clear, overall picture of the lie of the flatlands. Our next move was to ask apparently idle questions of the locals in the pubs. The Marsh is thick with pubs, if you know where to look, and what is more the local beers are excellent. The sites of these local inns date back to the Normans. Most of them were rebuilt in the eighteenth century, when smuggling was at its height.

The small coastal ports of New Romney and Rye have the oldest pubs, but many of them have been redecorated with phoney horsebrasses, Taiwanese Toby-jugs and Pakistani reproduction muskets. Only in the depths of the Marsh can you recapture the authentic atmosphere of the Levels. Here the small 'locals' primarily serve the farmers and agricultural workers. There are few residents in tiny villages like Ivychurch and they are usually Marsh-born and bred. We bought drinks for the locals, who seldom refuse a free pint, and chatted up the landlords, but got precisely nowhere. Marsh men, and women, are tight-mouthed and uncommunicative at the best of times, being reclusive by nature. They are perfectly willing to man the lifeboat at Dungeness and risk their lives in raging waves to rescue some poor souls in peril on the sea or to go out in a blinding snowstorm to help find some reckless visitor who has failed to return to his bed-and-breakfast at Rye, Dymchurch or New Romney. But the people of the Levels don't gossip much even amongst themselves. In comparison clams have more conversation. Edward has always said this habit is a relic of the old smuggling days.

Them that asks no questions isn't told a lie.
Watch the wall, my darling, while the Gentlemen
    go by!

Old Rudyard certainly knew the Marsh folk and they weren't too communicative even to him. After the war Edward asked a local blacksmith why the old roadsigns hadn't been replaced.

'Well, Squire, we took 'em down to fool them German parachutists and you *never* know,' the aged smith winked.

'Never know what?' the Squire asked curiously.

'Never know if they might try again! After all, we don't need 'em. *We* all know the Marsh, don't we? 'Sides, it 'ud cost a bloody fortune to put 'em back.'

The locals were particularly close-mouthed over the sort of happenings we wanted to know more about and no matter how casually we put our questions or how subtly we phrased them the Marshmen kept their mouths firmly shut, with their usual: 'I dunno 'bout that,' answer to everything.

I hadn't been down to the marshes for some years.

Patricia had loved them so much and the memories of us playing with Ian on Dymchurch Sands were so poignant that I had neglected visiting what really is one of my favourite places on earth. Once I get into the marsh-country itself, I find it a place for dreaming. Crisscrossed by the labyrinth of dykes and ditches, the reeds rustle mesmerically in the sea-breezes, and wildflowers and waterbirds are everywhere. However, after such a long absence, most of the old Marsh folk who were my friends were gone and I couldn't quote my longstanding friendship with Squire Tolsford as an introduction to the younger Marsh folk because Edward specifically wanted to be kept out of it until we had finished our survey. The upshot of it all was that we learned little to add to what we already knew or had sensed. It was baffling and frustrating.

Two other important places that we had to examine in the area were the nuclear reactor at Dungeness, for which visit Romola was getting us permission from the Central Electricity Generating Board, and John Aspinall's wildlife park set in the lovely grounds of Port Lympne, Sir Philip Sassoon's memorable home until his death during the war. This mystical jewel of an English country house would be sure to captivate Robert, so I intended to leave it till last, just before we both went to report to Edward.

I had allotted two days for these visits and when I radio-phoned Romola she told me that it was all arranged and that the CEGB's Construction Manager, Joe Seddon, and his Services Manager, Miles Jackman, would meet us for lunch in Rye at noon on the following day and take us around the power-station after the meal.

We spent the afternoon dowsing and came across the one really co-operative person we had met on the

Marsh so far. I first noticed the thick-set, active man in waders sloshing about in a dyke near some Saxon ruins, and when he hailed us Robert and I went over to speak to him. He was one of those cheery, sun-bronzed people who instantly convey an aura of friendliness.

'Good afternoon,' he said in a foreign accent. 'I haven't seen you before. Are you conservationists?'

I introduced Robert and myself.

'I'm Dr Isadore Cowan,' he said. 'I'm an archaeologist, researching the Saxon sites. There are a lot of their burial grounds on the Marsh. Fascinating place, isn't it? I've been here for the past two months. Gets pretty cold in the winter. Do you know it well?'

'My friend Dr Whiterivers doesn't, but I know it intimately. I've been coming here ever since I was a boy.'

The stocky archaeologist smiled winningly. 'It's all new to me. I'm from Israel. I'm writing a book on the Saxon seawall builders. They came soon after the Romans and kept up the good work. There are some very interesting remains here.'

I played a hunch. 'You probably know some friends of mine in Israel.' I mentioned their names.

Dr Cowan grinned, his deep-set eyes twinkling. 'It really is a ridiculously small world, Professor Fortune! I know *both* Professor Yadin and Dr Bar Lev.' He paused, trying to remember something. 'Aren't you *the* Daniel Fortune who wrote such a good book, *The Magical Rituals of the Ancient Egyptians*? It was absorbing.'

Dr Cowan was full of surprises. I was amazed that he had come across the book and delighted that he liked it. We authors are a vain lot!

'Yes,' I admitted. 'I am.'

Dr Cowan again searched his memory, which

seemed to be prodigious. 'You also wrote a fascinating book about the Nazis,' he said, 'that tied in well with what I have always believed. Those terrible people were up to their nasty pseudo-Aryan ears in the dark rituals.'

'They were, which was the cause of the horrors of the Holocaust. That was undoubtedly the most dreadful mass-sacrifice to the old dark gods in the history of the world.'

'I never thought of parapsychological books as being of interest to archaeologists,' Robert remarked.

Dr Cowan shook his head vigorously, 'Ritual is of prime importance in the study of ancient civilizations. Look at these supposedly Christian ruins. They're part of a pagan long-barrow. This Marsh has a number of such early burial-grounds. Those people were a sheep-rearing community and their fields and saltings produced fine flocks. They kept to the same plan of massive sluices and dykes that the Romans had dug, but they extended the seawall far beyond the original Rhee wall to the west which, by the way, I am certain is far earlier than the Roman invasion. At a guess, I'd say the Belgae, from the Netherlands, built that one. I assure you that when you're researching ancient sites you find that magic rituals are very much a part of it all.'

He chuckled. 'I see that you're dowsing. I saw you cutting fresh hazel-wands. I'm fascinated by that whole area of human abilities. Some of my colleagues use dowsers to check out underground chambers in old ruins. I can do quite well at it myself, but I use a pendulum. Most people think I'm a crank.'

With a broad grin, he pulled a 'Mermet' brass pendule from the pocket of his disreputable old tweed jacket. 'It works well for me,' he said.

'By the way,' I asked him, as an afterthought, 'have you ever been disturbed by any of the locals? Rowdies on motorbikes? That sort of thing?'

Dr Cowan rested on the stout shepherd's crook that he used as a staff for walking and, to judge from the graduations marked on it, as a measuring device as well. 'Funny you should ask me that. Yes, I have. The locals left me alone when they saw my Ministry permit to survey these sites, but a bunch of rowdies tried to harass me. They even tried to burn my tent.'

'Did you go to the police?' I asked.

'No, Professor Fortune, I didn't. With my Israeli army training I can look after myself pretty well. One of the bikers has no front teeth now and I think I broke the other one's arm. He yelled hard enough to wake the dead Saxons. Oddly enough, no one came to see what was up. These Marsh people certainly keep themselves to themselves. The bikers have left me alone since then, but I don't sleep out near the sites anymore. I'm staying in Rye, at the Mermaid. If you'd like a chat I'd be glad to talk some more. We must have a lot of common interests. Good-day, my friends.'

The meaning he put into those sentences implied that he might have something more to tell us. Robert and I both felt good about this man. As Romola would say, he was a *mensch*.

Back in the Winnebago that night Robert said, 'I'll take a bet that archaeology isn't Dr Cowan's only line of work. He's too quick on his feet and too ready to have a go at a set of thugs to be just a scholar. What do you think, Prof?'

'I'm sure you're right! One of the friends I asked him about, Dr Bar Lev, is an old colleague of mine from my MI9 days. He was a Professor of Hebrew Studies at the Sorbonne and he is a very brave man. He was also one of the founders of Mossad, the Israeli Intelligence Service. Did you notice how Dr Cowan smiled when I mentioned his name? I wonder if our good doctor is interested in the same sort of things that we are researching? Though why the Israelis would be interested in drug-smuggling on Romney Marsh beats me.'

Robert shook his head in puzzled amusement. 'Sometimes, Daniel, you really spook me! I picked up the same sort of reaction. One thing's for sure, he'll be on *our* side. Dr Cowan has got a great aura. Pure gold.'

Shortly afterwards, we turned into our respective bunks and slept deeply.

When the dawn filtered through the morning mist we both felt eager to be up and about. It was one of those magical days on the Levels when everything is stirring: the birds, the sheep, and such Marsh folk as are out at that orange-tinted hour.

I've taught Robert a fondness for porridge, eaten properly, with salt, on such a sharp morning.

'It's better than grits, Prof. This Scots porridge is really something. I'm addicted,' he chuckled, his cobalt-blue eyes twinkling with humour. 'I'm going to teach the Navajo how to enjoy this.' He finished off two bowls of that splendid cereal before tucking into his scrambled eggs, brown toast and local honey, washed down with coffee, while I stuck to the strong breakfast tea that Fortnum & Mason do so well.

After breakfast we set off on our trail-bikes and when we reached the sea the spring morning came to its peak. The long swaths of sand glowed in the sunshine and a thousand memories came flooding back.

'It's beautiful,' Robert said, simply.

Inside me, an emotional dam burst. 'Far more than

69

that, the bay itself generates its own forces. Out there on the horizon, beyond the shingle buttress of Dungeness, the water is broken into short, steep seas. But inside the sweep of the bay, low-crested waves roll onto the beaches. On windless days like this, at low tide, the sea seems to caress the sand with probing swirls of sun-warm water, but when the wind rises and the tide is at full flood the tempo quickens. This is the prelude to a gale and the gulls know it. They sweep inland, crying against the rising wind, to shelter among the water-meadows.

'The storm roars in from the west, its fury contained by the narrow straits between Dover and Calais. Wind-whipped into frenzy, the seas take on the grey sheen of steel. The thunder of their pounding shakes the beaches. Charging ranks of spume-topped waves crash against the wall of stone, hurling towers of grey-green water high over the top. Wind and water rise to a deafening crescendo.

'When the tide turns, the gale abates. The wind drops to a keening moan, and finally dies away in a whisper. With the ebb-tide, the waves retreat in seething confusion, like a routed army regrouping its ranks over the horizon. The storm clouds tear apart into moonlit lace. The wet sands gleam with silver light. All that is left to mark the passing of the storm is the smell of brine and the tingle of ozone in the air. A few torn scraps of seaweed litter the sands.'

As I spoke, I had lapsed unconsciously into quoting some lines I had learned by heart. My late wife Patricia had scribbled them in her diary after just such a day and night.

Robert was silent for a moment. 'This place must mean a whole lot to you, Daniel,' he said, with great gentleness.

'It does that,' I blew loudly into my handkerchief. 'Come on, let's go and see the lifeboat.'

My Navajo friend got on well with the lifeboatmen at Dungeness. These fine seamen are a special kind of person, most of them fishermen with a couple of professional engineers to keep that beautiful craft in trim. Their hard, dry hands gripped ours in welcome because instinctively they sensed that we knew about boats and the sea. From many years' close acquaintance with it, both Robert and I have a deep respect for the sea's moods and tantrums. Robert is an expert slalom canoeist and is also much in demand in yacht-racing circles around Santa Barbara and San Diego. He has crewed on one of the beautiful twelve-metre yachts that habitually bring home the America's Cup. That morning interlude when the boatmen proudly showed us over their superb lifeboat was a memorable one. It took me back over forty years.

By eleven o'clock we had left Dungeness and rode easily along the coastal road. We circled around the Ministry of Defence enclosures and past the golden Camber Sands, reaching Rye at a quarter to twelve, in good time for our meeting with Mr Seddon and Mr Jackman from the power-station. For me, Rye is always a pleasure to visit and for Robert it was a revelation. The cobbled slopes of the little port, which rise gently to the summit of the hill that carries the bulk of the town, are lined with small shops and happily untouched buildings. One of the five 'Cinque' ports that once dominated the south-eastern coast of Britain in the thirteenth and fourteenth centuries, the sea has long since left Rye high and sometimes dry, its only access to the English Channel being through the waterways that circle the ancient town. Rye and its smaller twin, Winchelsea, which is only a mile or so down the coast to the west, are two of my favourite spots. These tiny ports have seen much violence over the years, from deadly, flooding storms to raids from the French, which the locals returned with interest.

Cut off from the sea except for short periods at high tide, Rye is the more intriguing of the two towns and retains a magic that is rare in these materialistic days. During the season it caters for the tourists, including the French, who nowadays invade it peacefully, looking for bargains in antiques and local crafts, mainly pottery and painting. It is perched high above the Rother, that strange river which, in the fourteenth century, completely changed its course, cutting off the nearby port of Romney from the sea so that *New* Romney had to be built instead, to service the rich wool-trade. Marvelling, we made our way to the Mermaid Inn, riding our bikes through the arch of the old hostelry and parking them round the back. A few moments later we were welcomed by Mr Seddon, a quiet reserved Northerner, and Miles Jackman, a sturdy manager who exuded calm efficiency. Both men were enthusiasts who loved their work and the construction and engineering of the nuclear reactor on Dungeness in particular. Mrs Seddon, our attractively shy hostess, laughed when I commented on their kindness in inviting us to lunch and agreeing to take us to the power-station.

'Joe and Miles are only too happy to show off their beloved child. Miles came here eighteen years ago, when he had only a hut and a set of plans, and Joe has been hard at it for over eight years, installing the reactors.'

It was a good lunch, with plenty of laughter and interest on both sides. Our hosts didn't ask us why we were interested in their nuclear power-station, but the fact that we *were* interested opened the floodgates to their enthusiasm. I could see why when, on our trail-bikes, we followed their car to the great nest of concrete buildings that houses the pressurized reactors and services the generators.

I can't say that the building struck me as being aesthetically pleasing, but later, at night, from a short distance away, I could see what Joe and Miles meant when they described it as a cathedral of light. Forbidding by day, at night it cheers up the Ness with a sparkle of different coloured lights and glowing arc-lamps.

Both of us noticed that the wildlife seemed to be undisturbed and that seagulls circled the great buildings while many species of wildfowl nested in the water-filled shingle quarries nearby. Whatever was disturbing the Marsh, it wasn't caused directly by this nuclear complex or the wildlife would have been affected.

Part of the Marsh is reserved as a bird-sanctuary. On the gravel spit of Dungeness lies one of the nesting sites for England's gulls, who come from all over the country to this desolate spot. Safe in the cover of the shingle banks, among the scattered clumps of yellow gorse, thousands of seabirds bring their next generation into the world.

North of the Military Canal, the bird-life is confined to the conventional pattern of starlings and thrushes, magpies and crows, wood pigeons and blackbirds, sparrows and finches in abundance.

South, from the weed-choked Canal to as far as the seawall, lies the domain of the true marsh birds. Redshanks and sedge warblers and herons, with the occasional flashing glimpse of the blue kingfisher.

Many birds fly in from Europe and the Arctic Circle

to join the waterfowl population of mallard and moorhen, strutting guinea-fowl and tiny snipe. I remember one terrible day in the twenties when I stood, a horror-struck little boy of six, helplessly watching the pitiful plight of thousands of oil-soaked guillemots and gannets strewn dying along the Folkestone beaches, tragic victims of a careless tanker.

The skies above the Marsh are always filled with circling birds, just as the sea currents around Dungeness teem with fish. The ethos of the Marsh attracts far more than human visitors.

To be fair, the power-station wasn't operating at full strength. The first 'A' Station Reactor had come on stream in 1965, amid the usual protests from the anti-nuclear lobby, who, apparently, would rather see six conventional power stations belching out fumes and other sulphurous and hydrocarbonate by-products of oil- or coal-firing than have one nuclear power-plant whose system is safely enclosed and fumeless.

As Joe Seddon explained it to us, 'That was an earlier form of nuclear reactor, a Magnox. Dungeness 'B' was the first power-station to be ordered under the government's *second* nuclear power programme and is an advanced gas-cooled reactor. It first produced power for the national grid in 1983 but is not yet fully commissioned and is currently shut down for its statutory bi-annual inspection.'

Being a scientifically-trained person, I am not naturally part of the anti-nuclear lobby, but I certainly want to know how *safe* these nuclear power-plants can be made. That is plain common sense. We would all be happier if we could utilize some other way to provide the huge amounts of power that we need to run our complex civilization but, so far, attempts to harness the sun or the forces of wind and tide and the geothermal energies locked inside our planet haven't produced anywhere near the power that we require. It's a case of Hobson's choice.

That afternoon, nuclear engineers were actually loading the fuel elements into the 'B' reactor when we arrived. We stood in a gallery high above the top of the reactor's pressure vessel, facing the tall, superbly engineered loading tower that quietly moves over the pressurized reactor cores to extract the long core-elements from their graphite sheaths. The lofty proportions of this tall-windowed building reminded me of the huge pre-war Cardington airship hangar, built to contain Zeppelins. It had about it a strong clinical feeling, as though every part of it had been meticulously sterilized.

Dominating the busy scene on the floor below was that massively engineered moving gantry, a giant pressurized servicing robot straight out of science fiction. It looked like the armoured fighting citadel of a dreadnought battleship, radiating a sense of purpose and contained power. It was a breath-catching example of gigantic precision engineering, a remarkable piece of safety equipment, and an awe-inspiring glimpse of the twenty-first century. That plant and its pressure-vessels have been very carefully thought out, from the massive pre-stressed concrete shielding of the huge stainless-steel-capped pressure vessel to the stringently inspected and maintained complex of stainless steel piping which makes up the veins and arteries of the great reactor. From the heat exchangers to the massive turbines, this is engineering at its best, and I felt confident that Joe Seddon, Miles Jackman and their teams knew exactly what they were doing and, what is more, were doing it with total dedication.

When Robert and I left, at the end of a fascinating

afternoon, we felt that we had made more friends. Neither of us had any doubt that the Dungeness nuclear power-station posed no threat to the welfare of the Marsh. However, there was still the matter of the long overhead power lines that stretch from the nuclear complex right across the marshes, and the theoretical possibility that living close to these powerful lines of electrical force might be disturbing. However, we had dowsed large areas of the Marsh where there were no power lines but where the ethos had nevertheless been altered in some subtle way, so we dismissed the Dungeness nuclear complex and its power lines as possible causes of the Marsh's troubles.

There remained the wildlife park at Port Lympne. Could that be the source of the animal mutilations which Edward had been so hesitant to tell me about? Some wild animal could possibly have escaped or – a sinister thought – could have been let out *deliberately*; but then no wild animal, except a dangerously aberrated human, would have not only disembowelled another animal but also arranged its steaming entrails in a complex ritual pattern. Apparently some of the remains resembled the hideous mutilations performed by the infamous Jack the Ripper at the end of the last century.

Whereas the Dungeness nuclear reactors had impressed Robert and me with their massive engineering and sense of as yet unleashed power, Port Lympne, with its superb, matured-brick proportions, perfect landscaping and breathtaking views of the whole of the Romney Marsh, left us with an equally lasting impression, but this time it was one of peace and tranquillity. The gardens themselves are laid out with the consummate skill of some twentieth-century Capability Brown, their terraces and sweeping lawns kept scrupulously ordered by a dedicated team of landscape gardeners. One section is set out in the form of a giant chess-board, and the marvellous symmetry of the tall box-hedges, the dense yews and cypress groves complete the magic.

'Winston Churchill was a frequent guest of Sir Philip Sassoon and often painted here,' I told Robert. 'Several of his early works are hung on the walls. Noël Coward, whose own country house was close by along the escarpment, often visited. Rex Whistler, the painter and muralist whose work decorates the restaurant walls at the Tate Gallery, painted the magnificent 'tent-room', filling it with magical symbols. Other visitors included Charles Chaplin and Aircraftsman Shaw, better known as Lawrence of Arabia. In fact, during Sir Philip's tenure, royalty, great beauties, writers, scientists, actors, musicians, and statesmen visited the house, making it a real Shangri-la.

'My father often dined here and once I came to a children's party for the offspring of the pilots and their air-minded families who gathered at Lympne Airfield before the war for the Folkestone Air Races. I was a fan of Sir Philip Sassoon, who at that time was the Under-Secretary for Air and an ardent supporter of the Royal Air Force and its Naval equivalent, the Fleet Air Arm. He was an extraordinary man from a wealthy Parsee family and had won a well-deserved place in honest political life when he became personal private secretary to Lloyd George.'

Unfortunately, the present owner, John Aspinall, was not available on the day of our visit. He is a very busy man, dividing his life between his famous London club and his two private wildlife parks, at Port Lympne and Canterbury. Instead we chatted with the friendly management and got a good idea of the layout of the

250-acre park. The high chainlink fences seemed to us to ensure the secure enclosure of the animals roaming about inside the acres of downland. Certainly it all looked safe enough and Robert and I agreed that there was no way the animals could be involved in the general feeling of subliminal fear that seemed to stalk the Marsh.

We paused to admire the Rex Whistler Room, restored by John Aspinall to its former magnificence. 'Just look at those symbols, Robert! The symbolism of this great mural is unmistakable. Port Lympne is a kind of mystical Arcadia, with its shaded groves and magical symbols such as the statue of Hermes Pan in that "tree circle" of cypresses outside the east-front façade.'

The Navajo grinned, his hawk-like features lighting up like a cheerful bird of prey. 'Goddammit, Prof, you're a persuasive talker. What you are saying is that this whole place, and especially this room, is a kind of magical generator of light!'

'Precisely, Robert!'

'Agreed, one hundred per cent. It is a beautiful house and the marvellous grounds radiate peace. I can see why John Aspinall has spent a fortune on restoring it. It glows with great vibes. I'm sure you've got a point about its original owner. Sir Philip Sassoon, or whoever was responsible for all this beauty, has to have known a whole lot about the leys. Magically, psychologically, and even materially, this house is a beacon of light. I'll buy your theory, Prof. Sir Philip was a remarkable white magician, on the side of the angels. One thing is for sure.'

'What's that, Robert?'

'John Aspinall is certainly not a Companion of Chaos. The positive vibes coming from this house and its wonderful grounds tell us that.'

So we completed our survey of the ethos and the atmosphere of the Romney Marsh. We hadn't learned much, from an *exoteric* point of view, but *esoterically* we now knew that Edward was right. There was something dreadfully wrong with the ethos of the leys and it looked as though the atmosphere of unease and the subtle cloak of fear that hung over the marshes like a shroud were being deliberately engendered.

We were due to meet Edward at Tolsford Manor on the following morning. A note from the Squire had confirmed this arrangement. It said: 'Deborah is up to her eyes in the local gymkhana, all day. Come here tomorrow and have lunch with me. I'm anxious to know what you have found out so far.'

We filled in the rest of the day with a brief tour of Lympne Castle. This was the former home of the Beecham family, where Sir Thomas Beecham had once lived. Robert found this impressive stone fortress which dominates the Marsh below as fascinating as Port Lympne.

'It's haunted,' he declared. 'I can feel it!'

'Yes, it is disturbed. A Roman soldier, a priest and, strangest of all, a terrifying apparition of an eagle, with a skull for its head, have all been seen many times. Lady Beecham saw them all, and many other people have as well.'

The castle was built about eight hundred years ago, above the ruins of the Roman fort at Studfall, the remains of which can be seen below. Like the Roman fortification, the castle guarded part of the Marsh against attacks from the sea. There was a small Roman port below, as well, where the Hythe Military Canal now flows. Portus Limenis it was called and Roman galleys used it, coming right up to the base of the downs at high tide. Once the Romans had mastered the Channel tides, which were so different from their own near-tideless Mediterranean, they learned to use them well.

Looking out from the Keep over the lichen-covered limestone walls of Lympne Castle, we saw a sweeping panorama of the whole spread of the Romney Marsh, stretching from east to west till it disappeared into the sea mists that veiled the tip of Dungeness. We could trace the magical pattern of reeded saltings, the broad acres of rich pasturage and the rape-planted fields, intersected by the intricate maze of dykes, sluices and ditches.

It is a watershed of nature and has its own magic. A moment comes, on a lazy spring day, when the Marsh falls silent. In the stillness, nature pauses to catch her breath. The sea-breeze dies down to a sigh. The reeds cease their rustling chatter. For a space no birds cross the skyline; no gulls cry in their circling flight. The sheep stand alert beside their sleeping lambs. Nothing stirs on the Marsh in the mist of silence. That is the time to lie asprawl in the thick web of the downland grass. Press back against the warm chalk. Look up at the silver-blue vault and watch the cloud-stippled sky wheel overhead. For a magic moment you feel the earth turn beneath you and sense the infinity of space. Giddy with awe you clutch the reassuring clumps of rich grass around you. Arms outstretched, you ride the undulating back of the great green dragon of the downs.

Smoke was rising lazily on that warm, windless afternoon, hovering over the spires and towers of the ancient churches, while on the fog-bound horizon the long seawall dominated the scene with the sheer power of its purpose in holding back the ever-hungry sea from submerging these smiling lands.

Robert sighed at the beauty of the scene, taking in every distant detail. 'I can see now why you and Sir Edward are in love with these marshes. I confess I wasn't too impressed when I first saw them, but it soon gets into your bloodstream. There's so much goddamn history packed into such a small area. What size is it, Daniel?'

'About twenty miles long and ten miles wide, at its broadest part. The Romney Marsh teems with the subtle forces of past, present and future. It encapsulates the subliminal life of the ethos of this part of England. John Davidson, the poet, a contemporary of Swinburne, captured this feeling in his poem dedicated to the Romney Marsh. I learned some of it from Edward:

> 'As I went down to Dymchurch Wall,
> I heard the South sing o'er the land;
> I saw the yellow sunlight fall
> On knolls where Norman churches stand
>
> 'As I came up from Dymchurch Wall,
> I saw above the Downs' low crest,
> The crimson brands of sunset fall,
> Flicker and fade from out the West.
>
> 'Night sank: like flakes of silver fire
> The stars in one great shower came down;
> Shrill blew the wind; and shrill the wire
> Rang out from Hythe to Romney Town.

'Davidson was referring to the new telegraph wires that sang so eerily in the sea breezes.

'If a few miles of telegraph wires could so change the appearance and feeling of the Marsh, the relentless march of power pylons, bisecting the Levels, would have a far greater psychological effect. But what we're dealing with here is even more serious, the work of

81

black magicians, men and possibly women of power deliberately manipulating the dark forces of terror to carry out their plans. Smuggled drugs must be their richest currency, worth millions in street value for a comparatively small outlay. I believe that Dr Isadore Cowan might be able to help us. I'm sure that he is working for Israeli Intelligence. Meanwhile, tomorrow we report our findings to Edward.'

We got up early to face a grey day of drizzle, which dissolved into a mist once the sun rose towards the zenith. Tolsford Manor was only a few minutes away, just past the site of the forthcoming local gymkhana, set in a large field on the top of the downland. I told Robert that I intended to make a quick visit to where Deborah would, most probably, be overseeing the fences for the showjumping events.

'I want to take a look at her, without her seeing me. She doesn't know you, so there is no need for you to keep a low profile.'

Keeping discreetly in the background of trees while my colleague parked his bike and became an interested spectator, I used my binoculars and soon spotted Deborah. She hadn't altered in the few years since I had last seen her. Tall, slim and as coolly efficient as ever, she was evidently in charge of the proceedings. Her short, blond hair was set off perfectly by her riding 'hard-hat', and her figure was accentuated by the cut of her close-fitting breeches and riding boots. Deborah Tolsford looked every poised inch the Squire's beautiful daughter and an expert horsewoman.

I also spotted the gaggle of heroine-worshipping Pony Club girls, in their peaked caps, jackets and ties and jodhpurs; particularly one pretty lass who was acting as Deborah's personal groom. The wide-eyed look of teenage adoration on her fresh, freckled face spelt 'schoolgirl crush' to anyone who recognized the symptoms. What disturbed me was Deborah's evident enjoyment of the girl's infatuation.

I saw my goddaughter hold the pretty teenager close to her and stroke her long, pony-tail hair with an inviting smile that had me wondering if Deborah had lesbian tendencies. The little Pony Club groom was obviously a pliant partner in these subtle overtures, pressing herself tightly against her heroine's boyish body.

I happened to catch this disturbing interlude taking place behind the show-ring marquee, and I felt annoyed at being an involuntary voyeur of what could just as easily be construed as an innocent manifestation of the camaraderie of the show-ring.

I thought again about the estrangement between Edward and his daughter. My friend had also told me he was concerned that, at the age of thirty, his daughter did not seem to enjoy a normal relationship with male friends. However, it was not my concern, except as a godparent, whatever Deborah's sexual preferences might be. Catching Robert's eye, I motioned him to rejoin me as Deborah mounted her champion showjumper and rode out through the starting gate. She looked quite magnificent. Certainly, my colleague seemed to think so.

He watched in open admiration as she completed a clear round of the hurdles, fences, postern-gate and walls that faced her. Mount and rider moved as one entity in the joy of shared physical effort as they easily cleared the jumps. Robert was truly smitten by his first glimpse of Squire Tolsford's daughter. I couldn't recall seeing my colleague so enthusiastic about any girl before.

Like most North American Indians, he is reticent about his private life and the fact that he plays it cool is an irresistible attraction to the opposite sex. However, he is not a chauvinist, any more than I am. We both revere women, when they deserve to be so treated.

I found it odd that, with his ultra-sensitive instincts, Robert had not picked up what I had sensed in my goddaughter, and hoped that he would prove me wrong.

Five minutes later, we were at Tolsford Manor, which had been built originally about the same date as Bateman's and then, after a fire, rebuilt in Georgian style. The house is most appealing and many generations of Tolsfords have left their mark on its lovely proportions.

Edward's plump, motherly housekeeper, Mrs Waverley, an old friend of mine, greeted us and showed us into the large, elegant oak-panelled drawing-room. I was shocked to see that Edward was sitting in a wheelchair.

He waved aside my concern. 'Don't look so alarmed, Daniel. I crocked my ankle doing a bit of gardening. This is only temporary. It's good to see you both. You must be Dr Whiterivers. I'm delighted to meet you. Daniel has told me about you. Isn't Dr Kobrak with you?'

'No sir,' Robert said as they shook hands. 'The Professor insisted that Romola stayed out of the preliminary survey, so she is still in Dorset. She'll be joining us soon.'

'I see. Well, Daniel, what have you found out so far? Was I right?'

'Unfortunately, yes. There is something very nasty going on, and I'm sure you're correct in your assessment that these mysterious Companions of Chaos are behind it all.'

Edward looked even more worried than he had done on his dramatic visit to Wessex. 'I've prayed that I was wrong,' he said, his voice breaking with emotion. 'Can't anything be done?'

He was starting to wheeze heavily with the nervous strain and once more over-employed his inhaler to abort the asthmatic attack.

'Easy with that aerosol!' I cautioned as we waited for him to get his breath. 'Just calm down, Edward, and we'll tell you what we have found out.'

Sitting comfortably in that elegant drawing-room, we related what had occurred in our investigations and exonerated both the nuclear power-station and John Aspinall's wildlife park.

I quickly outlined our dowsing procedures, as they had once been taught me by my friend Colin Bloy of Brighton, a scholarly protagonist of 'ley' theories, and added, 'Every landscape generates its own atmosphere, as we know only too well in the case of the Marsh. Your instincts told you that certain influences had been at work, terrorizing the area. All we had to do was to pinpoint where these actions had affected the ethos of the Levels, to find the negative centres of force.'

My friend hung on every word as I went on, 'Colin has done some similar research on the Templar sites around south-eastern England. He showed me how these knightly ritual magicians of the twelfth and thirteenth centuries learned to manipulate the ethos by constructing abbeys, fermes, granges and manors, all laid out to precise formulae and using étangs (ditches) and other waterways as their boundaries, to channel the power.

'Apparently, the Templar system was based on a deep knowledge of earth-magic, and depended on the

85

exact pinpointing of springs, holy wells and other sources of underground water. Their knowledge, which was derived from the "gnosis" of the ancient civilizations, such as the Egyptians, Chaldeans, Greeks and Chinese before them, was part of the arcane wisdom. The secrets are contained in the system of "ritual-manipulation" of these subtle forces within the landscape. The art of earth-magic is still very much alive.'

'Then mineral masses must affect such forces,' observed Edward. 'How could these be manipulated to alter the atmosphere of a large area?'

'In ancient Britain stone-circles, tumuli, dolmens, megaliths and other massive mineral structures were ritually built to act as accumulators and condensers of these forces,' I explained. 'Nowadays your Companions of Chaos must know a great deal about the ritual methods of altering these natural lines of force which exist in the form of this great invisible grid extending over and under the surface of the whole earth.

'By performing certain rituals during the appropriate seasons, mainly at the equinoxes and the solstices, these adepts have apparently altered the ethos of the Marsh. It may seem crazy, but similar methods were used on a grand scale by the top Nazis to manipulate Germany during the twenties and thirties; by Mussolini, in Italy during the Fascist regime, and by every accomplished adept since the ancient civilizations first discovered the secrets of psycho-social manipulation by ritual means. The whole operation is really one of forcefully applied mass-psychology.

'By performing acts of terror and by ritually "charging" the ancient sites with the negative forces of fear and then letting it be known that this had been done, a coven of modern adepts have laid down a similar curtain of fear in this area. It works for evil in

86

the same way that the cathedrals and churches of the Christian era – all sited on the existing pagan centres of worship – dominate the region by ritual means, by psychologically changing the area's ethos. It's like any large-scale military operation, in which you take the high ground in order to dominate the scene of the action.'

Edward indicated that he followed my reasoning as I went on, 'Just as the Templars, like the Cathars and other gnostic groups before them, utilized the knowledge of their magical predecessors to manipulate the natural forces of the areas which they intended to subjugate to their regime, in this present situation, knowledgeable adepts have been at work, terrorizing the countryside by psychological methods such as their use of the bike-gangs, ritual animal mutilations, and their savage desecration of the old country churchyards.'

I coughed and Robert continued our report. 'We have also found indications, by dowsing, that they have actually succeeded in altering the layout of the earth forces generated by the great chalk escarpment backing the Marsh, by the natural springs, by holy wells and by the underground water systems of the Levels. We both believe that these Companions of Chaos have deliberately generated an ethos of chaos which enables them to carry out their work of drug smuggling undisturbed. Presumably, Sir Edward, their motive is to gain power over the region to make huge sums of money.'

We must have taken over an hour to tell him, in detail, these impressions of our first days on the Marsh, and we were just finishing the grim report when we were interrupted by one of the most savage thunderstorms I have ever experienced. The skies teemed down, with giant hail and a rainstorm of unparalleled fury. Lightning flashed incessantly and the atmosphere quickly changed from a subtle sense of menace to one of alarmed awareness of the frightening power of the earth's primeval forces.

The three of us are normally undisturbed by thunderstorms, unless we happen to be caught out in the open, but the ferocity of the wind was so unexpected that our nerves were set on edge. The sudden storm also caused an awkward change of circumstance. Edward had planned our meeting to coincide with Deborah's absence at the final rehearsal for the gymkhana. But now that event was being washed out by the thunderstorm and his daughter returned home unexpectedly.

Before the full possibilities of the situation had dawned upon any of us, Deborah Tolsford arrived at the Manor, drenched to the skin. She was badly upset, while we had been too engrossed in our discussion and the savage progress of the storm to notice her arrival.

Suddenly, she was standing in the doorway. 'Jesus Christ, Daniel,' she burst out angrily. 'Why the hell didn't you let me know that you were coming. Daddy's not a well man and your coming here is a bloody cheek!'

Poor Edward was very upset, as much by Deborah's startling rudeness to me as by the turn of events that made us three look like guilty conspirators.

'Deborah, how dare you talk to Daniel like that! Apologize at once!'

'I'm sorry, Daddy, but he's got no right to come barging in, unannounced. He damn well knows you're not well. Look at you — you're trembling.'

She turned to me before going to comfort her father. Her tone was icy. 'I'd appreciate it, Daniel, if you took your friend with you and left *now*. I'll ring for the doctor. I'm nearly out of my mind about my father's health and now look what you've done to him.' Her tirade suddenly stopped. 'Oh God, Daddy, are you all right?'

Edward, choking, was trying to rise from his wheelchair, an intense attack of asthma seizing him in its grip.

Terrified, Deborah screamed and tried to reach her father. His face became drained of blood and an awful gasping wheeze rattled in his throat. Robert and I were closest to him and both of us sprang forward to catch him as his bulging eyes rolled up and he collapsed back into his wheelchair, upsetting it with a crash.

'Deborah,' I shouted at my goddaughter, who was screaming hysterically, 'shut up or get out! Robert, phone for an ambulance! We need oxygen right away. For Christ's sake, keep that bloody girl quiet!'

As I rapped out these orders, I was examining my stricken friend and loosening his clothing. As I feared, it was a massive coronary.

My medical training automatically took over as I carried out the emergency procedures. But Edward's blue-lipped and contorted features told me the whole story. His breathing suddenly ceased and he suffered a total cardiac arrest.

Having phoned for the ambulance, Robert now held the sobbing Deborah back from her dying father, while I banged Edward's chest as hard as I could between my applications of mouth-to-mouth resuscitation.

Deborah unexpectedly went limp in Robert's restraining arms and would have slumped to the floor if my friend hadn't effortlessly picked her up and gently put her down on the sofa. During these few moments, when everything had suddenly turned into tragedy, I used every technique I knew to avert Edward's death.

'Get my medical bag, Robert. It's in the near-side

pannier of my bike,' I shouted, while I applied artificial respiration.

Robert was back in under a minute with that all-important medical kit. I took out a phial of methyl-nitrate and broke it under Edward's nose; filled a long-needled, disposable syringe with adrenalin and plunged it through Edward's chest, straight into the silent heart muscles. Without pausing, I went back to external heart massage, pressing as hard as I dared on my patient's ribcage while I anxiously scanned his agonized face.

After what seemed an age but could only have been a couple of minutes, my stethoscope picked up the first faint heartbeats as Edward started to respond. Robert took over the oral resuscitation while I continued with the pounding external chest massage. The miracle was happening. Edward was starting to respond; at first breathing faintly and then with a gasping intensity. We both supported him, semi-upright, to give him as much ease as possible, while we did everything we could until an ambulance arrived with the oxygen.

'How is he? Will Daddy make it, Daniel?' Deborah's pitifully contrite voice quietly implored me and, for the first time since the tragic emergency had developed, I was able to pay attention to my goddaughter, who had fallen on her knees beside me.

I put my arms round her and held her close.

'Oh God, what have I done?' Deborah said in an agony of remorse. 'Thank you, Daniel. You've saved his life. I forgot that you are a doctor. Please forgive my stupidity. I don't know what came over me. Oh Christ, Daniel, make him well.'

Her last three words reminded me of her when she was the little girl who had become a surrogate child to me in place of my own lost boy.

We comforted each other and waited for the

90

ambulance. Robert was calm and reassuring, with all the caring love of this big man evident in the gentle, crooning chant that he murmured as he held Edward in his arms.

All the underlying tension of the Tolsford family's long period of fear had at last come to this terrifying climax and had evaporated in the tears in Deborah's eyes. Whether death could be held at bay or not, the Tolsfords were reunited in love. Her former hostile attitude and the impressions that I had picked up so reluctantly at the gymkhana had also melted away in the deeply loving concern that had transformed Deborah into the girl of whom I was so fond.

CHAPTER 5

A Degree of Darkness

Edward's breathing was still irregular but was nearer to normal than I had hoped when, at last, the ambulance arrived with the oxygen.

It had raced over from Hythe. Folkestone and Ashford both have excellent hospitals and the driver and his assistant were experienced professionals. They immediately summed up the situation and decided on Ashford as the safest bet because it was fractionally nearer. Edward was now breathing oxygen and, under the transparent mask, I was relieved to see the blueness of his lips changing to a more normal colour.

'I'll go with you,' I said, more as a statement than a request.

'Glad to have you with us, doctor. The telephone operator said you were in attendance. Are you the family physician, sir?' the grey-haired driver asked.

'No, just a friend. I'm thankful I was here when the cardiac arrest occurred.'

I turned to my colleague, 'You stay here with Deborah, Robert. We must get Edward into intensive care right away.'

'I'm coming with you, Daniel. Please!' Deborah's eyes were pathetically pleading.

'OK, Miss.' The driver was in charge. 'But come on. Every minute counts.'

Moments later, we were on our way.

In the casualty department, an efficient young registrar took over and my patient was rushed into intensive care. Deborah and I waited miserably that long, rain-soaked afternoon as the consultant cardiologist fought for Edward's life.

At six o'clock that evening, in spite of everything the surgeon and the dedicated nursing staff could do, Sir Edward Tolsford, last baronet in his family, died. The battle against the dark forces of the Companions of Chaos had begun and the first tragic casualty was on our side.

Deborah was in the numb state of grief that nature provides when tears have washed away the shock of sudden loss. Dry-eyed, my goddaughter leaned over her dead father and kissed his forehead. She thanked everyone for their efforts and sat silently with me until the taxi arrived. She had not been with her father at the moment of death. It would have been pointless to allow her to be part of that grim tableau, surrounded by the electronic gadgetry of the complex life-support system, and I had stayed with her in the common-room, trying to comfort the girl, who cuddled up to me as closely as a child.

After the savage battle for Edward's life, however, the cardiologist took me aside. 'Sir Edward regained consciousness, momentarily,' he said, 'and mumbled a few words. I think I made them out correctly. They might be of significance.'

He handed me a piece of paper on which he had written: 'Marsden – Marsden – Deborah – Mary – love.'

Apparently, Edward was thinking about his late wife and his daughter and for some reason was also referring to the Royal Marsden Hospital in London, where Mary had died of cancer. Knowing the generous donation that he had made to the Marsden on that sad occasion, it was possible that Edward was trying to say that he wished to donate a further sum.

Back at the Manor, Deborah thanked Robert charmingly for his help and kindness and again unreservedly apologized. 'It was unforgivable of me,' she said.

'Please forget about it,' Robert replied. 'You were very worried about your father's health. Look, Miss Tolsford, it doesn't matter a bit that you got upset, with the terrific storm and us being here so unexpectedly.'

'Please call me Deborah.'

My tall colleague towered over my goddaughter, his fine eyes looking down at her drawn face. 'If there is anything I can do?' he continued gently. 'Deborah, I feel that your father is at peace and, like Daniel, I believe in life beyond death. I know it doesn't help at the moment. I just wanted you to know that I believe in the survival of the human entity.'

Her hazel eyes, which only a few hours earlier had flashed with anger, were now glowing softly. She smiled wanly at the look of concern on my colleague's handsome face. 'That's kind of you, Robert. As a Christian, I also believe in life after death.'

Robert smiled wryly, 'I'm a Navajo – not a Christian. My mother was an Irish Catholic but now, like me, she believes in the natural processes of Life and Death. The Navajo believe in God. I was brought up as a pagan by the medicine men of my people as much as I was indoctrinated as a Christian at school. We believe in a life after this one, not an *after*life but a co-existent life: before, now, and beyond death.'

He hesitated. 'I don't want to bore you with my beliefs at this time, you must be exhausted.'

'Please don't think that. I'm most interested in what you say, but I am very tired, so, if you'll both excuse me, I'll go up to my room. Goodnight, dear Daniel, you've been – you've *both* been – wonderful.'

She kissed me goodnight.

We sat up till after midnight, drinking tea. I had given Deborah a tranquillizer and a sleeping pill to ensure that she would get a good night's rest but neither of us felt sleepy enough to go to bed in the spare rooms in the west wing which my goddaughter had invited us to use. Originally she had intended having two of her friends from the gymkhana to stay, so the beds were already made up.

Robert seldom drinks hard liquor, not because he is a health fanatic, nor is he an alcoholic, but simply because, as he says, 'Fire-water, which is what the movie Westerns love to call it, has long been a weakness in my people. My own father is an example. We have little resistance to its effects. This weakness was ruthlessly exploited by the white settlers, and is the main reason, apart from superior numbers and weaponry, why they won their wars against us with such dreadful loss of life. I don't like hard liquor, though I do appreciate a glass of good wine with a meal, and an ice-cold beer on a hot day is great! I won't give those weak genes a chance by tempting Providence with the hard stuff, as my other ancestors, the Irish, call it. Mother, on the other hand, can drink most men under the bar; but she now prefers strong tea, brewed on the hob. She says that the caffeine in it gives her all the stimulants she needs and that there are no more hangovers.'

We discussed the significance of the day's tragic events and tried to formulate a new plan of action.

'We can't do anything until after the funeral, Robert. I hope we can hold that as soon as possible. As Sir Edward was a local dignitary and a squire, protocol will require a more public funeral than Deborah would want. I'll ask the vicar at Lympne to help me with the arrangements and then we can take some of the weight from her shoulders. She has been running the Manor for years by herself, but we can help a lot.'

Robert nodded his agreement as I continued, 'She told me that her father had been so upset when her mother died that his asthma became chronic. He withdrew from an active role in country life and started to brood.

'On these marshes a squire who is also a farmer has more to do than a City businessman. After Mary's death, Edward leased out most of his land to tenant farmers such as our present landlord, Eli Whitgift. Deborah has been running the whole shebang ever since. That's why she gave up her showjumping career, otherwise she would have been in this year's Olympic team.'

Robert nodded sympathetically. 'I guessed that. Jeez! That girl can really ride. She flies over those jumps like an angel. OK. What do we do now? It looks as though the whole reason for your investigation went with Sir Edward's death.'

'On the contrary,' I said. 'The same darkness hangs over the Marsh, all the more so since he died.'

I paused, deliberately, 'We've got to protect his daughter. I know she'll cope with everything practical but she desperately needs help with this other dreadful business.' I hesitated awkwardly. 'We know that her father suspected Deborah of being involved with these Companions of Chaos. *You* even thought that she might have been the informer who put these people on to us.'

'I certainly said those things. But now that I've met her, I can't buy that any more.' His eyes softened, 'She is such a beautiful girl. There's no way that she can be mixed up in all this mumbo-jumbo. She's spunky all right! She showed that when she was angry, but she's

humble enough to apologize. I like that in a woman. . .
I see what you mean. We can't turn back now. We've
got to keep on until we root out all this garbage.'

It was apparent to me that my friend was well and
truly hooked, and I was sure the feeling was becoming
mutual.

As I lay in bed in the guest room, Edward's last words
again came to mind and I wondered why his thoughts
had been of the Royal Marsden Hospital. Perhaps the
environment of the intensive care unit could have made
a mental link between the death-beds of both his late
wife and himself.

In spite of everything, all three of us slept well that
night and it was past nine o'clock before we woke. Mrs
Waverley had already heard the news from local gossip
and dutifully wept in sympathy. She obviously meant
the nice things that she said about the late Squire, and
she provided us with a good breakfast, which, as she
pointed out, we all needed if we were to face the day.

I was still reluctant to use the Tolsford phone in case
it might be tapped, a relic of my earlier days in
Intelligence, so I rode my trail-bike down to the
Winnebago and used my radio-telephone to contact
Romola.

Her first words were surprising, 'Daniel! Are you all
right? I tried to contact you all day yesterday and early
this morning. I picked up that there was something
terribly wrong –' She paused, her voice tense. 'There's
been a death, hasn't there?'

I should have known that she would have sensed the
turn of events. 'Edward died last night, after a cardiac
arrest. I didn't want you to be worried, so I didn't
phone you. You've picked it up anyway. Romola, I've
decided to bring you down here. I'm going to ask

100

Deborah if you can stay at the Manor. You'll like her, you're about the same age and she needs someone like you at this time, to help her over the worst of the hurdles that face her now that her father is dead. I didn't want to involve you directly, but we badly need you here.'

Romola was delighted.

'I also want you to contact Terence Naylor,' I continued, 'at Special Branch. Ask him if he has any information on an Israeli, Dr Isadore Cowan, an archaeologist. I have a feeling that he has something to do with the Israeli Intelligence Service. Also, tell Naylor there's smuggling going on around the Marsh and I need the name of a *retired* Customs and Excise man living near these parts, in either Folkestone or Dover. They usually retire near to the airports or harbours where they've been working, so there must be some around here.'

'Why retired? Won't a serving Customs officer do?' Romola asked.

'The retired ones might give me the sort of information I need, if it doesn't contravene the Official Secrets Act. Serving Excise men are very close-mouthed about their job. Of course, Terence will have to get me security clearance so that I can have full co-operation, but a word from Special Branch should do the trick. Incidentally, ask him if he has anything on a motor-bike-gang operating in this area.'

'Certainly. Do you want him to get you special co-operation from the local constabulary?'

'I don't think that would be a good idea at the moment. If I establish an official link with the local police, the Marsh folk will soon get to know about it and they're unco-operative enough already. I'm sure they'd clam right up.'

'When can I come down, Daniel?' Romola sounded as excited as a schoolgirl.

'I really don't like to bring you into this business, because it is dangerous and distressingly nasty, but I've got no choice. Please come as soon as possible.'

'Good!' said Romola gleefully.

'Deborah needs you, as a friend, and I want someone I can trust near her, day and night. I also want you to "remote-view" some places down here.' I thought for a moment. 'How about the day after tomorrow? Does that give you enough time to get ready?'

'Of course I can get myself organized by then. Daniel,' she paused meaningfully, 'I do miss you so much.'

'That's settled. I'll meet you at Folkestone Central; you can catch a fast train from Charing Cross at ten o'clock.'

'Take care, Daniel. I – I mean *we* love you very much. Don't take any chances.'

The funeral was fixed for Thursday and, at Deborah's suggestion, the service was to be conducted by the Reverend James Maitland, DSO, RN (Retd), the chaplain whom both Edward and I had known at Dartmouth and later on *Ark Royal*. We had enjoyed a long-standing friendship with this brave man and with him in charge we could give Edward a funeral service that he would have wanted, a Naval service even though he would not be buried at sea.

The Tolsford family vault lies in the grounds of the beautiful church at Lympne, overlooking Edward's beloved marshes. His daughter wanted her father buried there. Although Edward's soul no longer inhabited his body, I was sure that my friend would somehow help us fight the darkness from his new life beyond death.

102

When I told Deborah about Romola coming down, she immediately offered her the hospitality of Tolsford Manor. She welcomed the suggestion that my assistant could help her with the arrangements which her father's death would entail. 'That's very sweet of you both,' she said gratefully.

'You'll like her. She's a lovely person and she plays the piano beautifully.'

'That's marvellous. Daddy loved musical evenings. As you know, Mummy played well, especially Chopin. The Steinway hasn't been played properly since she died. Daddy wouldn't let anyone play it after that but, funny man, he always kept it tuned.'

I knew that she would benefit greatly by Romola's presence, and I was damn sure I would!

I returned to the Winnebago that night and again radio-telephoned Romola. She already had the information I required.

'I checked with Terence Naylor. He says you were right about Dr Cowan. He has been with Mossad and possibly still is. Terence says he's not sure what Cowan is doing right now but says that he is certain it's all right, as far as Special Branch is concerned. He told me he had worked with him before, investigating possible Arab terrorist attacks on Lord Sieff, the chairman of Marks and Spencer. He had nothing on any bike-gangs but will contact Folkestone police. He sends his best wishes and says you are to be careful. Oh, Daniel, I can't wait to be with you. All this business sounds so dangerous. I do so worry about you.' Her voice was full of concern.

'I'm fine, Romola. What about the retired Customs officer?'

'He's found you one who lives in Hythe; that's

practically next door, isn't it?'

'It is. Well done.'

'He's a good friend of Terence's. He used to cover both Folkestone and Dover harbours. His name is Arnold Bell and he now lives over his own antique shop in the High Street. He specializes in "nautical byones", whatever they are. Terence is ringing him to give you a glowing reference and to tell him that you will be contacting him. Anything else, Daniel?'

'No thank you. I'll see you the day after tomorrow. I'll probably be seeing Bell before then. Oh, and Romola. . .'

'Yes, Daniel?'

'Bring a mack and your wellies with you. It's pretty wet down here.'

The next morning, as Robert and Deborah seemed to be getting along so well together, both being keen horselovers and fine riders, I left them to enjoy a canter over the long green downland above the Marsh and took my trail-bike down into Hythe, where I soon located Arnold Bell's small cluttered antique shop.

He certainly specialized in nautical bygones. It was stacked high with ships' wheels, anchors, compass binnacles, port and starboard navigation lights of every size and shape, bollards, cleats, portholes and just about every other relic of the age of proud ships when Britain ruled the Seven Seas. It smelt strongly of tar and rum-soaked tobacco.

Mr Bell was a 'nautical bygone' himself, having served in the Royal Navy before joining Customs and Excise. He was a well-built, capable-looking man in his mid-sixties, who walked with the rolling gait of someone who has spent a lot of his life at sea. His crewcut grey hair had thinned under many years of wearing his Naval and Customs officer's 'fore and aft' caps, but his button-bright brown eyes missed nothing and his weathered face was shrewdly good-natured. As I stepped inside the low doorway, ducking my head to enter, I started to introduce myself.

'Good morning, Mr Bell. My name is. . .'

'Professor Daniel Fortune. Terence's descriptions of people are audible identikits. You're exactly as he described you, sir. I understand you're a good friend of his. Glad to know you, Professor. What can I do for you?'

Arnold Bell's appearance was matched by his voice, its subdued tones carrying a sense of vocal power which, I was sure, could still rap out strident commands audible over a full gale.

I found my hand grasped firmly in his large palm, the hand of a man who handles ropes and lines. I sensed that he was a small-boat enthusiast.

The shop was empty. I came straight out with the cover story I had planned. 'Smuggling on the Romney Marsh is the subject of a psychological study I'm writing. I'm particularly interested in methods used in smuggling by air. What can you tell me?'

'Not a lot,' Mr Bell sighed deeply. 'But what I do know, I'll pass on to you. However, there is someone in France, an old friend of mine from French Customs, the Douane, who is also retired and lives in Deauville. He could tell you about the French side of the operation and where the stuff comes from. Flying in the stuff is quicker and a lot harder to detect and intercept.' He paused to bring out a battered old briar pipe. 'Being retired, I'm under no restraint, other than the Official Secrets Act, and that only covers *our* methods not those used by the smugglers. I gathered that's why you wanted to see someone like me.'

Arnold Bell was no fool. I liked him. 'What method is being used to fly in the drugs?'

'Simple really. A light aircraft takes off from somewhere in northern France. It flies along their coast until it enters one of the mandatory airways, which are used by all aircraft crossing the Channel. It's perfectly legal up to now, except the cargo, of course. The take-off point could be one of the many private airstrips used by farmers or rich landowners anywhere between Deauville and Le Havre. Therefore no flight plan is made out, nor would the pilot have to book-out as he would from a flying club or a small aerodrome. That means the flight is unrecorded.'

'Why would the pilot use the official airways?' I asked.

'Because he doesn't want to risk his neck while crossing even the narrowest part of the Channel, which is about twenty-two miles wide. If he is in the official airway and gets into trouble, he can always radio his position and call "Mayday". A rescue boat or a helicopter, from either side, will pick him up. The chances are that a light plane will float long enough in calm weather for the pilot to get into his rubber dinghy. This will be equipped with lights and sea-marking dye and will give him every chance of survival.'

'What about the drugs?'

'Easy! He ditches them in a weighted bag. He'll be clean when he's picked up.'

'After he has crossed the Channel, what then?'

'Near Dover he dives out of the airway under cover of the cliffs, and turns west. Still below the clifftops he flies along the Folkestone–Hythe coastline safely concealed in the radar "clutter" and turns inland over the Hythe rifle-ranges or the School of Musketry to drop his package of drugs onto one of the many water-meadows of the Marsh.'

'Surely the parachute might be spotted by a casual observer, hearing the engine of the plane and looking up?'

'He glides in for the last mile or so, and drops the drugs in a specially padded waterproof container with the ditching weights removed and no parachute. He'll drop the container near a designated area. It doesn't have to be *that* accurate. All of it will have been arranged beforehand by letter, or phone, using some sort of code.'

'How is the package located?'

'With a small radio beacon.' The old Navy man's grin was triumphant. 'About ten minutes after chummy has flown back to France, a small impact-proof radio beacon starts to bleep. It's only got a range of a couple of miles, so it's unlikely that it will be detected by our official direction-finder sets. The pick-up man, most likely using a motorbike, like yours outside, which is ideal for cross-country work, will locate it with a small hand-held DF set such as yachtsmen use to get their bearings in bad weather. Once the stuff has been picked up, it can be broken down into smaller packets and concealed in the bike's panniers, or it can be hidden inside the hollow tubing of the machine's frame. It's a doddle!'

'What route would he take after that? Presumably he would make for London?'

'At three o'clock in the morning? I doubt it. The London traffic from the coast, at that time, is thin enough to monitor and there aren't many lone motorcyclists about then. Our blokes would nab him with police patrols. No. He's bound to lie low in a safehouse till morning and then run up to London in the rush-hour. No way could we search all the traffic at that time.'

'It's neat,' I conceded.

'All shipshape and "pusser" fashion, well-planned and almost foolproof. The bastards are getting away with murder. Ten kilograms of pure heroin can command a street value of over a million pounds, for an initial outlay of a fraction of that sum. That's big business: *filthy*, but profitable enough to pay for all that organization. Does that answer your question, Professor?'

'Perfectly! I still haven't got a line on the sort of people behind this whole operation. Have you any thoughts about them?'

Mr Bell scratched his head. 'That's the hardest question of all. My guess is that it isn't the regular mob. This doesn't *feel* like a Mafia operation.'

'Why do you say that?'

'Instinct, Professor. Terence tells me that you don't scoff at such things.'

'Certainly not. I use instinct myself a lot, and so do my colleagues and they are much more expert at using their paranormal abilities than I am. Instinct is something that we are born with, some of us being more sensitive than others, but basically these inherent powers of the mind are the greatest gift handed down to us by our ancestors. Sadly, the sort of routine tasks of schooling and the daily work round of our modern civilization tend to dull our inherited perceptions. Like any other ability or faculty, instinct can become atrophied if we don't use it enough. In your profession, I understand, instinct is your most effective weapon.'

'Nicely put.' The ex-Customs man nodded vigorously, his ample bulk shaking in agreement. 'Mine was sharpened by my years in the Navy, like yours, sir, no doubt, and later even more so in the Customs service. I caught many smugglers, professionals and amateurs, over the years, because they just didn't "smell" right somehow. My instinct tells me this isn't a Mafia job but an operation planned and carried out by some new lot, people who would normally be above suspicion.'

He paused, partly for dramatic effect, and partly because he wanted to muster his arguments. Then he continued, his voice dropping lower. 'This method cannot be used by terrorists because arms or explosives are too bulky and need a parachute and a small truck or estate car to carry them from the pick-up point. My guess is that if it isn't *terrorists*, it has to be hard drugs. I think it's private enterprise. Sounds sick, doesn't it? But that's my opinion. Sheer bloody profit motive. Because of the enormous sums involved. Whoever they are, they're a bunch of right bastards. Those drugs can wind up in the hands of young kids, some of them only twelve years old. What kind of filth would do that to children?'

Had we been at sea, I'm sure that Mr Bell would have spat, to emphasize his disgust.

'One more question,' I asked him, almost as an after-thought. 'Your French colleague. If I flew over there, would he talk to me? He lives at Deauville, I think you said.'

'I'm sure he would co-operate. His name is Jacques Dhery – D H E R Y.' Mr Bell spelt it out. 'What's the matter, Professor? You look surprised.'

'I *am*,' I laughed, with a whoop of joy. 'In fact, I am amazed and delighted. I'm sure I know this man; that is, if he is about my age, short, thin, with small features except for a large nose and mouth that always seems to be smiling. Blue eyes? Half his left ear missing?'

The old sailor continued, grinning broadly, 'Grey hair, thick, cut *en brosse*, speaks excellent English. Well I'm blowed. How do you know Jacques?'

'He was in the French Resistance. We were *copains*, mates, in Normandy, in 1944. We were both working on the underground side of the air-raid on Amiens Prison in February 1944. I haven't heard from him in years. He saved my life. Carried me on his back for three kilometres. Jacques is a hell of a fine chap! I should be ashamed of myself for losing contact.'

Mr Bell was enthusiastic. 'Why don't you nip across and see him then? I'm sure he'd be delighted. I'll telephone a mate of mine in the Douane and tell him you're coming. I haven't got Jacques' address, but I can find him for you. Phone me tomorrow, or the day after and I'll tell you what I've arranged. You can fly over from Lydd. It only takes half an hour from take-off to touch-down. Good old Fokker Friendships. Nice, comfortable little planes. Jacques could meet you at Le Touquet. Funny, isn't it, you knowing him? But before you go, is there anything else I can help you with?'

'Yes, there is. Have you ever heard of the Companions of Chaos?'

For the first time since our meeting, Mr Bell shook his grizzled head. 'No, I can't say that I have. Sounds like a pop group. Why? Do you think these Companions of Chaos are mixed up in the drug smuggling? Pop groups do go in for those hard drugs and they've got plenty of money.'

I agreed, but in defence of many decent young musicians, I said, 'Tragically, some do. In fact, I've had to treat a number of the poor devils.' I hesitated. 'My own wife and baby son were killed in a car smash, caused by a wealthy pop musician on a mescaline trip.'

Mr Bell grunted sympathetically.

'I found out from my patients that drug-pushers have made fortunes out of supplying pop groups with hard drugs and then blackmailing them. It's a foul business.'

110

'That it is,' agreed my new friend, sucking loudly on his old pipe.

I left him in the middle of his nautical hamster's nest and headed back to the Manor.

Robert had picked up a hired Ford estate car and the next day we drove over to Folkestone to meet Romola at the Central Station. On the way he talked enthusiastically about Deborah and it was obvious to me that they were falling in love. We arrived early and parked the car at the top of the long slope that leads to the down-line station. I remembered that station so well from many holidays spent with the Tolsfords and from my wartime visits to Dover and Folkestone. It brought back a flood of memories.

Robert ran over to help Romola as she jumped down from the high coach, lifting her small trenchcoated figure clean off the platform while she laughingly squealed her protests. She looked adorable with her long dark hair cascading down her back and her brown eyes alight with joy. My heart gave a leap at the sight of her.

When it came to my turn, I tried to make my cuddle as paternal as possible, but failed miserably when my lovely Hungarian colleague impulsively flung her arms round me and, with her trim body pressed close to mine, kissed me full on the lips.

It rocked me back and involuntarily I found myself responding eagerly. Then gathering together the last strands of my rapidly snapping control, I broke away and held her, admiringly, at arms' length.

'You look wonderful,' I said. 'I'm *so* glad to see you!' That was the understatement of the year.

Romola laughed happily. 'I would have been here a week ago if you'd only let me come to the Marsh. Tell

111

me everything! I'll ride pillion on your bike, Daniel; you ride so *conservatively*.'

I smiled at her gentle sarcasm. I ride *fast*. 'We left the bikes at the Manor. We've got a hire-car.'

Romola looked disappointed. 'That's extravagant, Daniel,' she protested. 'We could easily have put my bags, slung together, on either side of the carrier.'

'Not without bending the bike's frame,' Robert remarked as he lifted the two over-packed bags into the back of the Ford. I settled her into the front seat.

'I'll remember to bring a bike next time, Romola. I see you have your wellies!'

Romola's idea of suitable wet-weather gear was a brand new chic trenchcoat and a ridiculous pair of red wellingtons designed more for a fashionable garden party in inclement weather than for the storm-lashed Romney Marsh.

We chatted away on the drive back to Tolsford Manor, my little colleague giving delighted gasps at the passing springtime beauty of the Kentish countryside. By the time we got to the Manor we had given her an overall summary of what had happened up to then, and Romola had told us everything that she had learned at her end of the operation.

'I've been so worried about you, Daniel. I mean, about *both* of you. The night Sir Edward died, I had the most awful nightmare. I dreamed that we were being chased across the Marsh by a motorbike gang, only instead of heads, they had helmeted skulls. It was horrible.

'Then I left my body and found the Winnebago on the Marsh, parked near a farm by a dyke. It was empty; I didn't know where else to look for you. I woke up and got out my pendulum. I dowsed the large-scale map of the area that you left me for reference.

The pendulum traced your journeys for me, but went off the map in the direction of Ashford.'

'Well done,' I said approvingly. Robert grunted his agreement.

To someone unacquainted with the strange world of the paranormal, Romola's statement would have seemed like certifiable mumbo-jumbo. To Robert and me it was a simple statement of fact, as though our colleague had been using the telephone to find out where we were that night.

Deborah was at the front door to greet us and I noticed with amusement the two young women warily assessing each other. I could sense Deborah stiffening when Robert put his arm round Romola while I introduced my beautiful assistant to my goddaughter.

But Romola Kobrak has an indefinable quality of innocence that, like Orpheus, can draw 'trees, stones and floods', and, within an hour, Deborah had fallen as much under her honest spell as Robert and I had when we first met her.

I gave an inward sigh of relief that my hunch had paid off; or was it a hunch? Perhaps it was guidance from some loving discarnate spirit. I've seen too much in my eventful life to scoff at such a notion. Whatever the source or the motivation for that inspiration, between Robert's open and caring admiration and Romola's loving heart, Deborah Tolsford was now in good hands.

Naturally, I was very concerned about Romola entering the danger area, and my plan, unknown to either of those two determined young women, was to send them both off somewhere safe directly after the funeral while Robert and I got on with our investigations. This probably meant sending them to my house at Cerne Abbas. I should have known that it would be

113

a forlorn hope. '*L'homme propose. Les femmes disposent*', to paraphrase an old truism. No way could I persuade them to leave the dirty work to the men.

As it happened, events developed too rapidly for my plan to work. The new phase was initiated at the funeral. Deborah had been unable to keep the service strictly to a small private affair because of the popularity of the late Squire and his position as a Lord of the Levels.

Although, as Edward had told me, the practical need for these ancient traditional offices had been removed when the maintenance of the seawall, with its maze of dykes and sluices, was made a public responsibility, tradition dies hard in Britain. The funeral of such a distinguished Bailiff of the Levels as Sir Edward Tolsford required the august presence of all the remaining Lords, complete with their wives, to pay their last homage. The small church next to Lympne Castle was packed.

The day itself was funereal. A light drizzle increased the sombre atmosphere, but the dark forces had not allowed for the uplifting presence of my friend, Chaplain James Maitland, whose cheerful personality and breezy manner were those of one used to conducting Sunday morning Divisions on the flat-topped deck of an aircraft carrier.

God bless that splendid man! He turned that gloomy church service into a triumphant send-off for an old shipmate. He stood in the fine, carved pulpit to read the lesson and the rolling tones of a fleet chaplain rang out, filling the church with a feeling of sea-breezes. I felt the surge of the Atlantic against the grey sides of a great warship as the memory of many seaborne services came flooding back.

We could hear the gulls circling the ancient church as they sheltered inland from the rising gale out in the bay, their keening cries audible during the quieter parts of the service. I write the word 'quieter' deliberately, because one thing that I had always associated with Chaplain Maitland was his penchant for lusty hymns. Edward and I had often smiled at each other as we thundered out: 'For those in peril on the sea', and heard our chaplain's full-throated baritone voice rising above those of the rest of the crew.

It was typical of him to suggest 'Onward Christian soldiers', which we all felt was appropriate, and 'Abide with me', Edward's favourite hymn. We dissuaded him from including 'The Battle Hymn of the Republic', which he particularly enjoyed, and finally settled on 'Rock of Ages' sung with a great release of energy and emotion. It made us all feel better. Edward's funeral was an inspiring and joyous occasion and I could feel the darkness retreating from the wholesome air of loving respect for that fine man's return to his Maker.

Deborah sat between Robert and myself, Romola having declined the invitation to attend, and wept silently, but joined in the singing. Only during 'Abide with me', when the sun shone its rain-filtered rays through the east window of the church, did she falter.

I felt relieved that we had seen my old shipmate off in style, and outside, in the ancient graveyard, where Deborah had, by tradition, to undergo the ordeal of receiving the official sympathy of each of the 'Jurats' and their wives, the same feeling of fulfilment was evident among those who had attended the service. Even the vicar, who must have been a little put out at having to 'assist' at the funeral of such a distinguished parishioner in his own church, seemed as pleased as the rest of us with the choice of chaplain.

As we stood in a close supportive group around Deborah, I noticed that the rain had stopped. Through the intermittent cloud cover the sun shone fitfully. It was cold; more so than it should have been on that spring morning. I felt again the presence of evil and, involuntarily, I shivered.

Among the distinguished guests were a number of owners of local estates. Deborah introduced me to all of them as her late father's best friend and old shipmate, and presented Robert as my colleague at Wessex University. We were dressed in our best, mine being the formal suit which I always carry in the Winnebago in case I have to impress some local bigwig. Robert had no such dark clothes with him and, instead, wore his buckskin jacket, which, on him, looks splendidly swashbuckling but is more appropriate to a Navajo funeral than to a British one.

With his athletic frame clothed immaculately in this Navajo equivalent of 'Sunday Best', he dominated the whole scene. The women present couldn't keep their eyes off him.

Deborah had been somewhat startled by Robert's attire until he explained the situation and, as it was impossible to fit my broad-shouldered, deep-chested colleague with any borrowed dark jacket or coat, she gladly accepted his presence on his own terms. It was becoming evident that she welcomed Robert on *any* terms. I was delighted to see my goddaughter falling in love. Already she introduced him to other women with the sort of proprietary air by which a woman indicates to another: 'This man is mine!'

The long parade of civic dignitaries, local farmers and squires dragged on until, at the tail of the queue, three distinguished people paid their respects to Deborah. One of them was a tall, burly man with a younger face than his pace of movement implied. His hair had, I felt sure, been tinted from its natural white to iron-grey and his bland features had been the subject of skilled plastic surgery. I was also sure that he wore a corset. I didn't hear his name because Robert diverted my attention by suddenly stiffening his grip on my arm just as Deborah spoke to the elegantly tailored man.

He in turn stepped to one side to allow his female companion to speak to the Squire's bereaved daughter. This dark-haired woman was startlingly beautiful, not in the fresh-faced way of either Deborah or my lovely Romola, but in the sophisticated style of a leading fashion model.

'Rosamund Charnley,' she murmured, in the seductive voice of a confident woman of considerable presence. I bowed slightly as I took her hand, recognizing her as the sort of woman who makes a great courtesan. Her face was exquisite, with finely drawn features, which had almost certainly been cleverly improved by surgery. Her perfectly made-up mouth promised that hers was a very sensual and passionate nature. Her skin glowed with health, while her startling violet eyes, equally skilfully made-up, would certainly ruin the composure of most men.

It was obvious from the cut of her superbly tailored suit that she was a rich woman, or the mistress of someone in the multi-millionaire bracket. It never occurred to me that she was married. I felt that her relationship with her burly escort was that of mistress and lover, not of wife and husband. One thing was certain: she was very interested in Robert Whiterivers and she left Deborah and went over to talk to him, or rather to flirt with him.

The third member of this trio of guests now presented himself. 'Dr Sigismund Toddman,' he said in a low voice, bowing curtly, his gaunt face expression-less. 'My sympathies, *gnädige Fräulein.*' The Prussian courtesy form of address came easily to his thin lips.

Deborah shuddered as though a cold breeze played round her, while she graciously accepted this tall, sabre-thin European's tribute. Having completed his respects, the pale-faced man stepped behind the grey-haired leader of the trio. I seldom feel averse to anyone on a first meeting, but I didn't relish the idea of shaking hands with this strange man or, for that matter, with either of his two companions, even the stunningly lovely woman. The thin one disturbed me most. He wore gloves and seemed to be self-conscious about it but it was his pallid face and hooded eyes with a blazing brightness behind their heavy lids that troubled me. I sensed that Dr Toddman was a man to treat with caution.

The broad, expensively suited man now turned to me. 'Professor Fortune,' he said with a full-lipped smile. 'What a pleasure to meet you. Sadly though, under these circumstances. I have long admired your scholarship. I particularly enjoyed your book *Magic and the Mind*, a masterly work.' He was obviously given to pedantic superlatives and continued to lavish compliments on me.

'Recently I found your *Youth and the Drug Culture* to be another splendid analytical study.' He empha-sized his remarks by seizing my hand and shaking it vigorously. The timbre of his powerful voice indicated that he was a northerner who had received a good education and who tended to disguise his Yorkshire origins behind a carefully cultivated 'Oxford' accent. I am very fond of regional accents, especially those that have an honest richness in their tones, and don't warm to a person who deliberately disguises his.

'I'm sorry,' I apologized. 'In the many exchanges of sympathy, I failed to catch your name.'

'I'm Lord Marsden,' he said, 'Arnold Marsden.' I felt a chill race up my spine. Edward had *not* been referring to the famous London cancer hospital with his last murmured words.

Unless my guess was wild, I was now face to face with one, possibly three, of the Companions of Chaos. I felt it so strongly I could almost taste the flavour of evil. Unmistakably each of these people brought a degree of darkness and an alien sense of menace. I knew that I was in the presence of the adversary.

CHAPTER 6

Lines of Battle

As soon as we got back to the Manor, I made an excuse to Deborah and drove Romola and Robert over to the Winnebago. I wanted to talk to them alone. It wasn't that I didn't trust Deborah, especially now, but there was still the possibility that her father had been right and that his daughter had been involved somehow with the Marsden lot.

Inside the motor-home, I got straight down to discussing my fears. 'I want to know, Robert, how you felt about Lord Marsden, Mrs Charnley and the tall, thin doctor? You weren't there, Romola, or I think you would have been as disturbed by them as I was. I don't know about Mrs Charnley, except that I would rather not get involved with a woman like that, but Lord Marsden didn't smell right to me and that German doctor really gave me the creeps.'

Robert nodded. 'Strange you should say that, Daniel. I also noticed an odd smell about him.'

'Can you describe the smell, Robert?' I asked.

'Sure. It's not an actual odour or aroma, and I guess most people wouldn't notice it, because it isn't a physical thing.' He paused reluctantly. 'It's the smell of *death*.'

I was shaken by his statement but I couldn't fault it.

Romola said animatedly, 'I know exactly what Robert means. This psychic sense which manifests as a smell is often associated with a haunting. There was a presence at a country house which I visited as a child that manifested as an old lady. She brought with her the lovely smell of jasmine. It was the past association of her earthly life, expressed as a favourite perfume or the scent of flowers that she had loved. Only once have I actually sensed a smell of death, only to find out later that the man was a pathologist and had just come from his laboratory. I know how scrupulously clean pathologists habitually are and I'm certain that he would have scrubbed-up and showered. Of course, he wasn't wearing the same clothes. It was, as Robert has described it, a psychic sense of smell, caused by his close association with corpses.'

'Romola,' I said, 'I believe these three people are part of this filthy business and that they are members of the Companions of Chaos. What do you pick up, Robert?'

'Once again, you spook me, Prof. I was so upset by them that I clutched your arm. It was like a jolt of negative power. I've never felt such an antagonistic feeling against any woman. Rosamund Charnley's beautiful, all right. Most men would describe her as stunning. But inside, she's something else. I think the best term is *rotten*. How the hell did Deborah get to know that trio? She seemed to greet them warmly enough, but I guess that could be just your famous British politeness.'

'No, Robert. The Tolsfords knew Marsden and the woman well, but probably not the doctor, who is Swiss and lives somewhat as a recluse. Deborah told me that Marsden is a property tycoon who bought a lot of their land from them when things became difficult because of heavy death duties after her mother died. Marsden helped Edward out of financial difficulties and she feels obligated to him. She doesn't like Rosamund Charnley, who is apparently Marsden's mistress and social hostess.'

'She's a high-class hooker,' interrupted Robert. 'I was trying to define her in British terms but in American that's what the lady is, a high-class whore.

124

I've got nothing against an honest hooker, but that one I really do not like.' All of us were in complete psychic agreement.

We were about to leave when I had an inspiration. 'I'm going to make a phone call to Paul Brauner, my friend in the City. He is bound to know about Marsden if he is as important as Deborah says he is.'

I wasn't able to contact Paul but left a message on his answering-machine and I also made a call to Mr Bell, confirming the arrangements with our mutual French friend.

After a snack lunch I drove Romola around the area for a couple of hours, so that she would have some idea of the layout of the Marsh. It was her first visit to the Levels but, oddly enough, she confirmed just about everything that Robert and I had picked up about the Marsh, from the innocent involvement of the huge blockhouses of the nuclear complex to the psychic generation, by Port Lympne, of its sense of peace and tranquillity.

As we neared Tolsford Manor at the end of our short survey, Romola said, 'All the leys in this district seem to be badly disturbed. The whole Marsh still radiates the sensations and atmosphere that attracts you to it, I can sense that strongly. But overlaid upon its ethos there is something else and it is very frightening. This feeling of fear has surely been artificially generated. It's just not natural. It is all-pervading and it must be the work of evil men and women. I hate it! We must do something about it. I'm certain that Lord Marsden and that Charnley woman are mixed up in it, and I don't like the sound of the Swiss doctor at all. Please be careful, you are dealing with merchants of death.'

When we returned, Deborah had recovered from the

ordeal of the funeral and welcomed us with a large country-house tea. She told me, confidentially, 'Daniel, you've made a tremendous hit with Lord Marsden. He wants you to dine with him tomorrow. He says you have a lot in common and he wants to discuss the Romney Marsh with you.

'We were all invited but I told him that I couldn't go out just yet and he apologized. He's a bit of a rough diamond and came up the hard way. He was adopted, you know. Rosamund Charnley. . .' Deborah paused '. . . acts as his social hostess, but he made this invitation directly, himself. I'm sure he could tell you a lot about the Marsh that you don't know. He's been here for about five years but the locals still think of him as a "furiner". I think you should go, Daniel. Robert and Romola are both included in the invitation.'

Romola was quite firm about refusing the invitation. 'It's very kind of Lord Marsden, but if you're not going, Deborah, I'd much rather stay with you. We've got a lot to talk about.'

Deborah smiled her agreement. 'Of course, Romola. Actually I don't enjoy the Marsden dinner parties, principally because that odd Swiss specialist always seems to gravitate towards me. Frankly, he gives me the creeps!'

The dinner took place at Marsden's country house, the embodiment in bricks, stone and mortar of the words 'baronial hall'. Built recently without regard to cost, it was well-proportioned, if over-large, and had 'out-baroned' any hall that I had ever seen. From its half-timbering to the crenellated battlements, from its turrets to the mullioned windows, it radiated arrogant ostentation. The only things it lacked were a moat and a drawbridge. Marsden Hall was pure Disneyland, and it

126

suited its *nouveau-riche* owner perfectly. Like Marsden, it was considerably larger than life.

The evening was crowned, as Deborah had intimated that it would be, by an exquisitely prepared dinner, faultlessly presented by Marsden's chef, a Swiss *maître de cuisine* brought to Britain by Dr Toddman. Everything on the beautifully arranged table was new and expensive. Each piece of silverware bore Marsden's crest. It was hardly surprising that he had chosen a mailed fist holding a dagger. I could practically feel it aimed between my shoulderblades. Not only the food, but the accompanying wines were of superb quality, particularly the claret, a Château Margaux of excellent vintage.

From the copious amounts of Beluga caviar and over-generous portions of Scottish smoked salmon with its attendant fine Chablis, through the delicious guinea fowl with its stuffing of truffles, tangerines and chestnuts, to the spiced raspberry sorbets that followed, rounded-off by a selection of French cheeses flown in that morning from Normandy, the dinner was an overabundant masterpiece. I am ashamed to say that I ate far too much and enjoyed it all.

Marsden's appetite was more that of a gourmand than a gourmet. I knew that he would find dieting difficult, hence the corset. He ate rapidly without chewing his food and gulped rather than savoured his splendid wines.

Rosamund Charnley was a sparkling and alluring hostess who presided over the banquet with accomplished ease and great style. She drank sparingly and then only champagne. Obviously diet and body culture were a religion with her. Her looks were her greatest asset and her most powerful weapon and she preserved them assiduously.

But it was an unreal evening. The antipathy that we felt for one another made the occasion seem like a well-rehearsed play in which each actor knew his part and played it with professional skill. We were like two opposing armies, sounding out each other's weaknesses and strengths while we drew up our lines of battle.

As though to underline this *leitmotif* of tension, the conversation turned to the traditional occupations of the Marsh folk, smuggling and witchcraft.

'I bought this estate from a well-respected local family that once had a distant ancestor caught red-handed as a smuggler,' said Marsden, as an opening gambit. 'His name was Caleb Quested. The family name is famous among sheepfarmers on the Marsh. The sort of goods "run in" by the locals in those days was confined to conventional contraband, wines and spirits, silks and laces, in fact any dutiable goods that the Marsh folk considered that they paid too much money for in taxes.'

'This still goes on *today*,' I said, emphasizing the last word.

'I'm sure it does,' my host replied, as cool as the sorbet he was eating. 'After all, Professor, excise duties and value added tax are higher than ever.'

'I meant *drugs*,' I said, even more deliberately.

I could only admire Marsden's easy and relaxed manner as he continued, 'So I've heard. But nobody seems to know how it is done. Certainly no one ever seems to get caught.' He laughed.

'I'm sure they will be, given time,' I parried, feeling his mental blade rasp against my riposte.

'Naturally!' Again his coolness earned my grudging acknowledgement of him as an opponent. 'The Customs and Excise people are quite splendid.' Marsden smiled expansively, as he gave the authorities a verbal pat on the head. He reminded me of a Victorian actor. He was the archetypal wicked squire, the epitome of the heavy-framed, stony-hearted forecloser of mortgages on widows and orphans. There was nothing faintly comic in these similes.

We retired to the drawing-room, or rather the *salon*, an over-decorated octagonal room with white leather furniture and vast, Venetian chandeliers. I noticed that for a bulky man the Yorkshireman was very light on his feet. Because of his age he moved quite slowly, but with a studied grace. He was conscious of the effect and, like the Charnley woman, used his presence as a focus. I was sure he took dancing lessons. Over coffee Marsden set the ball rolling again. 'Professor, I was fascinated by our conversation at dinner. Sir Edward is a great loss to us all: a splendid man, who loved and served the Marsh all his life. I know that you were at Dartmouth together. It was he who loaned me your books. He was proud of having such an accomplished author as a close friend. I returned them to him and replaced the borrowed volumes with new copies of them all. I consider them a splendid addition to my library. I have an extensive collection of works on the occult or, as you learned parapsychologists prefer to think of it, the paranormal.'

I nodded in acknowledgement. 'I noticed some outstanding books and beautifully bound manuscripts while we were having our sherry in the library. I see you have works by Honorius, Eliphas Levi, Beckford, Lytton, Paracelsus, Cagliostro, Apollonius of Tyana, Trithemius of Spanheim, St Germain and, of course, all Liddell Mathers' and Aleister Crowley's books on ritual magic. May I congratulate you on a magnificent collection of magicalia!'

Marsden almost purred with satisfaction. 'Coming

129

from you, Professor, that really is a compliment. You may have wondered why I invited you to dinner in such tragic circumstances?'

'I did indeed, Lord Marsden.'

'Well, the fact of the matter is that I wish to further the cause of parapsychology by adding a grant to the one that you already enjoy at Wessex University.' Marsden leaned forward, his well-preserved face devoid of emotion and his expertly capped teeth exposed in what he intended to be a warm smile.

I was caught offguard by the man's impudence. He was actually trying to bribe me! 'How generous, Lord Marsden. I'm sure the faculty would be most interested.' I kept my tone as even as possible, although I was seething inside. His eyes shone balefully behind his tinted contact lenses as he said, slowly, 'I wasn't thinking of approaching the faculty *directly*. I was considering offering you a *personal* foundation to help fund your own all-important research, Professor.'

I had to admit that Marsden had style and the bloody nerve that only a multi-millionaire could have acquired from years of buying people and their talents.

'I'm sorry, but I couldn't possibly accept such a generous offer personally. Ethically it would be impossible. But, as I said, I'm sure that Wessex, or any *other* university, would be only too delighted to consider your generous proposal.'

Marsden accepted the snub without a qualm and continued to smile as he quickly pondered his next move. He tapped the arm of his chair impatiently. 'Of course, Professor, how remiss of me. I should have considered the ethics of the matter more carefully, but, like Rosamund here, I am a creature of impulse. Forgive me if I have in any way offended your sensibilities.'

The words would have sounded pompous coming from anyone else, but spoken by Lord Marsden they were more like a threat. He had made an offer and I had refused what was really an ultimatum.

The conversation switched back to the paranormal and we discussed the past and present history of witchcraft and folk medicine, for which Romney Marsh has long been renowned. It emerged that Marsden was very well informed on the occult, so far as a working knowledge of witchcraft or magic went. He was arrogant in his carefully acquired scholarship and contemptuous of those whose knowledge was less than his own. For me, however, he had a grudging respect; indeed he credited me with more than I actually knew. He was certainly not a man whom you would try to bluff. The life peer was no intellectual, but he had a hell of a shrewd mind.

I felt that he was carefully sounding me out, and was finding me an opponent worthy of his attention. It was as if we were two players sizing each other up before commencing a game.

For Robert, he seemed to have a certain contempt. I detected a strong streak of racism in Lord Marsden and felt that if ever there was a candidate for Nazism, or the National Front, it had to be this bigoted Northerner. To counteract this feeling of hostility I told Marsden something of Robert's brilliant academic background. However, it was when I mentioned Robert's remarkable psychometric abilities that I hit the jackpot. The life peer suddenly became enthusiastic.

'By God, I'd like to see him try his hand at that game with me.'

'Very well,' Robert agreed. 'Please give me something personal that you have worn or carried with you for some time.'

131

Lord Marsden handed the Navajo his watch, a fine gold half-hunter of nineteenth-century origin.

'See what you make of that, Dr *Whiterivers*,' he said, emphasizing Robert's last name.

'Certainly,' Robert concentrated hard as he passed the watch from one hand to the other. 'This belonged to an elderly man; tall, well-built, thin grey hair and a big moustache. Let's see now. He was not your father, but you treated him as though he were and he was very proud of you.'

'Yes,' admitted our host, almost grudgingly, 'Anything else?'

My colleague continued, 'This man loved horses and was himself a fine horseman, but he'd had a bad fall and suffered from a crippled, . . .' he paused '. . . left leg.'

'Correct,' breathed Marsden, now intensely interested. 'Go on, Dr Whiterivers.'

'I see a large grey-stone house, near to a busy manufacturing town. It's situated on the hills above, dominating the town, and I get the name "grey-fire", no! It's "greyfriar"! Yes, Greyfriar's Hall. Apparently it was the subject of a joke between you; something to do with a boy's comic paper — "greyfriars". Does that mean anything to you, Lord Marsden?'

'Quite amazing,' admitted the now deeply impressed owner of the watch. 'Can you see into the future as clearly as you do into the past?'

'Sometimes,' said Robert abruptly. 'For instance, I can tell you this. You will not own this watch very much longer. I'm sorry,' he hesitated, then handed it back to Marsden. 'The impressions have become unclear.'

'Remarkable,' said the tycoon; but I noticed that he didn't thank Robert.

'Please try something of mine,' Rosamund Charnley gushed with genuine excitement. 'Take this pendant. See what you pick up from that.' She held out a beautiful piece of jewellery which was an excellent example of enamelled Art Nouveau set richly with diamonds and rubies.

Robert handled the piece carefully and for a moment looked deeply into the beautiful woman's violet eyes, which were now alight with anticipation. Rosamund Charnley certainly made a picture of desirable womanhood in her expensively severe gown of dark blue silk. Then Robert spoke without hesitation, 'This piece was made for a Russian countess, by Fabergé. I sense that this was just before the First World War. I now see Paris, soon after the Russian Revolution. This pendant has been given to a wealthy Frenchwoman by a French nobleman. I see a château: great wealth. . . Ah, now this piece of jewellery goes to someone else, another woman. Some bargain is being struck. The time is now the Second World War and the Germans have recently occupied Paris. This pendant is in the nature of a bribe, in exchange for a permit, a pass, something like that. The new owner is an actress; she is the mistress of a German general. The general gave the other woman a *laissez-passer* to get her out of occupied France into Switzerland in exchange for this piece of jewellery. The scene changes. The Allied invasion is now in progress and the German general is escaping from Paris. His French mistress takes the pendant with her. They are driving fast along a highway, trying to get to Germany. The French will kill this woman if they catch her. She is a *collaboratrice*. I feel myself rushing along a tree-lined road. Suddenly, there is the sound of a diving plane. It is an Allied fighter. It strafes the general's car. The car crashes; I feel terrible fear and. . .' Robert stopped

133

abruptly and apologized. 'I'm sorry, Mrs Charnley. Please take your jewel back.'

Rosamund was stunned. 'Incredible!' she gushed. 'This piece was given to me by my late husband, Victor. He told me that it had belonged to a famous French actress, or rather, an *infamous* one, who had been killed, with her German general lover, when their car was shot to pieces by an Allied plane. Victor had acquired it from a Parisian jeweller. He told him how the pendant had been sold to him by a witness of the crash, who had found it near the wreck. It's quite unbelievable that you picked all that up so clearly. Can you read my mind?'

'No, Mrs Charnley. Just the pendant.'

'You're right about it being a Fabergé piece and I believe that it was originally made for a Russian countess. Victor had a picture of it somewhere.'

She turned to the silent doctor. 'Come on, Siggy, give Dr Whiterivers your watch.' The Swiss physician handed my colleague his watch, another well-made gold chronometer, of European manufacture. He was still wearing his white gloves.

'You must excuse Siggy's gloves,' gushed Rosamund. 'His hands were badly burned during the war, rescuing wounded men from an aircrash.'

'Forgive me,' rasped the doctor in a low voice. 'I do not like to reveal the scars. This watch I have had for many years. Please take it and tell me about myself.'

Robert held the fine timepiece almost reluctantly, once again passing it quickly from one hand to the other. Finally, he said, 'This watch is not yours, doctor; not originally, anyway. I see war, a prison camp, with barbed wire and watchtowers.'

'Of course, you would see these things,' the doctor's voice rose perceptibly in pitch and volume. 'That is hardly remarkable. I was in the war, in a prison camp.'

'Naturally, sir.' My big colleague hesitated, then abruptly handed the watch back to Toddman as though glad to be rid of it. 'I'm sorry,' he said. 'I'm tired and can't get a clear impression. But I still pick up that the watch is not yours.'

'Your powers must be failing you, young man,' the Swiss said, with a slight sneer on his taut face. 'The watch is *mine*, look!' He pressed the side of the timepiece and it sprang open. 'It says so here: presented to Dr Sigismund Toddman on his graduation from Heidelberg, 6 September 1934.'

To ease the situation, I said, 'Two out of three is not too bad an average. Dr Whiterivers has been over-working and he is not infallible; and now, if you will excuse us, we have to catch an early plane to France. Tomorrow we're flying over there to see an old friend of mine from the Resistance days, at Le Touquet. Thank you for a wonderful evening. It has been most enlightening.'

Our host and hostess looked the picture of genial hospitality as they stood politely in the doorway of that imposing entrance, framed by the portals of the great carved-oak double doors of Marsden Hall, but the illusion was shattered abruptly by the sound of a shotgun being fired and, instantly, the grounds of the whole estate burst into a blaze of light as Marsden's complex security system sprang into operation.

'It's that bloody poacher again,' snarled the peer. 'After my prize deer. Get him, Hammond!' The last sentence was barked as an imperative command to a man in chauffeur's uniform, who appeared, carrying a shotgun, from the east side of the Hall. Without a word, the chauffeur started in pursuit of a shadowy figure, who now broke cover in the background and

135

ran towards the distant chainlink security fence.

'Don't let the bastard get away,' shouted Marsden, cupping his hands to form a megaphone.

I felt Robert's hand grip my arm as his exceptionally keen eyes first spotted the fugitive in the distance. Then he was off, like one of his native mountain-lions, racing after the chauffeur in hot pursuit of his quarry.

All three of them disappeared from view behind the bushes lining the long drive, to appear momentarily between the trees. As they vanished there was the sound of a shout followed by a shot, another shout, a second shot, and a yell of pain. After this there was a short silence until Robert reappeared, the chauffeur's inert body slung over his shoulder. He was carrying a shotgun with a broken stock in his free hand.

As he approached us, a young girl appeared in the front doorway. She screamed and started to run towards my colleague and his unconscious burden.

'Damn,' cried Marsden and started after her, catching her arm so that she stumbled and fell onto the grass. Rosamund Charnley and I hurried forward to help, just as Robert, who moved deceptively fast, dropped his burden none too gently in front of Lord Marsden, who was, with Rosamund's help, restraining the hysterical young woman who, I noticed, was wearing only a nightgown. As she screamed in thwarted rage, Marsden slapped her face hard enough for her to stop abruptly. She burst into tears and collapsed, sobbing, against the tycoon's broad chest. It was a puzzling tableau.

Then Robert spoke, with clear emphasis on each word, 'Sorry about your chauffeur, Lord Marsden, but in the excitement he nearly shot me. I had to hit him to stop him taking a second shot. He'll be all right. But he'll have a sore jaw for a few days.'

The multi-millionaire grunted his understanding with a total lack of concern for his semi-conscious underling. 'Hammond probably mistook you for the poacher's accomplice.'

'Possibly,' Robert said.

'Did the poacher escape?' asked Rosamund Charnley as she prepared to lead the sobbing girl away.

'Yes,' said Robert. 'He climbed over the fence in double quick time and disappeared into the trees.'

'Pity,' commented Marsden. 'I apologize for my daughter Miranda's hysterical behaviour. She hasn't been too well lately; that's why she didn't join us for dinner. She's very fond of the servants. Miranda is always concerned for the welfare of others. She must have thought that some harm had come to young Hammond.'

Robert had, by this time, lugged rather than helped the bewildered chauffeur to his groggy feet. The man was furious.

Marsden spoke, 'All right, Hammond, ask Melvyn for the first-aid kit.' He turned to me, 'My butler will look after him. Thank you, Dr Whiterivers, for trying to help, but I'm sure Hammond could have dealt with the poacher by himself.'

Robert grinned, 'He was about to shoot him point-blank. The gun went off, narrowly missing the man. Your chauffeur then swung round on me and fired again, so I kicked him in the side. The shot smashed into a tree beside me. To stop him trying again, I hit him on the jaw.'

'So you told me, doctor. Again, my apologies for the incident. Still, as no one was seriously hurt, I think we had best consider the matter closed.' Marsden paused. 'Hammond's shotgun was only loaded with rock-salt. It's an old gamekeeper's trick. It stings badly, but it doesn't kill. Good-night, gentlemen.'

His attitude was so coldly dismissive that we turned and got into our hire-car without shaking hands with our host and drove off, passing through the security gate which automatically opened as we approached.

'What the hell was all that about?' I asked.

'Beats me, Daniel,' growled Robert. 'That bastard of a chauffeur tried to kill me; by my reckoning, for the second time. He was the one at Bateman's who fixed the Winnebago's brakes.'

'I thought he might be,' I replied. 'Why did you think he was trying to kill you? The shotgun was only loaded with rock-salt.'

'Rock-salt, my ass! That gun was loaded with buckshot, or something close to it. He nearly winged the poacher when I hit his arm and spoiled his aim. If I hadn't done so, he would have blown him in half.'

'How can you be so sure?'

'Because when he fired at me and I screwed up his aim the second time, he hit the sapling beside me...'

'Well?' I asked.

'He blew the tree to bits.'

'Then he really did try to kill you.'

'That's what I've been trying to tell you, Prof.'

'Why did you stop him firing at the poacher?'

'Because I like the poacher and I don't like the chauffeur. I *know* the poacher. I recognized him, even at a distance. If your eyes were in better shape, Prof, you would have recognized him too.' He paused, maddeningly, then said, 'The poacher was Dr Cowan, our archaeologist friend.'

'What on earth was he doing roaming around the grounds of Marsden Hall at night?'

'Beats me. He sure as hell wasn't digging. I saw him throw something over the fence before he jumped up to climb it.'

'A gun?'

'Nope. But you were close, Prof. It was a gun-mike; the sort you use for listening at a distance.'

I was even more puzzled. 'Why would our Israeli friend use a gun-mike to eavesdrop on the Marsden entourage?'

'I don't know, Daniel, but I guess your hunch is right. Mossad is interested in Lord Marsden, or in what he does.'

'Or perhaps in Dr Toddman?' I said in a flash of inspiration. 'Maybe, just maybe, Dr Toddman is the person who interests Mossad. A war criminal perhaps? He's old enough and, wait a minute! Suppose he *isn't* Toddman but someone else?'

'I don't follow you, Prof.'

'Robert, you said so yourself. Your words were, "This watch is not *yours*, doctor!" '

Robert gave a low whistle. 'So I did. What does it all mean?'

We turned into the narrow lane leading to our motor-home. 'I don't know yet, but as Sherlock Holmes used to say, "The game's afoot!" '

That may have sounded anachronistic, but it fitted the situation perfectly.

139

CHAPTER 7

Some Enemy Activity

Our consciences must have been clear that night, because we both slept without stirring until the first light of dawn crept through the Winnebago's east-facing windows. Since the Whitgifts had gone away for a few days there was no home-baked bread for our breakfast, but at Lydd Airport we downed coffee and excellent bacon sandwiches before boarding the Fokker Friendship bound for Le Touquet. This is a vintage aeroplane and has been in service for well over twenty years, a viable short-haul transport as safe as Dutch technology can make it. It made me feel secure.

The climb away from the small airfield was made in clear visibility and it gave us a panoramic high-angle view of the Marsh. The long sweep of the seawall stretched from the tawny shingle beaches fronting the rifle ranges of the Hythe School of Musketry round the gentle curve of the pale golden sands of Dymchurch until it vanished into the jutting pebbled bulk of Dungeness. Re-emerging from these shingle banks it curved back north-west, past the sand dunes of Camber beach to come to an abrupt end on the south side of the river Rother facing the ancient town of Rye.

'From the air it looks a big area,' commented Robert, 'but on a map it seems so small. That's one of the fascinations of the place, Daniel, the way its size keeps changing, relative to your position on the Marsh.'

'Believe me,' I said, with feeling, 'if you get caught out there, in the bitter white-out of a Marsh snow-storm, it suddenly seems as big as Greenland. Edward and I got lost in a blizzard when we were boys and nearly bought it. If he hadn't recognized a Saxon ruin that we had blundered into, we wouldn't have found our way back.'

Robert abruptly changed the subject. 'Why did you tell Marsden about this trip to Le Touquet?'

'I wanted to be sure that he knew about it; to see what he would do. So far, we have both been going on our instinctive reactions against these people. We haven't got a shred of proof that they are involved in this strange business. Last night's episode with the shotgun could be interpreted in quite a different way. The loads might have been an accidental switch. Hammond may not have been aware of it when he took a shot at the poacher, and he could have swung round on you instinctively.'

'Like hell, Prof! That murdering bastard is involved in this caper up to his Neanderthal head. So is his employer *and* Rosamund Charnley. As for Toddman, do you know, Daniel, that Swiss zombie has practically no aura?'

'I'm sure you're right about them all, Robert, but we still have no solid lead back to them from the drug smuggling. Nothing we "feel" about them, paranormally, would stand up in a court of law, especially in Britain, where precedent is everything. We could hardly accuse these dreadful people of complicity in drug smuggling and the terrorizing of a whole district on the grounds of our instinctive reactions to their negative auras. I'm hoping to draw Marsden, who is obviously the brains behind it all, into the open. I want to see how he reacts to our trip to France. I doubt whether he thinks we're doing it for a spot of Continental shopping, or a flutter at the Deauville casino. He'll have us followed and watched and, if he does so, that clinches it for me, but we'll still have to go a long way

144

to get something concrete on that wily gentleman.'

We were soon in the approach pattern to Le Touquet airport and our small stable Fokker gently touched the runway as though the pilot was flying in crates of eggs. Five minutes more and we had swung off the runway and were standing on the concrete apron in front of the airport buildings.

I stepped out of the aircraft and once again a flood of memories swept over me as the immediately recognizable figure of my wartime Resistance comrade ran forward to greet me in Gallic fashion, with a back-pounding embrace and a bearded kiss on both cheeks. I knew the warm hug from years before, but the beard was new. On Jacques Dhery it looked good, giving that cheerful old pirate the air of *un vrai Corsair*.

'Daniel, *mon vieux, tu n'as pas changé. Cheveux gris, oui, mais rien d'autre. Ta jambe? Ça marche, copain?*'

Jacques pointed to my leg, which had been the reason he had carried me to safety all those years before.

'It's great to see you, Jacques. This is Dr Whiterivers, my colleague and friend, and don't bother about my leg: it's fine.'

Jacques hugged the large frame of the Navajo with his usual enthusiasm but, as Robert towered over him by a good six inches, found it difficult to embrace him on both cheeks.

With my ex-Resistance friend in charge, Customs and Immigration were waved aside as unnecessary formalities and, chatting away in an interchangeable mélange of French and English, we drove in Jacques' battered old Citröen, to *un très bon petit restaurant* in Le Touquet.

The twin towns of Le Touquet and Deauville form a

combined holiday resort for French and foreign visitors alike. The style of architecture is predominantly Norman-Swiss, an odd mixture of half-timbered Norman farmhouses and Swiss mountain chalets, and many of the villas have porcelain doves and pursuing china cats perched on their roofs. Red dragons and other gargoyles abound on many gable-ends and neo-Gothic turrets and spires adorn the more adventurous late nineteenth-century mansions of the merchant princes which line elegant pine-clad avenues. In every respect the towns are Normandy's answer to Britain's Brighton and Hove.

Our meal was light and laughter-filled, in stark contrast to the overabundant banquet we had enjoyed the night before. Jacques and I drank a fresh Muscadet with the sole, a lusty Burgundy with the poulet de grain and a robust Marck, the brandy of Burgundy, with the coffee that followed the wonderful chocolate and calvados sponge cake.

Robert apologized and drank mainly Vittel, from the Auvergne.

'No kidney stones with this *eau minérale*, my friend,' Jacques pronounced. But Robert did join us in a small sip of each wine, and lauded them with enthusiasm.

We took our *café-filtre* outside, to enjoy it in the warmth of the surprisingly sunny spring afternoon, and sat in the shelter of a glass screen which effectively protected outdoor diners from the chilly Channel breezes.

'So, Daniel, you did not fly here just to have a long-overdue lunch with your old comrade! I owe you much, my friend. How can I help you?'

'Listen to Jacques,' I cried. 'He carried me a couple of miles on his back, with Germans shooting at everything in sight, especially us, and now he says that *he* owes me! You saved my life, *mon vieux*, and I can never repay you for that.'

Jacques went red with embarrassment and muttered into his rakish beard. 'Your splendid RAF risked their necks to breach the walls. But it was your message to the British, coupled with the pleas of the Resistance, that made the Amiens raid possible.'

'I thought it was a failure,' interjected Robert. 'Weren't a lot of French hostages killed in the bombing?'

'That was no fault of the Mosquito fliers, my friend,' Jacques fiercely defended the RAF. 'The ground was frozen hard and some of the bombs skipped, like flat stones on water. But we got out over two hundred hostages who were about to be shot. About a hundred escapers finally made it to safety, so it was *not* a failure. *Jamais!*' The Frenchman banged the marble-topped table, making the cups rattle.

'My fiancée, Marie-Thérèse, was one of those hostages and she escaped. That is what *I* owe *you*, Daniel. We married, as you know, and we have two sons, both fine boys. One, Jean-Marie, is a *flic* in the *Police de l'air*. He flies helicopters. It's all so different from our day, *hein*, Daniel?'

I nodded.

'The other one, Pierre, is in the Douane. He is a Customs officer at Calais, so he knows about the drug traffic. In my day such things were rare. Nowadays it is big business.' Jacques' eyes hardened. '*Salauds!* I understand from my friend Bell that you are investigating these things, Daniel? So! You are still in *le service de l'Intelligence, hein?*' He banged my shoulder.

'No, I'm not, but I am investigating drug smuggling, cocaine, heroin, etc., on the Romney Marsh. Have you any thoughts on that, Jacques?'

'A few, *mon vieux*, but so far as this parish is

concerned the drugs are going *out* of France, not *in*, so the *Police de l'air* and the Douane are not so concerned. We have our own problems. However, we do pass on any useful information to our friends.'

Jacques laid one hand across his sleeve, meaning *A travers la Manche* – across the Channel. It was a wartime play on the words like the Highland gesture to the King 'over the water' and had first been made popular by Maurice Chevalier, who had started it at a German troop concert.

'Jacques, can you tell me how the drugs are brought into England?'

My friend nodded and then repeated almost word for word Mr Bell's analysis of the situation. But he added the locations of the small airfields in France and other useful details which I could pass on to Special Branch. It certainly wasn't a wasted trip.

'They are private airstrips, you understand, Daniel, with grass surfaces, situated between Dunkerque and Le Havre. The grass shows signs of *light* landings, with unloaded aircraft, and heavy scuffing of the grass where the pilots have used their brakes to run up the engines to full power before take-off. That means heavy loads in fuel and cargo. It's not only drugs but arms and explosives also, for your terrorists.'

'You mean for Ireland? For the IRA?' asked Robert.

'The arms used to go into Ireland via the Channel Islands, using them as a way-station from Libya. Small, multi-engined aircraft were used for the long sea crossings. Now the Channel Islands are too well protected and the terrorists are seeking other routes. But our friend Bell knows as much about that as I do. Is there any other way I can help you?'

'Who are the people behind it all? Is it the Mafia?'

'No, we are certain that neither the Mafia nor the

148

Union Corse, our own home-grown gangsters from Corsica, are involved. We think it's a very different set-up. More like private enterprise, a commercial venture by men who have *no* criminal record.'

'And the arms?' I asked.

'KGB, for certain. They are supplying left-wing terrorists everywhere with arms and explosives. I think the two operations are separate. The KGB operate through Libya for the arms, and some private group in Britain is in business with the hard drugs. There are millions involved, Daniel. *Pounds*, not francs.'

'That's what we think, too. It's a foul business, but worth a fortune. By the way, do you know anything about the Companions of Chaos? Or an Englishman named Lord Marsden?'

Jacques scratched his Musketeer-style beard. '*Les Compagnons de Chaos*. No. But your English milord, Marsden; he is a familiar face at the casino at Deauville. He has his own private jet. He is a very rich man and plays the tables. He seldom wins; *en effet* he loses a lot. But it doesn't seem to worry him. Is he involved in this?'

'Perhaps that is how he pays for the drugs, by passing money over the casino tables?' Robert interjected.

'Hardly, Robert,' I pointed out. 'The French *state* owns the casinos. But Marsden would have no difficulty transferring the money with all the resources of his Group behind him.' I turned to Jacques. 'Anything else you can tell me about him?'

The Frenchman pondered for a moment. '*Eh bien*! He is always accompanied by a beautiful woman, a Madame Charnley, I think.'

'Rosamund Charnley is his mistress, Jacques.'

'He also brings guests, very important people from

your country. Some of them high up in your government. He picks up the bill, *l'addition*, for everyone. He is a generous man, no?'

'Sounds more like pay-offs and bribery to me,' I remarked, disgustedly. 'It figures, Jacques; all that money, especially in hard cash, has to come from somewhere. Though I suppose he can write some of it off against business expenses.'

The Frenchman shrugged. 'He also hires some very expensive girls. They are not local, you understand. Our hookers are seasonal. Like little birds, they migrate here only for the summer; but milord's ladies are very chic, very Parisienne and very expensive! They must cost him a fortune, those *poules de luxe*.' Jacques flicked his fingers in that typically French gesture that illustrates burnt fingers.

'Does he bring an elderly Swiss doctor with him? A tall, thin man?'

'No. I don't remember anyone like that.'

'You've got a great memory for everything else,' laughed Robert.

'It is, or rather was, my business to keep my eyes open. We in the Douane miss very little. It is the same with our friends in the British Customs, *n'est-ce pas?*'

Jacques' smiling eyes suddenly narrowed and he said quietly, 'There is someone very interested in us, Daniel. He is across the road having a drink outside the café. He can't be too warm there. The sidewalk is in the shade.'

'That doesn't surprise me, Jacques. What does he look like?'

'He's sitting, but I should imagine he is tall. Young, about thirty years old; weight around eighty kilos. He's built like a boxer, looks like a man of action, an ex-soldier, perhaps?'

'Hammond,' breathed Robert.

'Precisely,' I said. 'Jacques, we'll have to leave soon to catch the plane back and on the way I'll fill you in on the action so far. It's been wonderful seeing you again. So many memories, old friend! Thank you again for everything.'

We drove slowly back to the airfield while I told Jacques the basis of our investigations. Several times he whistled in surprise.

'*C'est la magie noire*! It's not unknown in Normandy. There are plenty of local country people who believe in witchcraft; but these Companions of Chaos, as you call them, surely they are a rich people's witches' coven. There are also such bored, wealthy degenerates in France who indulge in the same kind of revolting practices. This is a Catholic country, so we are more aware of such things. Our priests accept the presence of evil as a living thing. I think you have stirred up a nest of hornets.'

'We have. Special Branch can't help us much and neither can the police, until we've got something concrete as evidence. Rumours of witchcraft, terrorism and extortion have got to be backed up with facts; but I may still get milord Marsden to tip his hand. He's an arrogant bastard and is bound to overstep the mark.'

'You have such delightful clichés in English, Daniel. Now this chauffeur, as you call him, do you want him *delayed*? I can. . .' he paused, savouring the idiom, '. . . tip the wink – I like that one – to our *Police de l'air* and then we could easily find some irregularity in his passport – mistaken identity perhaps? You know the sort of thing. You want him . . .' he laughed outright '. . . in the nick? That is one of my favourites.' Jacques has an infectious guffaw that would bring a smile to the face of the Sphinx.

'No thank you. But I would appreciate anything else you can give me on Lord Marsden. He's the fly in the ointment.' I deliberately chose a hackneyed cliché.

We left Le Touquet with a genuine feeling of regret. Jacques insisted on kissing Robert on both cheeks, standing on tiptoe to reach him. He stood waving us goodbye as we taxied out for take-off, blowing his nose in his red-spotted handkerchief and, I'm sure, with tears in his eyes. I know mine were watering.

Robert summed it up for me. 'You don't often meet someone like that. We're lucky to have met two in the last week. Dr Cowan has that same happy knack of radiating warmth. I'd call them both *gay* people if that word hadn't already been pre-empted. I think your friend Jacques is a great guy. I like him a helluva lot.'

I sighed nostalgically. 'We went through some rough times together.'

The flight back to Lydd passed quickly and Mr Bell must have had a word with the Customs officer on duty, because he waved us through with a grin. We only had the usual allowances of spirits and perfume with us, but it was a nice gesture of confidence. It made us feel more official in this strange game, where we were working with the authorities but had no authority ourselves.

As we left the aircraft I noticed a private jet on the way back to the hangar. It had 'Marsden Group' painted on its side. Obviously, Hammond had already returned and was on his way back to his master, to report that we had lunched and talked with a middle-aged Frenchman who was probably a policeman.

It would confirm Marsden's suspicions about our activities, though he had surely already employed private investigators to dig up as much information as possible about both of us. My records would, at the very least, show a link with British Intelligence, and a few discreet inquiries by a private eye would elicit the information that, from time to time, I was still associated with the police as an expert witness. Putting two and two together (another idiom that Jacques would have enjoyed) Marsden would then begin to get worried and I hoped he might overplay his hand. We were now a definite threat and that might force him to take more violent steps, using his strike-force of motorcyclists as the weapon.

'He won't try to hit us at the Manor, but he might attempt to scare us off the Marsh, so keep a sharp lookout, Robert. We could have visitors!'

As it happened, Marsden made his move that night.

At the Manor both Romola and Deborah greeted us with unashamed warmth. Romola ran into my open arms and hugged me close while, to my delight, Deborah ran to Robert, who picked her up and kissed her, a brotherly kiss that quickly turned into something warmer and less fraternal.

By midnight Robert and I were on our way back to the Winnebago. We had given the girls only an edited summary of our lunchtime conversation, but after dinner Romola had drawn me aside to tell me that she had been down to the motor-home and that there was a message on my answering machine. Paul Brauner would be in Hythe the following day and would meet me around ten thirty at the terminus of the New Romney, Hythe and Dymchurch Railway. I chuckled when Romola told me the choice of venue. It was typical of Paul, who could never resist a fascinating toy. That marvellous, miniature public railway is undoubtedly the world's greatest model train-set.

Robert and I had just come off the downs road,

leading to Ivychurch, on the way to the farm when we first heard the thrumming of powerful motorbikes ridden in a bunch. At the same time we both sensed the presence of evil. A swift glance behind us in the light drizzle confirmed that we were being followed at a distance by a dozen bikes, their headlights grouped closely together.

Our crash-helmets are equipped with radio transceivers, which we can boost to a full power range of ten miles from the radio-telephone packs in our panniers. We normally use these intercom helmets to chat to each other, or to talk to our pillion passengers on long runs. It makes riding any distance less boring and is useful for keeping contact on an area survey.

We reacted to that first warning by checking each other's impressions. Then we started to ride for our lives. *Not* towards the Winnebago and the farm which was deserted, the Whitgifts being away, but as fast as we dared go on those twisting roads for the coast and Dymchurch.

'Follow me, Robert. We may have to go cross-country. Step on it!'

My companion gave me a curt, 'Roger, leader,' and we quickly wound up our trail-bikes, racing over the treacherous, serpentine roads which were glistening evilly in the drizzle.

I heard the mass acceleration of the pursuing bikers blare out behind. They were pounding along, a mile or so back, and though their powerful choppers could catch us easily on the straight, they were no match for our trail-bikes on that maze of narrow roads and tracks. I thanked God that, during the past week, I had relearned the Marsh's intricate patterns.

I had no plan except to try to keep as much distance as we could between ourselves and the murderous young thugs behind. I knew that the only chance we had of avoiding a beating-up, or worse, was to make for the nearest village, in this case Dymchurch. At that hour it would be firmly closed, but there might still be some late departures from the pubs. We needed witnesses. Whatever we might find there, it would be better than being caught out alone on the open Marsh.

Flat-out, our bikes could do over eighty. Their gearing had been modified to match the super-traction of their special trail-tyres. The result was a pair of highly manoeuvrable machines that could race up steep slopes or career down muddy tracks, and do practically anything that their riders could manage without coming off.

At my age, it seems crazy that I still enjoy motorbiking, but I have done so ever since I was a youngster. Although I have come to grief on conventional machines, I have managed to stay on my trail-bike. Robert, being so well co-ordinated, stuck to his machine like glue.

Our powerful headlights cut yellow swaths through the drizzle as we roared headlong towards the seawall. Behind us we could hear, even through our helmets, the thunder of the pursuit. We rounded a right-hand bend, catching a glimpse of the bunched headlights of the hunters at our backs, and saw that they were closing the gap. Apart from the roar of our machines, the Marsh was silent as death. No lights showed in the scattered houses and nothing else moved on the wet roads.

As we approached Dymchurch, we 'poured on the coals', skidding with shrieking tyres on the winding bends, taking them as fast as we dared. I blessed the instinct that had told us to ride wearing proper trail-boots, with their metal-reinforced toecaps. We also wore heavy, one-piece padded rainsuits over our clothes. These protected us perfectly from foul weather and possible 'road-burns' if we came off.

In minutes, I was running with perspiration. My mind raced ahead towards the next move. A slithering turn round a nasty corner gave us another quick glance at the pursuing bikers. They were much nearer.

'Robert!' I spoke louder than necessary. 'We'll never make Dymchurch before they catch us. There's an old bridge across the dyke in the next field. We'll swing off there and take the short cut to the railway line. We'll ride down the maintenance road beside it. I'll tell you when.'

A taut 'Roger' came from Robert, who was enjoying the chase.

We swung off the road, as I shouted 'Now!' and in an instant we were bounding over the large meadow beyond.

This confused the pursuit. One bike skidded and crashed into the side of the bridge. The rider's yell was drowned out in the grinding thunder of racing gears as the pursuing choppers changed down to follow us across the fields.

Our luck held. We bounced over the deep ruts criss-crossing the meadow which marked the ancient divisions of common land.

I was tiring fast, though the excitement kept me alert. My leg also started to give me trouble. It didn't like the bouncing about, nor the constant need to 'toe' the bike round the sharp corners and turns.

'The railway lines are ahead,' I gasped into my head-set.

'Can see! Take it easy.' Robert's voice was calm. 'Is your leg holding up?'

'I'll manage,' I muttered.

'They're getting too close, Prof. I'm going to split them up.'

As we hit the narrow road beside the railway track, we opened our throttles to the last notch.

The bikers were only halfway across the field, making heavy weather of the unexpected ruts. A loud crunch and an upward-waving headlight beam told us that a second rider had crashed.

'Nothing trivial, I hope. With any luck the bastard could have hurt himself. That's two down. Ten or so to go. Here's where I leave you, Prof. Make for the Hythe School of Musketry. They're bound to have security there.'

Robert's retentive mind had come up with the answer, provided I could hold my lead on the narrow trackside road.

Before I could protest about splitting up, the Navajo had jumped his bike over the railway lines, slithered through a half-open gate and was racing flat-out down a narrow gravel track towards Dymchurch.

The bikers skidded to a halt as their leather-clad leader sized up the situation. Three of them started after me while the other seven raced in pursuit of Robert as he hurtled towards the coastal road.

Obviously the leader of the bikers thought that three thugs were enough to deal with the 'old man'; but he was playing safe with the rest against my big colleague. I switched the radio-booster control to maximum power, to keep in contact with Robert for as long as possible.

'I'm making for the seawall. *Now*!' I could hear my colleague's excited breathing as he left his transmitter open.

I concentrated on keeping my bike on the narrow service road. Behind, in single file, the three riders quickly gained on me.

Robert's voice crackled through again, 'I'm up on the seawall. They're coming after me. Good luck, Daniel!'

'God be with you, Robert,' I muttered into my mike.

The glare of the three pursuing headlights was filling my wing mirrors. Ahead of me appeared a small crossroad. I jumped the bike over the railway lines and swung onto the narrow-gauge track, bounding crazily from sleeper to sleeper with the pebble ballast in between shooting up showers of gravel behind me.

The pursuing bikers tried the same tactics. One hit the points of a siding. The bike spun out of control and crashed, throwing the yelling rider over the handlebars into the dyke. Two to go.

The holiday campsite appeared ahead, to the right.

'Are you OK, Robert?' I shouted.

His voice sounded faintly in my head-phones. 'I'm making for the sewer outfall.'

My colleague was going to ride out into the sea, where his swimming skills would outdo his pursuers. He had a good chance.

His transmission ceased as he yelled, 'Here goes nothing!' Then silence. I prayed and jumped my bike off the railtrack, racing to the right over an undulating field towards the silent holiday camp.

The two bikers did the same. The campsite hadn't opened yet for the season. We raced between rows of empty chalets with the echoes of our snarling machines bouncing off their wooden walls.

One last effort and I skidded through the gate onto the coastal road, just short of the eastern Marsh's main sluice. Only a hundred yards separated me from my hunters. Flat out I hurtled down the main road towards Hythe.

The bikers had to slow down to clear their road-tyres of the clogging mud while my bike settled to its top speed of eighty, the exhaust deafening. It took two miles before the bikers shed the bulk of the mud and gravel picked up in that wild cross-country chase. I heard them change up to get the best out of their powerful choppers.

I wondered if I was going to make it, and I prayed for a miracle. Suddenly, ahead of me, it appeared: a heaven-sent convoy of army trucks, carrying guardsmen on night manoeuvres, driving up the main road from the camp.

The soldiers cheered what they thought was a manic road-race, and so daunted my otherwise unshakeable pursuers that they slowed down.

With a muttered blessing on all army trucks I sped on past the convoy and turned, with a tyre-wrenching screech, into the long avenue that leads to the guardroom.

The guards were armed and brought their Browning rifles up to challenge me as I skidded to a breathless halt. The two pursuing bikers gave up and spun their choppers round, roaring back up the coastal road towards Dymchurch.

'Blimey, mate,' gasped one of the guards as I removed my helmet. 'You must be mad, riding like that, at your age. Bloody nutter!'

Fighting for breath and with my leg aching like hell, I agreed, then told the sentries I had been chased by a bunch of lunatics and showed them my ID. They realized that few middle-aged professors race around late at night on motorbikes without a good reason.

'Shall I call the police, Professor?' the corporal asked, in deference to my grey hair and status.

'No thanks, Corporal. Those bastards will be miles

away by now. I'm worried about my friend. They were chasing *him* into the sea.'

I accelerated away in a shower of mud and rode fast back towards the last position, near Dymchurch, that Robert had given me.

All was silent as I mounted the seawall. The rain had stopped and the night was windless. I halted and swung my handlebars round so that the headlamp served as a searchlight. Not a soul was about on the long pale sands. They glowed in the moonlight as it shone out from behind the rain-clouds, illuminating the shore right down to the low-tide mark.

'Looking for me, Prof?' asked a familiar voice.

My heart gave a leap of joy. Behind me, from the shadow of a Martello tower, stepped Robert, dripping wet and grinning like a hyena. 'The sons of bitches thought I'd drowned,' he chuckled. 'They don't like water, those unwashed assholes.' Robert only blasphemes or swears when he's really roused.

'Jump on,' I said, as he bear-hugged me. 'We must get you out of those wet clothes. Where's your bike?'

On the leisurely ride back across the silent Marsh, shouting into my ears, his helmet-radio having packed up as he hit the water, Robert told me what had happened.

He'd thought he'd had it until he saw the sewer outfall. Riding along the top of its slippery wall had been no mean feat and he'd raced the slithering bike into the sea, diving clear only as the sloping walls met the waves.

At low tide there was still plenty of water at that point, more than enough for Robert to disappear, and a few powerful strokes brought him beyond the end of the outfall into deeper water. He was still wearing his waterproof coveralls and boots and had found swimming difficult, even for his powerful body, but he had swum inshore under water to come up in the shadows of the eastern side of the sluice. 'They must have thought I was drowned; certainly the damned bike is! Sorry, Prof. It was a bloody good machine.'

'Never mind, Robert, we'll ask the lifeboatmen to salvage it for us.'

We got back to the Winnebago at half past twelve. The whole incredible episode had taken less than half an hour. We were lucky to be alive.

We were soon showered and changed into warm, terry-towelling bathrobes, with both of us enjoying a steaming mug of cocoa. This was the real 'Ki' of the Royal Navy, complete with four spoonfuls of brown sugar and a hefty tot of Navy Rum. After that we fell into our bunk-beds and slept the sleep of survivors: deep, healing and dreamless.

CHAPTER 8

Knowledge Is the Best Weapon of All

Early the next morning we rode up to the Manor and put Romola's mind at rest. Once again she had picked up the dramatic tension of the midnight chase and had experienced a frightening repetition of her nightmare of pursuit by skull-faced helmeted bikers. When she rang the Winnebago the answering machine was still on, so she had passed an anxious night till I phoned her at eight o'clock to say that we were all right. I resolved next time to tell her right away, no matter what time it was.

'For God's sake bring in the police, Daniel. These devils will kill you,' Romola pleaded.

'On what charge, darling? We were just chased by some crazy youngsters on motorbikes; nothing else happened, thank God, because we were too quick for them. We've lost a bike in the sea, but what case can we actually bring to court and against whom?'

'I see your point, Daniel, but please do be careful. They'll try to kill you for sure.' She held out her arms to me in mute appeal. Suddenly the dam burst and Romola flung herself at me, crying uncontrollably as I held her close.

I am only human and the closeness and vibrant warmth of her young body was too much for me. I gave in completely. Without considering the future, which could well be a short one in the circumstances, my lips found her beautiful mouth and I kissed her with all the tenderness and passion which had been so long pent up inside me.

Romola kissed me back, making my senses reel with the eagerness of her moist young mouth. My hat went

165

sailing over the moon as her lovely firm breasts pressed themselves against my body. So much for all my resolve and good intentions.

'Christ,' I said, with blissful blasphemy, 'that's torn it! Oh God, my darling, I love you with all my heart. I've loved you ever since I first saw you. I can't help it, darling. I'm crazy about you.'

Laughing and kissing breathlessly, we hugged each other until Robert came in and coughed loudly.

'I wondered how long you two would hold out,' he chuckled. 'I'm sorry to break it up, my friends, but you've got an appointment with Paul Brauner at ten thirty.'

Romola and I, both suddenly shy, kissed a gentle goodbye and I drove the car, with Robert, down to Hythe in a haze of happiness.

At the station, Paul's vintage Rolls-Royce, a magnificent black tourer, was waiting. We arrived ten minutes late to be greeted by my distinguished friend looking more than ever like the popular idea of a City business tycoon.

'Well,' he said, his hazel eyes twinkling, 'Daniel, you look as though you've hit the jackpot. Either you've won the football pools or you've been to bed with a beautiful woman.'

'Damn you, Paul! You're too bright this early in the morning. Neither, as yet, but I'm in love.'

'Well done, Daniel, it's about time you married the lovely Romola Kobrak.'

'You've never met her! How do you know about her?'

'I keep an eye on your comings and goings.'

'You sly old warlock! Tell us what you've found out about Marsden and his crowd.'

'On the train, Daniel. I'll tell you in the buffet car.'

Paul had virtually chartered the train, for the line would not open officially until the end of the month. Altogether, with the three of us – Paul's chauffeur, Tim, having left to pick us up at the other end of the journey – there were only six people on board: the driver, the guard, Robert, Paul, myself, and a pretty girl who was behind the minute bar of the world's smallest buffet-car, in which the three of us sat enjoying our coffee and a brandy while Robert stuck to 7-Up.

'Marsden is an interesting bloke,' remarked Paul, his slight European accent, derived from his German father, accentuated by his choice of the ultra-British word 'bloke'. 'Apparently he is a bastard, in spades.'

'That we know, Paul. What else?'

'Settle back, gentleman. It's a long story.' Paul pulled out a set of typewritten notes and as we rattled along the narrow track beside the weed-choked Military Canal, he read them out with evident enjoyment.

'Arnold Marsden, now Baron Westenhanger, was born on 16 October 1914 at Pontefract in Yorkshire. He was the illegitimate son of a gypsy horsedealer called Josiah Ackersley. His mother was Harriet Victoria Larston, the niece of Arnold Marsden, a Yorkshire mill-owner. She died when her son was four years old, during the Spanish influenza epidemic of 1918.

'She had been seduced by Ackersley when he was working for her uncle as a groom: the hobby of Arnold Marsden the elder was horse-breeding. After Harriet's death, her uncle secretly adopted the child and sent him to various boarding schools. He paid off the father on condition that he would never return.

'Mr Marsden was a devout Methodist and put about the story that his grandnephew's father had been a

gallant soldier killed at the battle of Mons in 1914. . .'
Paul paused. 'Not bad for a quick private investigation
in a couple of days? It reads like a Victorian novel so
far. There's even better to come.'

As the small train swayed round a long curve, Paul
resumed reading. 'Little Arnold, now officially the
adopted heir to the Marsden fortune, did well at school
and won a scholarship to the Manchester College of
Technology, now Manchester University.

'He graduated at the age of twenty-one and settled
down to work for a small building firm which his
benefactor had started as a sideline, and during the
years 1936-9 Arnold Marsden, Junior, became a full
partner in the firm, which expanded rapidly when he
personally won a large contract for building the so-
called "Shadow Factories" for the British Government.
These were widely dispersed factories, constructed for
use during the coming war which, by then, seemed
almost inevitable.

'Throughout World War II, young Arnold, safely
ensconced in a "Reserved" occupation, made a large
fortune by building airfields and runways for the
rapidly expanding RAF and American 8th Army
Airforce. By 1945, his uncle had died of a stroke, and
young Arnold was a millionaire.'

Paul wiped his glasses as the Green Goddess, the
scale-model locomotive pulling our train, clattered
loudly over an open girder bridge spanning a bullrush-
lined dyke, then he continued, enjoying the suspense,
'By 1946, now thirty-two years old and considered to
be the whizz-kid of the construction business, Arnold
Marsden, Junior, was contributing heavily to Union
and Labour Party funds. The Labour Party was now in
power and Arnold won a series of extremely lucrative
contracts during the post-war council building boom.

'When socialism fell to the Tory assault in the fifties, his firm, Marsden Construction, became the Marsden Group and, through large contributions to *Tory* funds, "the Yorkshire Wizard", as he had become known, was chosen to build sections of the new expanded road systems.

'Arnold, Junior, had become plain Arnold Marsden and, as a multi-millionaire, had decided to concentrate on a programme of social-climbing. To this end he started off by marrying Rebecca, the pretty widow of a war-hero, Wing-Commander Sir Donald Stanford who had been killed in a raid on Berlin. But he saw the route ahead with great clarity and it certainly wasn't either strait or narrow. That is when he went into witchcraft. He became associated with another social climber, a young physiotherapist, named. . .' Paul paused.

'. . . Stephen Ward,' I finished his implied question for him.

'Exactly. We've spoken about him, eh Daniel?'

'We have indeed. I knew Stephen quite well as a physiotherapist, at which he was excellent. He tried to get me to join the coven of satanists which met at his leased cottage at Cliveden.'

'Precisely,' continued Paul, 'and this is where Marsden gained a lot more influence in high places, by moral and probably actual blackmail. Some of the members of that coven were from some of the most important families in Britain. VVIPs in fact.'

'I knew that Ward was practising some form of satanism,' I replied, 'but I felt that he was an inept performer and I am sure that the necessary scholarship was woefully lacking. He had little Latin, less Greek and no Hebrew whatsoever. So his ritual incantations must have been inaccurate and skimpy. From what he told me, his magical operations all centred on sex-magic and orgiastic practices of a sado-masochistic character. The satanic part was conducted by a small number of the more adept members of the coven. That's obviously how Marsden fits in. He would have had much more book-learning than Stephen Ward.'

I could see that Paul was impressed as he went on, 'It certainly suited Arnold Marsden down to the ground or, rather, down to the bed. Apparently our Arnold is quite a performer himself, very much into the black leather and whips, highboots and bondage.

'His marriage was largely a matter of convenience, on both sides of the marriage bed. Marsden wanted her name and social background and his wife wanted his money and the luxuries of life. They went their separate ways after their daughter, Miranda, was born. She, poor child, like her father before her, was packed off to boarding schools at a very early age.

'In 1954, Rebecca Marsden died in the crash of a private plane at Lympne. The plane was Marsden's, but the pilot was Rebecca's current paramour, an ex-RAF buddy of her first husband's. Arnold observed a brief period of mourning before returning to the social scene.

'By 1956 the Marsden Group was heavily engaged in many activities outside its prime role in construction and engineering. Its chairman had become involved with publishing and, inevitably, took a profitable part in the commercial television boom. In the same year, Marsden was knighted, under a Tory government. By now, according to my sources, he was deeply into the study of the occult and the owner of a fine library on the supernatural and kindred subjects.'

'I know, Paul. I've seen it. Marsden must have spent a fortune on those rare books and manuscripts. Yet he really hasn't got the scholarship behind him to understand half of them. I feel that his coven must be a bit like Stephen Ward's, but on a far richer scale.'

Paul sipped his drink, thoughtfully. 'He's a rum one, all right. I'm sure he isn't into all that madness only for the social blackmail that it can offer on wealthy associates. My impression is that he *believes* in it. He's a satanist, not just a sensationalist.'

'No doubt about it, Paul. Please go on.'

'Our hero, or rather villain, switched political loyalties again during the period of socialist government before Mrs Thatcher took over the reins. Sir Arnold traded some more of his ill-gotten gains and became a life peer. His choice of title was Lord Marsden of Westenhanger, an odd one, when you think about it. Westenhanger has only two claims to fame. One, it is the site of the Folkestone Races, a small race-course which rose to eminence between the wars and has had a chequered career since then, and two, you'll like this bit, Daniel, Westenhanger was the place where Fair Rosamund, the Rosa Mundi of the Plantagenets' "magical set" and the mistress of Henry II, was kept hidden in a tower away from the wrath of Henry's wife Eleanor of Aquitaine. What's more, Daniel, the place where the noble Lord has settled down, is at Westenhanger close to the presumed site of Rosamund's Tower.'

'I've been there. Robert and I dined with Marsden and some of his entourage, his mistress and a most alarming man, his Swiss doctor, Toddman.'

'Then you met fair Rosamund Charnley and the unspeakable Dr Toddman, Marsden's guru, physician, plastic surgeon and Mephistopheles all rolled into one. They're a weird crew.'

'You know about Toddman then?' interrupted

Robert eagerly.

'Only what rumour relays,' said Paul sadly. 'He sounds the most interesting monster of them all.'

The little train rattled on over the narrow track sandwiched between the thin coastal strip of retirement bungalows below the seawall and the broad acres of grazing land to the north.

'Is it possible,' I asked, 'that Marsden, who must spend money like water, is also mixed up with drugs?'

'Almost certainly he uses them in moderation but, by his well-preserved appearance, I think he mainly dispenses them to others. He makes them available to his coven, or to those whom he wishes to manipulate later by blackmail.'

'I'm sure of that. I meant, do you think Marsden is involved in drug smuggling? We know it's going on in these parts, in the most sophisticated way, using light aeroplanes to bring in the stuff and then air-dropping it.'

Paul looked solemn. 'Frankly, Daniel, I don't know. My researchers are excellent, but now you are speaking of a far deeper sort of criminal investigation. That's out of my line of business.'

'Well, what about the fair Rosamund Charnley? I bet your investigators have done us proud there. It's very kind of you to have come up with so much material.'

'Shucks! T'weren't nothin',' he replied, lapsing into a Western drawl. 'I have got quite a bit on that shrew. She's stunning, isn't she? Her life is the pure essence from which television soap operas are made.'

At this moment the Green Goddess blew off steam and pulled slowly out of Dymchurch on the final run to New Romney – where Tim and the Rolls were waiting.

Paul took a second file out of his pigskin briefcase. 'Rosamund Charnley was born, surprisingly when you

172

see how alluring she is, on 18 April 1934.'

'That means she's fifty!' Robert interrupted in surprise. 'She doesn't look forty.'

'No, she doesn't,' Paul continued. 'She's the daughter of the Reverend Peter Mansfield and Miss Rose Copley, a governess, whom the curate of St Michael's and All Angels, near Sherborne, Dorset, married when he found out that he had made her pregnant.

'Rosamund's mother died in childbirth, leaving her child to a grim upbringing by her father, who found his guilt overpowering and whose spinster sister, Bedelia, shared his tortured views. Rosamund was brought up in a loveless and ultra-strict atmosphere.

'On her father's death, appropriately from cancer of the testes, she left home and her hated aunt. She took a job as a hotel waitress in Bournemouth. Rosamund was by then a very pretty girl, and well read as well (she devours books, like other people gourmandize on food), so she made a lovely and interesting companion for any young man handsome enough or, alternatively, rich enough to take her out and screw her.

'Charles Whittaker-Brown, the wealthy only son of a rich Dorset family, fell madly in love with Rosamund. She saw her chance and made certain that she became pregnant by him. Despite his family's objections, she married him within three months of their meeting.

'As soon as she was safely Mrs Charles Whittaker-Brown, Rosamund had the unborn child secretly aborted, nearly dying in the process. Her husband, who adored her, poor sod, believed her story of a miscarriage and took her to the South of France for a long convalescence.

'At St Paul de Vence, Rosamund, who was by then barely twenty years old, fell in love with a wealthy friend of mine, Victor Charnley, a suave fifty-year-old socialite and international banker. The girl used her abundant charms to ensnare my chum, who fell for her like a ton of gold bricks.

'Whittaker-Brown was, as usual, the last to know of his beautiful wife's affair, and when she refused to break it off, he shot himself. Victor was very upset by the tragedy and, to avoid scandal, took Rosamund away on an extended trip to South America. Six months later they returned to the Mediterranean and Victor married her, on Aristotle Onassis' yacht. My poor friend thereby signed his own death warrant.'

Once again at a crucial point in his story, Paul paused to heighten our anticipation, while the midget train clattered past a large flock of sheep and playful lambs.

'How did Victor die, Paul?' I asked impatiently.

'In bed, and, no doubt, in ecstasy. A rare condition these days. Rosamund literally screwed him to death. She was insatiable. He told me so himself. The poor devil died of a heart attack, brought on by his use of methyl nitrate to delay ejaculation. It happened in the bedroom of his villa on Lake Como.

'I was at the funeral, so I can tell you that his widow looked breathtaking in black. Of course, she inherited his considerable fortune, well over two million pounds, plus a house in London, another in Monte Carlo and the villa on Lake Como and, oh yes, I forgot, a chalet in Switzerland as well. Not bad for a woman of twenty-three. Rosamund Charnley waited a full year before emerging onto the international social scene, except for the odd, discreet affair, such as the one with her late husband's accountant, who gave Rosamund most of his excellent financial advice in bed.

'Since then Rosamund has been the decorative companion of many wealthy men and the mistress of a

174

lot of them, but she has managed to retain most of her youthful beauty and *all* of her seductive charm. She first met the newly ennobled Lord Marsden about five years ago, and must have liked what she saw. Here was a man as thoroughly selfish, as wicked, and far richer than herself. He also had an equally insatiable sexual appetite and, by all accounts, possessed an aberrated imagination for sexual fantasies that matched her own.

'She was introduced to him by her Swiss plastic surgeon, the man mainly responsible for preserving her remarkable beauty.'

'Dr Toddman,' broke in Robert.

'Give my Navajo friend a cigar,' applauded Paul. 'As you say, Robert, Dr Sigismund Toddman, about whom I know practically nothing, except that he was responsible for saving Miranda Marsden's life and good looks after a high-speed car crash. Miranda was fifteen years old at the time and was apparently a right little raver. Rumour has it that she had become drug addicted while at her Swiss finishing school. Marsden's daughter nearly died and Toddman's success with her facial reconstruction made him the number-one plastic surgeon so far as her father was concerned. Marsden funds all Toddman's expensive research into anti-senility techniques and, to judge by the ignoble Lord's well-preserved appearance and apparently still-potent sexual prowess, he benefits hugely from his tax-deductible investment. So does his established mistress and sexual hostess, Rosamund Charnley.'

'Sexual hostess?' I queried.

'Rosamund looks after Marsden's most important guests, on whom her lord and master wishes to have something blackmailable. My investigators tell me that all the latest gadgets are installed in Marsden's country mansion; two-way mirrors, video cameras, tape recorders, et al. It's the perfect set-up for blackmail, copied, I have been assured, from the KGB, who are masters at that game.'

'You mean that Marsden is mixed up with Soviet Intelligence?' Robert asked.

'If it suits him, he will form an alliance or do business with the devil himself.'

'Which is what we think he is doing,' I added. 'If ever there was a prime candidate for the Faustian pact, it has to be Lord Marsden.'

'Of Westenhanger,' Paul completed the title with a cynical smile. 'That's all I've got.' He closed his briefcase with a snap of its combination locks as we pulled into New Romney station. To Paul, timing is everything.

Robert and I both spontaneously applauded him and he bowed his head in grinning acknowledgement.

'All that information in just over three days?' I asked in amazement.

'My sources are, as usual, impeccable. Of course, I already had a fair-sized dossier on Marsden, because he has been a business rival in one or two big deals over the years. It's really been a question of updating my files, but my investigators have done well.'

'Brilliantly!' I agreed. 'One other question, Paul: why did you hire this train?'

He burst out laughing with a surprisingly boyish guffaw. 'I love toys, as you know, and this one in particular. It gave us complete privacy. If Marsden's as good as I think he is, he is having you watched closely. I'm sure that by now he knows a lot about you both.'

'He *is* having us watched and he does know quite a lot about us. Twice he's nearly had us killed.'

Paul whistled. 'My God, Daniel, you are really playing for high stakes. Why?'

In the Rolls I told him the outline of the story as Tim drove us out to Dungeness. Great ships passed within hailing distance of us on their lawful occasions, or were close inshore swinging at anchor, awaiting clearance through the overcrowded Straits of Dover, while we enjoyed a typical Brauner picnic, from cold roast pheasant to fresh peaches flown in from God knows where. The whole *al fresco* banquet was washed down for Paul and me with a crisp Piesporter Goldtröpchen and Dow's vintage port and for Robert with copious draughts of British gingerbeer, which, by some personal witchcraft, Paul had discovered was a firm favourite with my near-teetotal friend.

Paul never ceases to amaze me, by his wit, his shrewdness, which is psychic, and by his generosity, which is endearing. My friend doubtless has a few business enemies, but he also has some good friends, one of whom, Colin Bloy, was the man who taught me dowsing, and it was he who introduced me to Paul.

By two o'clock in the afternoon we were back at Hythe Station.

'Take care, Daniel,' Paul said, with unaccustomed seriousness. 'Yon Cassius may not have a "lean and hungry look" but he's bloody dangerous!'

Then Paul beamed his irresistible smile. 'Nice to have met you at last, Robert. Look after Daniel, there's a good Navajo.'

Robert nodded, with a grin. 'I will! I suppose you know a lot about me too?'

'A *lot*,' laughed Paul. 'All good!'

He warmly embraced us both. '*Auf wiedersehen*, my friends. Daniel, kiss the luscius Romola for me. I'm longing to meet her.'

177

With a whisper, the Rolls whisked him away, leaving us wiser men.

Paul times his exits, like his entrances, perfectly.

CHAPTER 9

A Little Night Battle Music

We told Deborah a modified version of Paul's character summaries of Marsden and his mistress and later, alone with Romola, I filled her in on the missing pieces of information. While we were talking Robert and Deborah joined us, their faces glowing from a strenuous afternoon gallop over the downs. We spent the rest of the evening lingering over supper and discussing everything we could think of except the grim subject of Lord Marsden and his eerie companions. It was eleven o'clock before Robert and I left for the Winnebago, and well after midnight by the time I had completed rewiring Robert's helmet so that once more we had a viable short-range communication system.

While I worked away at the electronics Robert told me how the Navajo would handle a similar confrontation with such demonic forces. 'We make a special sand-painting to invoke the forces of light. We pray to Changing Woman, our Earth Mother. She is the equivalent of your archetype the Virgin Mary, or Egypt's Isis, China's Kwan Yin, Greece's Gaia, the *maternal* side of humankind. The medicine man, our shaman, is a "chanter". He "sings" along with his assistants inside the secret place. This is located in a six-sided hogan, a lodge, hidden from all eyes except the chanters'. Here they make the magical painting, using earth-colours set out on the sandy floor.

'They form a geometric cosmic pattern, mentally, spiritually and materially, a visual picturization of the problem. In the paintings, the symbols for man, woman and beast, gods and goddesses, and the elements of fire, earth, air and water, are all part of a mental discipline which is given potency by the chants and by the very act of making the paintings.

'It is the same as the famous prehistoric cave paintings in those deep caves in the Dordogne valley. Their effect on tribal society was as far-reaching, 50,000 years ago, as the great cathedral's influence on medieval times. The hidden depths of the caverns and the secret-places of the hogan lodges both represent the womb of nature. By acting out the hunt or battle, the healing or the planting, a psychodrama is created, dealt with magically and finally resolved.

'It's like creating a building. You draw the plans and then go ahead and build it. The "chant" is the accompanying discipline, *aide-memoire* and driving force; its remnant today is the humming, whistling, or even rock music that forms the background for so many workers' efforts. From Musak to reggae and hard-rock, the chant is still with us in one form or another.

'In the sand-painting ritual the unifying influence of the chant directs the motivation of the painting and therefore is the essence of the ceremony. Sand-painting is a "journey together", expressed audibly and visually. Romola's clever doctoral thesis on Music and its Effect on History says it all. We know the universal impact on our lives made by symbols, from the cross to the swastika, from the crescent of Islam and the Star of David to the advertising logos of Madison Avenue.

'When they put music *together* with the symbols, the Navajo have the potential to deal with any situation. In the worst possible way, that's what Hitler did, with the music of Wagner and the Nuremberg rallies. They were living sand-paintings, complete with the Nazi chants.'

'Did you use peyotyl when you took part in the rituals?' I asked, knowing the importance of the

182

peyote-based hallucinogenic to the Navajo.

'I have taken it, under the direction of my medicine-man, Blue Hawk, but I found the mescaline content nauseating and depressive rather than an enhancement of my psychic senses. I believe that the less stimulation, by chemical means, that we use in our quest for self-knowledge the better. If only the young would learn to trigger the latent powers in themselves *without* all that drug garbage. Daniel, it's tragic — the sheer waste of good minds, needlessly destroyed by drug-taking, when the answer to all their problems already lies within the mind. I found that I had no need for drugs because the chant and the sand-paintings did it all for me.'

'Didn't you tell me your mother is an accepted authority on the subject of these paintings?' I asked. 'How did she get into the ceremonies?'

'She didn't! Mom took pictures of the copies, not the originals. They're beautiful, all right, but the originals were destroyed as soon as the rituals had been completed. Once the chant is finished, the painting *must* go. The power is too great to leave lying around.

'The paintings that you see on sale in Sedona, Flagstaff, Sante Fe or in the reservations, even the finest, are copies for the tourists. The rugs and tapestries are often made up from patterns and symbols brought into our culture by the white man. Our sand-paintings, the real ones, are far too valuable to us, from a religious point of view, to risk profaning them. So we make copies, without the "chant". That way there is no *power* in the paintings, only the artistic value.'

'Which is marvellous, Robert. I treasure my Navajo rugs and the pictures of sand-paintings you and your mother gave me. I wish I could attend one of the chants.'

'Perhaps you could, Prof. Who knows? I'll talk to

Blue Hawk and see what can be done. You are one of the few white men on this earth who would fit in perfectly with the spirit of the chant. But you are not Navajo, not even half, like me. Blue Hawk may not allow it.'

It was almost another hour before I had finished reinstalling the helmet's headset and tested out the new pannier power-pack which Robert would take with him to fit into a hire-bike.

We were both dog-tired and slept deeply, needing to renew our energies. But I woke suddenly to the sound of a shout. Someone was calling my name. At the same time I heard the drumming of powerful motorbike engines. There was also another sound, which made my heart miss a beat. It was the unmistakable crunch of a breaking bottle, followed by an explosion: the horribly distinctive noise that for me spells Molotov cocktail. I knew it only too well from my days with the French Resistance.

The 'whoosh' of the blazing petrol came immediately after, as the petrol-fed flames spurted over our motor-caravan. Roaring fire covered the rear end of the Winnebago, filling the interior with a sinister orange glow as the long tongues of flame licked up the aluminium cladding. Before I could shout a warning, Robert was out of his bunk and climbing up through the skylight to emerge onto the roof of our motor-home, carrying two fire extinguishers.

'Watch it, Daniel,' he shouted. 'They're using sling-shots.'

The impact of heavy ball-bearings, shot from powerful catapults, thudded against the side of the Winnebago. There were also the loud spurts of the extinguishers' carbon-dioxide propellants as Robert, crouched behind the two large fibre-glass luggage containers on the roof, directed the jets of fire-smothering foam down onto the flames.

In seconds he had put the blaze out under a thick blanket of bubbles. The immediate danger was over. And luckily the fibre-glass insulation between the outer aluminium shell and the inner plywood panelling prevented the heavy missiles from penetrating the caravan body, and the shatterproof polycarbonate windows, installed after a hideous experience of poltergeist phenomena, stopped the rest of the ball-bearings as they crashed against our walls. There is a barn-door modification to our side entrance. I flipped down the top part of it while I stayed safely under the cover of its bottom half.

A quick glance over the top showed me an eerie parody of a Red Indian attack on a Western wagon train. The sinister leather-clad, helmeted riders sat anonymously astride their stationary machines in a loose circle round the Winnebago as they fired their fusillades of steel.

'There's something wrong with this scene,' yelled Robert above my head. 'According to the movies, *I* should be out there circling the wagon and the white men should be inside. All yours, you little bastard!'

His last words accompanied the sound of the whirring of the 'sling of David' that he was spinning round his head. As he released one of the stones the sound of a breaking headlamp indicated the accuracy of his aim. One of the bikers cursed and the fusillade of ball-bearings redoubled.

At this point, I joined in the battle. I strung my powerful steel bow and grabbed a box of aluminium-shafted arrows from my small store of archery equipment.

A shooting glove was already on my right hand and I

had slipped the elasticated leather arm-guard over my left forearm. With a silver shaft 'knocked' onto the string, I quickly knelt upright and loosed an arrow towards the circle of lights, smashing another head-lamp with a heart-leap of satisfaction.

A second stone from Robert's sling thumped loudly on the helmet of one of the bikers, who yelled incoherently and tumbled to the ground. He had involuntarily accelerated his bike when he was hit and the powerful engine jammed at full throttle, plunging the roaring machine across the concrete hard-standing, to fetch up in a heap on the edge of the dyke.

The other bikers let out a flood of obscenity and started to circle the Winnebago, making themselves harder targets. This manoeuvre stopped them shooting as they needed both hands to control their bucking machines.

My second arrow was aimed at the windscreen of one of the circling thugs, but I hit the petrol tank instead, piercing it clean through and missing the rider by an inch. The biker screamed in terror and hurriedly laid his machine over.

The petrol spilled onto the red-hot exhaust and immediately exploded into flames, rivalling the blaze of the Molotov cocktail. That was enough for the rest of the gang. Screaming curses they took off in a panic-stricken bunch, leaving the stunned rider lying beside his still roaring machine. The petrol-soaked biker whom I had brought down was immersed up to his neck in the nearby dyke, where he had hurled himself on fire.

As the bikers roared off into the darkness Robert nearly brought down another retreating thug with an echoing hit on his crash helmet, which probably saved his worthless young life. The dyke-soaked biker dragged his singed leathers into the bushes and, dripping with slime, disappeared from that brief battle, leaving the sole remnant of the attacking force lying unconscious beside his now silent machine. Robert jumped down like a great cat and ran over to bring the man in.

I then realized something alarming. Instead of using the blunted arrows, I had seized the box of target arrows with their pile-ends made out of solid, sharpened steel. Had I hit any of the gang, I would have skewered him like a shish-kebab, and a badly wounded or a dead biker would have been awkward to explain to the police.

Robert stood over the fallen thug. Suddenly he threw up his head, spread his arms to the sky and gave a great shout, '*Todiieh ii nii ei nishli! Baa yoonech!*'

'What the hell does that mean?' I shouted back.

My Navajo friend gave a loud bark of laughter. 'I'm of the clan of the Bitter Waters, and don't forget it! Don't worry, I was just *reverting*, Daniel.' His grin resembled that of the Cheshire cat. 'What a night, Prof. That *really* got the adrenalin going.'

Obviously he had enjoyed himself. I was still shaking with nervous reaction. 'Bring the little bastard inside, Robert. I want to ask him some questions under hypnosis.'

My colleague had trussed the unconscious biker's wrists with the thongs of his rawhide sling. He draped the limp body over his shoulder and, neatly negotiating the caravan door, dumped the body on to a spare bunk. I turned the biker over on his back and shone a powerful reading lamp into his bleary eyes, while Robert coiled himself down into a chair.

I didn't have time to waste in employing normal techniques to induce hypnosis. Instead, I used a radical

187

method, which I do not recommend to anyone else. I applied pressure to the biker's carotid artery, a very dangerous thing for a medically unskilled person to try.

Immediately, the youngster lapsed back into unconsciousness. As he went under, I took over control of his mind. 'You will obey me in everything,' I started off. 'Do you understand?'

The half-conscious biker woozily replied, 'Yes, I understand you. I will obey you.'

'Good! Tell me who you are.'

'Harry Fagg,' he said mechanically.

Robert gave a whoop of joy. 'Don't ever use that name in America. It's a slang word for a homosexual!'

'Fagg is a local name, Robert, like Whitgift. Now shut up! I want to concentrate.' I turned back to the biker. 'Tell me the name of your gang.'

'The Riders of Chaos.'

'The name of your leader?'

'Pete Hammond.'

'Marsden's chauffeur,' breathed Robert. 'That makes sense.'

'Where are you based?' I asked.

'Maidstone.'

'Did your gang smash the stone crosses in the churchyard?'

'Yes, we done it.'

'Did it,' I automatically corrected him.

'Did it,' he repeated.

'Who pays you?'

'Hammond.'

'Where does *he* get the money?'

'I dunno.'

'It's obvious. From his master,' Robert interjected.

'Who is his master?' I asked.

The answer was surprising, coming from a semi-

188

literate thug.

'The Lord Satan is our master.' The atmosphere took on a sudden sinister chill.

'Jesus Christ!' Robert muttered, partly as an invocation.

The biker's face started to twitch as though he suffered from a nervous 'tic'. He shrank from us in terror. 'Don't say that name!' he screamed.

'He's a satanist. Look at him, Robert. He's scared stiff.'

His features had become contorted with fear. Foam dribbled from between his shaking lips.

'Peace. Be still!' I commanded. 'Listen to me. You hear only my voice. Do exactly what I tell you. Obey me!'

'I will, M-M-Master,' he stammered. His face relaxed, the lines of terror fading until his grubby, fear-twisted features became those of an ordinary, acned young man.

'Now, sleep,' I said, in a gentler voice. 'You will wake *only* when I tell you. You *will* obey me, Harry. You *must* obey me.'

'I will obey you, Master!'

'I am not your master, Harry, I am your friend. You trust me completely. Do you understand?'

'I understand . . . I trust you . . . You are my friend.'

I bent close to him. 'When the police arrive, Harry, you will tell them nothing about what we have been doing here. You will only tell them what your gang has done. Do you understand that?'

'I understand.'

'Now sleep, when I count to three: one-two-three.' I snapped my fingers on the final count. The young man instantly fell into a deep sleep, his breathing slow and regular; a healing slumber that would help to eliminate

189

the shock he had sustained from his night's mishaps.

'Well done, Daniel,' Robert patted me on the shoulder. 'You really are a whiz of a hypnotist!'

'It wasn't difficult. The lad was half under already.'

Suddenly there was a loud knock at the door and we spun round to meet any new threat that it might imply.

'Hi there!' said a cheery voice. It was Cowan, the archaeologist. 'Quite a night,' he grinned.

'Come in, Dr Cowan. You're more than welcome.'

His bulky figure almost filled the caravan doorway. 'Who's the sleeping beauty?'

'One of the bully-boys,' I replied; then a memory chord sounded.

'It must have been *you* who shouted that warning before the petrol bomb exploded.'

'Right on the button, Professor. We've been keeping an eye on you ever since you were first hunted across the Marsh.'

'We? Who exactly are we?' I asked.

The Israeli smiled. 'Do you mind if I shut the door? It's an old habit that I find hard to break.' He closed the door, sat down on a bunk, and looked solemnly at us. 'By we, I mean my colleagues in Mossad. But you had guessed that.'

'Yes. How did *you* know that?'

He chuckled, a deep rumble, low in his throat. 'Terence Naylor told me.'

'The rotten sod! He could have told me too. So you two have been in collusion, eh?'

'Correct, Professor. We work a lot with Special Branch. Mutual help, you know. By the by, I'm called Lev by my friends. Isadore is such a mouthful.'

'OK! Lev it shall be.' Robert extended a large hand which our Israeli friend grasped warmly. His smile was like a beam from Dungeness lighthouse.

'Thank you, Robert, for saving my life. That meshuggenah Hammond was all set to blow me in half as I climbed the fence. You saved me from a messy end.'

Robert laughed. 'My pleasure, Lev. What the hell were you doing with that gun-mike at Marsden's place?'

'Listening. What else? I particularly enjoyed your psychometry. You must read *my* watch some time.'

'I'd be pleased to. Do you understand these things?'

'Of course. It was Mossad who gave Western Intelligence the first information on Soviet research into the application of paranormal powers for espionage and mind manipulation. We Israelis are an ancient and mystical people, Robert. You must have read the book?'

'What book?' asked my puzzled colleague.

The Israeli laughed with delight. 'The Holy Bible!'

We laughed, mainly with relief that we had come off so lightly. Things could so easily have gone the other way.

I made a suggestion, 'Why don't we all have a celebratory drink and you can tell us whatever you feel we should know. What will you have?'

'How about a hot chocolate Ki, mixed with rum? Your favourite Navy drink, Daniel?'

'You really do keep a close eye on us, Lev. I'll make it right away.'

'I've got a good idea of what you two are after – and I approve. We're all fighting the same kind of dark forces. We Israelis recognize the presence of evil and, God knows, there's enough of it about in the world and especially around Marsden and his degenerate coven. The Companions of Chaos, that's a fit name for them. That is your department, fighting them on the

191

esoteric level. You understand the satanic side of things better than I do.'

He paused, silent for a moment. When he looked up, all trace of humour had gone from his unexpectedly grim face. 'It's Toddman we're after.'

'I thought so,' I said. 'We all feel that one is the very embodiment of evil.'

'Toddman is a Nazi war criminal,' Lev said. 'His real name is Werner Kuttner. He was a young doctor, brilliant in his own twisted way. He graduated from Heidelberg at the same time as a good man, Dr Sigismund Toddman, whose name and identity he later assumed.'

I can still picture the scene, that night, inside the lately beleaguered Winnebago. Robert's big bulk was hunched up in a chair as he listened, fascinated, while I leaned forward, my eyes seldom leaving the Israeli's serious face. The good-humoured features of the Mossad agent were, for once, without a trace of a smile.

What he told us was grim. 'Kuttner was the son of a chemist, born in Stettin. After he graduated from the Hochschule, he went on to gain a brilliant doctorate at Heidelberg, in 1937. There's no doubt that he is a first-rate physician and surgeon. At that time, the Nazi party was in control of Germany. It had been elected by an overwhelming majority and had then marched into the Saar, reoccupied the Rhineland and was in the full flood of its insane career, aimed at world-conquest and the reign of the thousand-year Reich. Kuttner was a fanatical member of the Hitler *Jugend* and went on to become a fully-fledged initiate of the Schutzstaffel, the SS. He joined the notorious Death's Head Regiment after a mystical initiation by Reinhard Heydrich the evil Reich-Protector himself, at Wewelsberg Castle in

1939. Kuttner fitted the insane Nazi game like a surgical glove. He was brilliant, but his aim was not the healing of the sick. His perverted dreams were those of a black magician and a master alchemist. He was trying to discover the legendary Elixir of Life, in order to win immortality for himself and his Nazi masters, and certainly by the look of the beautiful Rosamund Charnley and the well-preserved Lord Marsden, he has gone a long way towards finding new techniques for staving off the effects of age.'

'I'm beginning to see why Marsden is so involved with this man,' I said with riveted interest. 'Both he and the Charnley woman utterly depend on him for their illusion of youth.'

'Exactly! Kuttner, now Toddman, injects them with his elixir. That sort of interference with nature requires enormous sums of money for research, as well as a special source of supply for making the elixir itself.'

'You mean that the legendary *elixir vitae* actually exists?' Robert's voice conveyed his disbelief.

'Marsden, Charnley and Toddman think so, and I suspect many others do as well, especially those for whom physical life is everything. Kuttner, as he then was, sold the idea of prolonging the lives of the Nazi hierarchy indefinitely to Heinrich Himmler, who was deeply into every aspect of the occult. He, in turn, told Hitler, who approved the plan.

'The Reichsführer authorized large sums of money for Dr Kuttner and, far more important, Himmler gave the would-be Pygmalion *carte blanche* to experiment on any of the "Enemies of the Third Reich".

'Kuttner's sinister plan blossomed into appalling action. He set to work in the concentration camps.' Lev paused. 'As a child, I was one of those prisoners. Thank God I was not one of that monster's victims.'

193

'What techniques did he use?' I found myself asking. 'Was it anything like the work of Switzerland's Dr Niehans? He had quite a success with injections formulated from extracts of cells taken from the placentas of baby lambs.'

'Indeed, Daniel, Kuttner pursued a similar line of research to both Dr Niehans and Professor Zoranoff, the pre-war scientist who used monkey glands to increase sexuality and potency among the rich. In both cases their results were mainly psychological. In Kuttner's case, however, the approach was different. Instead of employing animals, he used *human beings*, the younger the better!'

Again, I felt the unmistakable chill of evil.

'By the time that he was beginning to show results, the war had come and the concentration camps were filled to overflowing with Jews and other "Enemies of the Reich". This meant a bonanza in human suffering for sadists like Kuttner, for the doctor's dedication to science is accompanied by a sadistic enjoyment of human terror and pain.'

'How monstrous!' I said, and felt the taste of bile rising in my throat. 'It seems inconceivable that a physician and surgeon could experiment on children. It is against every principle of our Hippocratic oath.'

Lev grunted his agreement. 'Kuttner wasn't the only one to do these appalling things. There were many such monsters, like the infamous Joseph Mengele, the so-called Angel of Death, who injected helpless prisoners with all kinds of substances to observe the results. Their surgeries in those concentration camps, like the laboratory of H.G. Wells' Dr Moreau, were houses of pain.'

Robert was carried away by shock and disgust, 'Why don't you just kill the bastard?'

'As a last alternative? Yes. Of course he must pay the supreme penalty; but for a trial indisputable proof is necessary before such poisonous vermin as Kuttner can be executed. And people are all too ready to neglect the lessons of the Holocaust. It is very important to bring these facts to light continually before the International Courts of Justice.'

'Lev is right,' I said. 'It is too convenient for people to forget the horrors of the six million Jews and an even larger number of others — gypsies, socialists, homosexuals, the disabled — who were exterminated. Big business doesn't like to be reminded of these crimes. It is bad for international commerce! "Forgive and forget" is their pragmatic motto. Especially forget!'

'Daniel, in this case we are dealing with a criminal psychopath, a sadistic pervert who thrives on his power over others. Kuttner even manipulates his financier, Marsden, and Rosamund Charnley. There is no trace of humanity in that appalling man. Kuttner's work is unholy. He is a practitioner of the Black Arts, truly demonic.'

I agreed with everything Lev had said.

Lev looked directly at Robert. 'It's incredible what ordinary, decent people allow to happen to others. You know only too well what the early American settlers did to your Indian people. They damn nearly wiped them out, herding the survivors into reservations on poor land. Those areas were forms of open concentration camps from which the Indians were forbidden to move.'

He turned to me, 'Britain did similar things in the Boer War, boxing up their prisoners in concentration camps. The words themselves were coined by the British military. The Americans stole the Indians' land and the British took over large parts of South Africa, which had already been annexed from the African Zulus and Matabeles by the Dutch. If it hadn't been for the twentieth-century oil strikes on Indian land, the bulk of the American Indians today would be poverty-stricken. As it is, like the African peoples, they are second-class citizens.

'But I must get back to Kuttner's curriculum vitae. There are plenty more horrors to tell. When the invasion came and it seemed that the Allies would win, Kuttner realized that his crimes against humanity would catch up with him. By sheer chance, he happened to be present when the real Dr Sigismund Toddman, his humanitarian contemporary at pre-war Heidelberg, was shot for refusing to torture Allied prisoners of war. These unfortunate prisoners were captured members of Allied Intelligence and their maltreatment and torture is a matter of record.

'Dr Toddman was a gallant Wehrmacht Major in the Medical Corps, who had been badly burned while trying to rescue German wounded from a transport plane during the retreat from Moscow. His face and hands were scarred, but he could still operate as a surgeon.

'The Allied forward troops were only days away from the concentration camp when Kuttner decided to switch identities with Toddman. They were about the same height and build and, from Toddman's records, Kuttner knew that he was an orphan with no close relatives.

'What Kuttner did was typical of his meticulous Teutonic approach. He deliberately burned his face and hands, making sure that his fingerprints were eliminated so that future identification would be difficult, and he inflicted various other surface trauma on himself to duplicate Toddman's war-wounds. He

196

accomplished all this under local anaesthetics, administered by his dedicated assistant nursing sister, who was also his mistress.

'When he had recovered sufficiently he eliminated his mistress with an injection of cyanide. He then hid for a few days in his Westphalian cottage and finally surrendered, complete with Toddman's military records, to the Allies, who, in this case, were British troops. As an ethical Wehrmacht medical officer of considerable ability, with an impeccable war record, he was employed by the British Medical Corps to treat wounded German prisoners-of-war. He accomplished this with such professional skill that he became a favoured member of the German POW fraternity. In fact, the British loaned him to the Americans, who were short of German medical staff. Eventually, when Toddman, as he was now known, had successfully passed through the so-called "de-Nazification programme", he was released on the grounds of his fine humanitarian record.

'In those months succeeding his switch of identities one man nearly unmasked him. A patient who had known the real Toddman expressed naïve surprise at how much he had changed in the intervening years. That patient only survived for a few hours before the "new" Dr Toddman disposed of him by injecting air into a vein, creating a fatal embolism.

'After the period of "non-fraternization", during which many Nazi war criminals quietly melted into the background of their homes in the remoter parts of Germany, the new Toddman was allowed to leave the fatherland in order to visit mythical surviving relatives of the Nazi persecution who were supposedly living in Spain. These fake family ties were the fabrication of the infamous Odessa organization, which looked after

Nazi refugees who had escaped their just deserts and were in need of new identities and a place to go till things cooled off.

'Toddman travelled to Spain with a case of heavy orthopaedic appliances and prostheses. This equipment, which he had hidden in his small cottage in Westphalia, had been made specially for him by skilled inmates of the concentration camp in exchange for certain privileges. Actually they were constructed out of pure platinum. This nest-egg enabled him to make another fortune in Brazil, where he used his undoubted professional skills to preserve the fading beauty of rich South American women.

'He returned to Europe in 1960 and opened a small clinic in Switzerland specializing in gerontology and plastic surgery. It was filled with wealthy clients anxious to preserve their beauty and sexual potency, and he made a great deal of money. One of his satisfied patients was Rosamund Charnley. Toddman also treated Miranda Marsden for the facial injuries she suffered in a car crash in Switzerland.'

'Yes,' I interjected. 'We heard about that, and from her behaviour last night I'd say she is still controlled by drugs.'

'It's tragic, I agree,' Lev said. 'And it was through Miranda that Toddman met her father and found in Marsden not only a rich benefactor for his researches, but also a kindred spirit, in fact someone who was basically as evil as he himself. His own knowledge of alchemy and ritual magic soon opened doors to the Marsden coven, which I'm sure you know exists among the peer's wealthy circle of friends. These dreadful people allow the darkest forces within them to govern their lives in return for great temporal power. The illusion of extended life and continued, even

198

increased, sexual potency was the lever which Marsden used to blackmail his powerful but aberrated friends into their Faustian pact.

'Ostensibly Toddman, who now has a laboratory in an old flintstone house next to Marsden Hall, treats Lord Marsden and others with his revolutionary elixir, a course of injections based on the extracts supposedly obtained from newborn lambs from the Romney Marsh.

'It all seems perfectly legal and above board, except with the anti-vivisection lobby, who rightly condemn cruel animal usage in experimentation. But the reality may be more appalling still. It is possible that Toddman uses the organs of newborn babies to carry out his foul work.'

'Oh, my God!' Robert exclaimed in disgust. 'But how would he get hold of babies for work like that?'

'There are ways, if you have enough money and no scruples,' said the Israeli. 'Even in England, newborn babies disappear. Isn't that so, Daniel?'

'Tragically, yes,' I was forced to agree. 'Dozens of newborn infants vanish every year and are never found.'

The three of us paused and breathed a silent prayer for those murdered babies.

'These monsters must be stopped,' declared Robert, putting all our thoughts into words.

Lev nodded vigorously. 'As you say, my friend. They must be stopped; but to do so we need *evidence* to put Marsden behind bars and to ensure Toddman's execution in Israel.'

Lev's tone of voice became urgent. 'Toddman, being so thoroughly German in methodology, will have kept records, and if we can get hold of those from that dreadful laboratory of his at Marsden's place, we could alert Special Branch and Interpol and bring their whole obscene house of Tarot cards tumbling down around their pointed ears.'

'How the hell are we going to do that?' asked Robert.

The Israeli immediately supplied the answer, 'I've got to break into the laboratory at the Marsden place.'

'It's called the House of the Four Winds, and I happen to know it,' I said. 'It is the twin of another flintstone house, at Beechborough, only a couple of miles away. Both were built in the early nineteenth century by the same man, a wealthy dilettante who was deeply into magic. He established a coven similar to Marsden's modern one, made up of wealthy perverts living in the area. The same eccentric scholar probably also built a temple on top of Summerhouse Hill which was later used by an elderly handicapped lawyer who loved fox-hunting and used to follow the progress of the local foxhounds as they crossed the countryside far below. Both the flint houses have been used for magical purposes, but at different times. Parapsychologists believe that flintstone, being quartz, carries subtle charges of electricity and can store bio-electric patterns of people and past events within its dense solid-circuitry. Any sensitive person entering an old flint-walled house can feel the atmosphere almost immediately.'

Lev Cowan leaned forward eagerly. 'If Robert can assist me to break into that laboratory, I think I can get the proof that we require. You, Daniel, could best help by, somehow, keeping Marsden busy, if possible somewhere well away from the Hall. Perhaps you could persuade Deborah Tolsford to invite the Marsden clan over to the Manor for dinner. But, whatever we do, we will have to move fast. It's coming up to the full moon and Beltane's Eve and, as sure as the devil has horns, the Marsden coven will meet there for a full-scale Black Mass.

'That's when they'll make a blood sacrifice, and some poor little baby will be the victim. That way they will satisfy their perverted lust for blood ritual and, at the same time, supply Toddman with the living organs that he needs for the extraction of the *elixir vitae.*'

'Oh, sweet Jesus!' swore Robert. 'I can't stand this filthy group of sub-humans. Let's get in there and smash up the whole thing. It's a blasphemy against nature to let it continue.'

'I agree with Robert. For God's sake let us have done with it, once and for all. We'll help you, Lev. I'll get Deborah to arrange that invitation as soon as I can make sure that she is now entirely on our side.'

I caught the look on Robert's face. 'Don't worry,' I smiled. 'I'm really sure she's one of us. Otherwise you wouldn't have fallen in love with her.'

CHAPTER 10

Paranormal Techniques

Soon after dawn the police arrived. It was obvious that our cover had been blown from the very violence and size of this attack, so after calling Romola to assure her that all was well, I had taken the precaution of telephoning the officer on night duty at Special Branch. He must have contacted Terence at first light who, in turn, had passed on a request for discreet police assistance from the local constabulary.

'You'll be bringing charges of assault and wilful damage, of course, sir,' the detective sergeant stated rather than asked.

'Certainly,' I said. 'But against whom, besides that young thug?'

The sergeant, a solidly built Kentish copper, gave a discreet cough. 'I don't think we'll have too much trouble interrogating this young man. He looks as though he might co-operate with us. We'll find out who the rest of them are.'

The policeman looked slyly at me. 'You two gentlemen seem to know how to look after yourselves, like Dr Cowan here. I remember that he saw off a couple of hooligans who attacked him earlier this year. Very commendable!'

Lev slapped the side of the Winnebago, which was deeply dented and holed in some places, his voice suddenly authoritative. 'As you can see, Sergeant, those holes were made by heavy ball-bearings shot from powerful catapults, and the Molotov cocktail that they used to try to burn up the motor-caravan must also be considered as a deadly weapon. I hope to see those young monsters in court before a really tough magistrate.'

The sergeant sighed regretfully. 'Too often we bring these young criminals before the bench only to have the little perishers put on probation; but the catapult attack and that dangerous incendiary device may do the trick. I'm confident that we will get the information we require on this bike-gang. They've got away with it for far too long. We'll have them in prison this time. Good-day, gentlemen!'

The sergeant had accepted the Israeli's story that he had been passing and had witnessed the whole incident, and this cleared the air of any awkward questions as to *how* we had bested the dozen or so bikers who had attacked us. There were no arrows evident and it appeared that we had driven off our tormentors with a few well-aimed stones.

In any case, I was certain that Marsden would not dare to set any more of his bully-boys onto us. He now knew that he could neither scare us off nor buy our co-operation. He either had to take more drastic steps and contract someone to remove us permanently or try, at the highest possible level, to put a block on our investigations. I wanted to know just how high up the ladder of power Marsden could go. Either way, the Companions of Chaos knew that they were now vulnerable.

As Lev Cowan said, 'We've got to get hard evidence from that laboratory, and quickly too. If they are becoming as worried as I think they are, Marsden will want Toddman to clear his medical papers out of there as fast as he can. You must help me to get inside that estate. My only colleague is keeping a close eye on Marsden's private jet in case Toddman makes a sudden dash to Switzerland. There's no Customs control at Lydd Airport except during normal flying hours, and I can't let him slip through my fingers that way.

'Help me get into that laboratory, Robert, while Daniel and the ladies keep Marsden, his mistress and the doctor engaged at an impromptu dinner party. Toddman is the key to this whole business. At least, the Marsden lot believe that. Without their mad doctor's injection their elixir of life will quickly go sour on them. They dread that almost as much as they dread death itself.'

'I'm sure you're right, Lev,' I said. 'But they may not fall for the bait, especially as they will be suspicious of Deborah's connection with us. Such an unexpected invitation to dinner, so soon after Deborah's father's death, at short notice and just after the attack on our motor-home, could look very like a trap. However, I'm counting on Marsden's curiosity and arrogance, that he'll be too anxious to find out how much we *really* know to resist an opportunity to outwit our "puny" minds at dinner. He's so cocksure of his own omniscience.'

'Good point, Daniel,' Robert chimed in. 'I sense that he also wants to see Romola in action as a remote-viewer. His worries about our investigations are mainly centred on just how effective we actually are as operators on the *paranormal* level. He feels that in his unassailable position in public life, surrounded by powerful, blackmailable allies on whom he can put the squeeze, if necessary, he can wriggle out from under most of the threats that we pose. But he is anxious to find out how good we are paranormally, in case he has to do battle with us on the astral plane. All this isn't too esoteric for you, Lev?'

'On the contrary,' said the Israeli, 'I follow your line of reasoning completely. Marsden is a raving megalomaniac and he believes that he is a great magician with a near godlike ability to manipulate people and circumstances according to his own "divine" will. Of course he is bound to want to know exactly what he is up against. He has already seen Robert in action as a psychometrist, and he's sure to want to find out what the rest of you can do esoterically. For all he knows, you have other equally paranormally gifted allies backing you up. I agree with Robert. I'm sure that Marsden will accept a dinner invitation. He's arrogant enough to believe that you, Daniel, might be having second thoughts about joining him after the savage attacks that he has ordered on you. He may also believe that you have changed your mind about that large foundation grant you told me he offered you.'

'It all depends on how far we can trust Deborah,' I said. 'In other words. . .' At that point I saw Robert's lips tighten and hurriedly continued, 'I believe that the time has come for Edward's daughter to either trust us completely and tell us everything she knows, which I *believe* she will do, or alternatively, for Deborah to back out and join Marsden as one of his Companions of Chaos.'

'It's got to be the first alternative, Daniel,' Robert broke in angrily. 'I'll go bail for Deborah with my life.'

'Of course you will, Robert. I love the girl too. She's my goddaughter. I certainly don't want to put her in such a terrible dilemma but now there is no alternative.'

Fifteen minutes later we were back at the Manor, having promised Lev that we would try to get Marsden to dinner within the next forty-eight hours. It was going to be a gamble, but if Deborah came up trumps it would be well worth it. We also promised the girls that we would stay in spare rooms at the Manor, instead of returning to the Winnebago.

208

I had a trump card up *my* sleeve and I believed that the time had come to play it. I decided to use narcotically induced hypnosis on my goddaughter and, for once, I didn't confide in either Romola or Robert. I *had* to know just how deeply Deborah was involved with our adversaries.

The opportunity to do so came after supper. Romola had been telling us how she had been badly disturbed once again, in her sleep, at the time of the bike-gang's attack but she had sensed that we were all right within minutes of the failure of their night-raid. It had come as no surprise when I rang to tell her that all was well. Deborah, also, was deeply concerned over Robert's safety. She had no such safety valve as Romola's remote-viewing, and we all sensed that the poor girl was being torn between her love for Robert and her affection for me on the one hand and any previous involvement with the Marsden crowd on the other. I asked my friends to let Deborah spend some time alone with me in the library.

This peaceful book-lined room with its fine collection of works by the world's greatest writers and philosophers had been one of Edward's favourite places, his special retreat where he could renew his energies and think out any problems. It was the ideal setting to induce a calming effect. I wasted no time and poured us both a brandy and soda, handing Deborah the glass that I had prepared beforehand. We drank slowly and I broached the subject that we both knew had to be faced.

'I want you to tell me everything you know about Lord Marsden. I know that you are *very tired* and I appreciate how *exhausted* you must be with all these emotional upsets. Just *relax* and tell me about these people. . .' I could see that the tranquillizer which I had administered in a weak solution of alcohol was already affecting her, and I felt fully justified in using this method.

'Sit back and *relax*, Deborah – you are feeling *sleepy*, *tired* and *sleepy*. *Relax*. You have nothing to worry about. *Sleep*, Deborah. *Deeper*, *deeper*, and when you wake, you will feel refreshed and well. You understand me?'

'I understand you, Daniel.' Her eyes had closed.

'Good girl. *All* you will hear from now on is my voice. Do you hear me?'

'Yes, Daniel.' Her breathing was becoming deeper.

'Very good! You will answer all my questions. Do you understand that?'

'Yes. I will answer all your questions.'

'You will fear nothing. Any suggestions which have been put into your mind by others will be forgotten. You have no further mind-link with Lord Marsden. Do you understand?'

My goddaughter was now under deep hypnosis and was responding totally. 'Yes. I will forget all other suggestions.'

'Except mine.'

'Except yours.'

I heaved a sigh of relief. It was going to be much easier than I had thought.

'Relax, my dear, and answer my questions. Go *deeper*. You are *not* afraid.'

'I am not afraid.'

'When did you first become a friend of Lord Marsden's?'

'Four years ago. He had bought some of Daddy's land when we were in financial trouble, and I felt grateful to him. I wanted to be friends.'

'Of course you did.' I paused deliberately, then

210

continued, softly, 'Did you become *more* than friends?'

'No.'

I gave another sigh of relief. 'Did he want you to become more than just a friend to him?'

'Yes, but I couldn't bring myself to let him touch me. He made me feel so uncomfortable. I couldn't bear him too near to me. His smell was. . . was. . . unpleasant.'

'Yes, Deborah. He smells *wrong*! Like an animal smells?'

She looked upset. 'But like an animal smells when it has *killed* something,' she said.

I could see lines of distress on her face and quickly reassured her. 'Don't be alarmed, Deborah. You're quite safe. I am guarding you.'

'I know.' Her features relaxed again.

'Do you mean that Lord Marsden smelt of blood?'

'No. . . not blood. He smelt of *death*.' Again she showed signs of alarm and started to shiver.

I calmed her. 'Sleep, Deborah. Go deeper — *deeper*! Can you hear me?'

'Yes.'

'You are quite safe and you feel well and happy.'

'I feel well. I am happy.'

'Good girl! When you were reluctant to allow Lord Marsden to come close to you himself did he try to suggest that you might prefer loving relations with someone of your own sex — one of the Pony Club girls, for example?'

'Yes, he did imply that. . .' Deborah hesitated.

'. . . but somehow it never felt quite right,' I finished for her. 'Forget about it,' I insisted firmly. 'It was just a silly idea, and not your true self at all.'

'Yes, I'll forget about it,' my goddaughter replied contentedly.

'Did he ever give you a drug or anything like that?' I

asked next.

'Yes, but I wouldn't take it.'

'Well done! Did he ever try to hypnotize you?'

'He did. He said it was an experiment.'

'How many times?'

'Three times.'

'Do you remember what he told you?'

'It was very strange. He told me that we had known each other in a previous life; that we had been lovers, and that we would be lovers again.'

'But you now know that that is not true.'

I repeated the suggestion. 'Nothing that he told you is true. Do you understand me?'

'I understand, Daniel.'

'Good! Did he ask you to do anything for him?'

'He asked me to tell him all about you and to keep him informed of every move that you made. Did I do wrong?'

'No. All that is in the *past*. From now on you are going to be free of Lord Marsden and all his associates. Do you hear me, Deborah? You are *free*! Tell me what you are.'

'I am free. I am free. I am *free*!' Her voice had a new joyful ring.

'Very good, Deborah. You will now wake and remember nothing of what we have been saying, except that you will never, *ever*, listen to any demand, or command, or suggestion, that Lord Marsden may make on you or to you. You hear me?'

'Yes, Daniel.'

'Good. When I count to three, you will wake up, feeling well and happy and at peace. We love you, Deborah, and you have nothing to fear. One-two-three-wake!' I snapped my fingers.

My goddaughter woke, her face completely free

212

of stress.

'Oh Daniel,' she said cheerfully. 'Do forgive me! I must have dropped off for a moment.'

'So you did, but only for a moment.'

'Now, what did you want to ask me?' she said, her lovely face relaxed and smiling.

'I want you to be a kind girl and invite Lord Marsden, Rosamund Charnley and Dr Toddman to dinner, if possible tomorrow night, or the next night, but anyway as soon as possible.'

'Of course, but why bring me in here to ask me that?'

'You might have said no, my dear, and I didn't want to embarrass you in front of the others.'

Deborah smiled and kissed me. 'Daniel, you are a funny old thing,' she said with a chuckle.

When we rejoined the others, as though nothing unusual had happened, I knew that the hold Marsden had once obtained over Edward's daughter was neutralized. I had won this round hands down.

It was such a weird situation, and so frustrating to know who the villains were and why they were perpetrating such dreadful crimes and yet be in a position where we could bring only our *suspicions* to the authorities. As Lev Cowan said, without concrete evidence we had nothing with which to fight.

Our only trump card was that Marsden did not know for certain how much we knew, or whether we were working for some police agency or security service. He also knew nothing of Toddman's real identity. And in that lack of knowledge lay his greatest weakness. All we could do was to pray that he would take the bait and bring his small entourage to dinner, when we planned to lay on a demonstration of paranormal powers which would unsettle his arrogant complacency.

The next morning Deborah phoned Marsden Hall and spoke to Rosamund Charnley. Marsden was away in London on business but, to our relief, Rosamund phoned back after an hour to say that they would be delighted to join us on the following evening.

That left the rest of the day for us to make the preparations. By the afternoon Robert, Romola and myself had settled our plans. I would drive Robert to Folkestone Central station as though I was seeing him off to London. He planned to leave the train at Ashford, where Lev Cowan had arranged to meet him at a motel and brief him on the coming attempt to break into Toddman's laboratory. My plan with Romola was to keep the Marsden party interested for as long as possible by demonstrating my little Hungarian colleague's extraordinary powers of remote-viewing.

We had twenty-four hours' grace before our confrontation. Robert and Deborah went for a long ride over the downs. When they returned, I didn't need to be clairvoyant to know that somewhere up on the hills they had found the place and the opportunity to make love. Their faces were radiant with their experience. I was delighted.

In the atmosphere of danger and uncertainty, my feelings for Romola had also taken a new turn and I was more concerned than ever for her safety. The stakes we were playing for were so high that our personal feelings had to step down to second place. The lives of many young people would be saved if we could smash the drug-smuggling ring. The unspeakable horrors of the child murders would be stopped, before the next hecatomb of the innocent, if we could destroy the coven and remove Dr Toddman. All of it depended on luck, timing and our total dedication to the task: truly a part of the work that the Great Architect of the Universe seemed to have placed before us. Either we would win and the forces of light would triumph, or we would fail and pay with our lives the price of that failure. In those few hours before the encounter I have never felt so strongly the presence of a guiding force, a holy guardian angel. But once again, that night, I dreamt the same appalling nightmare that I had experienced on those three consecutive occasions in March. This time I woke up screaming, bathed in a muck-sweat of horror, with the ghastly impression that I was the rider of that doomed motorbike and that Romola was my tragic pillion passenger.

By a fierce effort of will I wiped away my terrors and exorcized the nightmare visions of Romola screaming as we crashed to our deaths on that roaring motorbike. I recognized these images as the products of a distorted Feng-shui: perverted projections of the twisted minds of our adversaries. Even in my dreams they could reach out and haunt me.

In the morning another sickening incident occurred to remind us all exactly what we were up against.

My first indication that something was dreadfully wrong was a woman's terrified scream. Still in my dressing-gown, I dashed downstairs and found Robert supporting Mrs Waverley, who had fainted.

Robert's voice was hoarse with disgust, 'Look at the visiting card those bastards have left.'

Stretched out on the green slope of the east lawn were the pathetic remains of a mutilated lamb, its entrails meticulously arranged in a black magic pattern.

The Tolsfords' housekeeper, normally the cheeriest of souls, had happened on it when she arrived. She had screamed and run into the house, collapsing in the hall.

I hurried back inside, found a sack in the understairs cupboard and used it to cover the little corpse. An over-reaction by a confirmed lamb-eater? I don't think so, because I know that the slaughter of those spring innocents is normally as humane as possible. It was the cold-blooded efficiency with which the lamb's still-steaming entrails had been arranged that had sickened me. What sort of person could perform such a thing; a deliberate act of demonic sadism?

'Supposing these lunatics attacked one of the girls,' snarled Robert furiously. From then on I found it hard to persuade him to leave the Manor, according to plan.

'They're not going to attack the Manor itself,' I tried to reassure him, 'nor commit murder if they can possibly help it, *at the moment*!' I emphasized the last three words. 'They can feel a net starting to form around them and this dreadful episode is their way of saying "Lay off".'

Luckily, neither Romola nor Deborah had seen the mutilated lamb and thankfully I had been able to calm the housekeeper by a mixture of applied psychology, light hypnosis, some glib lying and a stiff brandy. Of course, she didn't understand the hidden implications of the sacrifice. She accepted my explanation that one of John Aspinall's wolverines had got loose and later been safely recaptured.

The brave lady stoutly volunteered to continue to help Deborah with the dinner preparations for that night. 'Just so long as it isn't lamb!'

After I had seen off the very reluctant Robert at Folkestone Central I drove slowly back to Tolsford Manor while I considered a number of possible

216

scenarios as to why Marsden had ordered the lamb's ritual sacrifice on Deborah's lawn.

I was passing Lympne Castle when the answer hit me so hard that I gasped. Marsden wanted to make sure that we would stay close to the Manor for the next few nights rather than be out on the Marsh in the motor-caravan or roaming it on our bikes! He didn't dare order his chauffeur/bodyguard to use the bike-gang again as, by now, the police would be looking for them.

Suddenly the logic stared me full in the face. *There must be a run or an air-drop scheduled for the coming night.* That was why Marsden had agreed to dine with us at the Manor and to keep us indoors with him for as long as possible. The lengthy dinner party into the small hours would be his alibi should the air-drop go wrong. As he could no longer rely on the bikers to pick up the drop, he would have to use Hammond as the courier.

I gave a whoop of elation as the solution popped into my mind. Marsden had no suspicion that Lev Cowan would strike again, and even if he had recognized the archaeologist in the previous raid on his estate, he knew nothing about Cowan's Mossad connections; nor had he any inkling of the Toddman/Kuttner switch of identities. I was sure that if he had known of Kuttner's previous war-criminal record he would never have taken him into his entourage, elixir or no elixir. It was all so ridiculously simple. *Both* our purposes would be served, the longer we could keep the Marsden bunch at the Manor.

If we were to present a united front in our coming confrontation, now was the time to explain to Deborah what our adversaries were all about. With Romola present to bear me out, I presented my goddaughter with the facts. 'You must first understand that there are certain people for whom power is compulsion, in the same way that gamblers become addicted to their drive to risk everything on the turn of a card or the fall of the dice. You must have known people in the world of showjumping and horseracing who have lost everything because they just could not resist that thirst.'

'Very much so, Daniel,' Deborah agreed, her lovely eyes alight with interest. 'I begin to see what you are driving at. Marsden *is* a compulsive gambler. He plays the horses and has taken a whole party of us over to Deauville to play the tables at the casino.'

'Jacques Dhery confirmed that for us,' I said. 'In Marsden's case, it is certainly all part of his aberrated sex-drive and his sado-masochistic tendencies. That man's psychological make-up is so complex it would take years for a therapist to unravel it. Did you know that he was a satanist?'

My goddaughter looked startled. 'I knew that he was mixed up in some strange goings-on at the Hall and periodically has parties of people down from London who have stayed the weekend without going out at all. They were not the usual socialite crowd who, during the season, come down for a point-to-point or the county fair. All of them were wealthy, judging by their cars, and the whole party kept very much to itself. They didn't dine out and only occasionally would a small party of them fly over to Deauville in Marsden's private jet. I thought he was involved in Scientology or one of those Maharishi cults.'

'Far more than that, Deborah. Marsden is a black magician.'

My goddaughter shivered and Romola put her arm round her. 'He's a terrible man,' she said. 'I'm sure that any attempts he has made to drag you into his sadistic

218

practices have met with failure, otherwise your aura would be quite different.'

Deborah looked puzzled. 'How so, Romola?' she asked. 'What do you mean by a *different* aura.'

Romola smiled. Her voice was eminently reassuring. 'Your aura is blue and gold, an aureole of light which denotes a kind and caring nature like a positive aurora borealis. Had you been tainted with the sort of malevolent vibrations given off by Lord Marsden and his corrupt associates, your aura would have been murky and dull. So I know that you are untouched by their negative influence. However, your aura has been clouded, in part, by your tragedy and by the worry and guilt that you have been suffering. Don't be upset, Deborah. You are quite safe in Daniel's hands.'

My goddaughter sighed with relief, kissing Romola on the cheek. 'Thank God for that! I nearly got involved in one of their strange quarterly meetings, or whatever they were up to, but Daddy persuaded me not to go. I remember we had a terrible row about it. I was very upset at the time. I can't forgive myself for the anxieties that I must have put my father through.'

Romola cuddled her closer like a loving sister while I continued, 'His coven, the Companions of Chaos, are a bunch of wealthy degenerates, besotted with aberrated sex and jaded in their normal appetites. They seek new sensations, new thrills and complete carnal self-gratification. That is their driving force, the source of all their compulsive desires. *Self* is the sole object of their existence, to the exclusion of all other interests. Furthermore, they are all terrified of growing old.

'This dedication to their own self-interests and the gratification of every twisted desire are the basic building blocks of the Faustian pact. In return for the satisfaction of every carnal desire they are willing to sell their souls to the Devil or, if you prefer to think of it more logically, to sink down into the foulest depths of human depravity that their tormented souls can conceive.

'Satanism is a state of mind in which the devil-worshipper throws off all the decencies of humanity to wallow in every perversion that the abnormal brain is capable of dredging up from the dark pit.' I deliberately emphasized every word.

My goddaughter was shocked, but I had to make things absolutely clear. When the confrontation came, Deborah must have no doubts whatsoever as to which side she was on.

'It's all right,' I reassured her. 'You have not been contaminated by them in any way, and we are here to protect you.'

'I know that,' she said huskily. 'And I'm deeply grateful to you *all*.' She looked at my little colleague affectionately.

'Dear Romola,' she smiled. 'I'm so glad you came here. You've helped me enormously. I always wanted a sister, just like you.'

'Satanism and devil-worship are not new,' I went on relentlessly. 'They go back to the earliest times, when our primitive ancestors evolved from being just an advanced animal, struggling for existence, into a much more complex entity within a growing social structure. With the expansion of the tribal environment came organized religion, which taught the stern necessity of service to others for the good of the community. At the same time ritualized evil became the attractive secret alternative. It is no coincidence that clandestine activities like espionage, sabotage and subversion are usually mixed up with secret cults and rituals of a fanatical and often demonic kind. Take Fascism in

Nazi Germany and Italy, the Falange in Spain, the Black Hand in the pre-World War I Balkans, Thuggee in India, the Assassins of the Middle East, Mau-Mau in Kenya, etc. They are all examples of such twisted cult activities. All of them became grossly perverted and drew sadists, murderers and torturers towards their ranks. Their secret rituals were designed for that end: to kill without mercy, to generate terror and pain, suffering and total subjugation of the people that they controlled.

'Sadism and terrorism go hand-in-hand. I'm not overstating the case, Deborah. These social parasites span the *whole* political spectrum and a quick review of some of the corrupt politicians, civil servants who accepted bribery, and unscrupulous industrialists and financial entrepreneurs of the past three decades will tell you that the guilty ones came from every level of society, irrespective of race, colour or religious and economic background, and independent of any professed political creed.

'That is why the Marsden mentality makes such apparently irreconcilable allies. The extreme right goes along with the extreme left, the ultra-Capitalist with the fanatical Marxist, all in the name of pragmatism. Now do you see what you nearly became mixed up with?'

Deborah nodded miserably.

I felt badly about making my final point but I had to be sure that my goddaughter fully understood the situation. 'These people were responsible for your father's death,' I added. 'They are the sinister Companions of Chaos. They killed him just as surely as if they had driven their witches' daggers into his overstrained heart.'

There was a tense silence, then the glowing logs fell,

221

crackling, into the bottom of the fire. I thought I had gone too far.

Deborah raised her head and, though her eyes were glistening with tears, they now shone with resolve. 'I agree absolutely with what you have told me, Daniel,' she said in a clear, steady voice. 'These dreadful people *owe* me my father's life. I want all of them to pay that debt in full.'

I breathed a silent prayer of thanks. Deborah Tolsford was now one of us.

CHAPTER 11

The Mad Hatter's Dinner Party

Just before dark I drove over to the Winnebago to make a phone call to Special Branch. Terence answered the call himself and I told him in outline what I believed might happen that night.

'It's too late to order anything massive in the way of a countermove,' he said regretfully. 'In any case that bloody Marsh is far too big to patrol properly without rousing suspicion in the minds of the ungodly and then "Chummy" will surely cancel the drop, or the run, whichever method they're going to use, by air or sea. I'm sorry, Daniel. You'll just have to do your best while I organize whatever I can at such short notice.

'One thing is certain. Things are hotting up fast. So for God's sake be careful. I don't want the death of two distinguished parapsychologists on my conscience. I'll come down to see you early tomorrow morning, but if Romola calls me in an emergency, I'll try my damnedest to get there before dawn. I'll also bring some marksmen with me. If Lev Cowan is right and your findings are correct, we are dealing with something very bad and very big. This time we might be able to pin charges on this Marsden lot.'

'You've got something on them already, Terence?' I asked.

'Let's say we're keeping an eye on some of them. One or two of Marsden's cronies are paedophiles. They are a really nasty lot. And we do have a couple of interesting tip-offs from a reliable grass that could have connections with Marsden and the sort of terror operation which you believe he is masterminding. This talk of their free use of shotguns disturbs me. As I said,

I'll bring marksmen, just in case. However, when you are dealing with VIPs like these you have to move very carefully. One wrong step, or too hurried an unsubstantiated charge, and the police would be laughed out of court. We must be absolutely sure that we've got a watertight case before we move in and press charges.'

'What about the motorbike gang?' I asked.

'Small fry. The local constabulary will deal with them. But if you can come up with something solid in the way of evidence on the ringleaders we'll back you right along the line. As you know, it must be concrete evidence, Daniel. I'm sorry I can't do more. I'm certainly going to get our commander to have a word with the Director of Public Prosecutions and he, in turn, should contact the Home Secretary just as soon as I get word from you or Romola that you've got the goods. Keep your head down, Daniel. Woa Mohammed!'

Before joining the police, Terence Naylor had been with the Special Air Service. That was their old warcry!

I drove straight back to the Manor and closeted myself with Romola in the library. It was the ideal place for viewing, with Romola stretched out on the long leather sofa, comfortably relaxed in the glow of the early afternoon sun. I have found the exclusion of light to be a handicap rather than an advantage while inducing hypnosis, because the lack of light often generates a nervous reaction in the subject. Even Romola, with whom I have perfect rapport and mutual trust, still likes to feel the presence of light as she goes into the trance state.

We had already discussed the area that Romola would view and I maintained hand contact with her forehead during the session while I alternately listened to her description of the projected 'mind-journey' and directed her to a specific area of Marsden Hall. Simul-

226

taneously I recorded the whole session on tape.

It may seem incredible in these times of advanced electronic technology that two people closely attuned emotionally could, without instrumentation, form a bionic link that allowed the mind of one of them to roam about at the will and direction of the other. Yet that is exactly what we were doing, as we had done successfully many times before. The mental connection between Romola and myself was now so complete that I could almost see what she was 'viewing'.

In this case, the astral part of Romola's mind quickly left the confines of her body and entered the grounds of Marsden's estate, passing above the landscaped lawns and through the walls of the ultra-secure baronial hall, which for all its protective gadgetry, was completely insensitive to the presence of this invisible intruder.

This is the mind technique that the superpowers are engrossed in perfecting for purposes of ultra-espionage, in which all secrets, no matter how they are protected electronically, or how thick the steel walls of the vaults that surround them, are open to the mind of the remote-viewer who is entranced, perhaps, thousands of miles away.

Romola, under my direction, scanned each room in the lower part of the sprawling building while I checked out her description of their layouts with my memory of our recent visit to Marsden's home.

Her powers are uncanny. Her description of the library was extraordinarily accurate as she reeled off the title and author of book after rare book exactly as I had noted them.

'De Gabalis, St Germain, Lytton, Beckford, Crowley, they're all there, Daniel. Marsden must have the biggest collection of magicalia and profane literature outside the British Museum and the Ashmolean.' Romola shivered. 'There is a very unpleasant feeling in this library, Daniel. May I leave it now?'

'Of course, the unease that you feel is generated by *misuse* of those scholarly works rather than by the books themselves. Go now to the upstairs rooms. I want to see if Marsden has a special study up there.'

'He has a large mirror,' Romola continued, 'set in the ceiling over his huge bed. It's even bigger than king-size, I suppose that emperor or dictator-size would be more appropriate. The bed has black satin sheets. I don't like the implications there, Daniel. Other large mirrors are set on the sides of the bed and I pick up that they can be moved to any angle electronically. The "vibes" are very dark. I feel fear and pain. I think this bedroom is more of a torture chamber than a place of rest and pleasure. Can I leave it now? Please!' Her tone was urgent.

'Right away, darling. I'm sorry to have to subject you to this. Can you move out of the main building?'

'Yes, Daniel, I am now outside, hovering above the orangery, a beautiful building which I feel has been transported here and re-assembled.'

'Spot-on, darling. Marsden told me how much he paid for it when he bought it from a stately home in Northamptonshire.'

'It's such a shame to waste this beauty on the dark side of people,' Romola sighed sadly. 'What a healing atmosphere could be generated inside its warm, sunny walls among those lovely plants.'

'Move on, Romola. You should come to the House of the Four Winds. It's the square, flintstone building with the small octagonal lantern skylight on the top.'

'I see it, Daniel. It has splendid proportions, but somehow I don't seem to want to enter it. The quartz in the flintstones stores the energies generated inside and the feelings coming from them are very unpleasant.'

'I'm sorry, darling, but I must know what it contains.' I felt very badly about this, but time and lack of opportunity were both against me.

'Very well, Daniel. I'm sorry I'm such a coward.'

'Nonsense, Romola. You're as brave as a lioness. Please enter the building. It is the twin of another house that I knew well as a boy. That one had lovely vibrations.'

Romola made a courageous effort of will and passed through the thick, flint-clad stone walls into Marsden's House of the Four Winds.

'The walls are painted white, but the atmosphere is one of clammy darkness. I sense a stifling cold. Oh, Daniel, I don't like this at all.'

I held her hand tightly.

'Trust me, darling,' I said. 'I love you very much, and that will surely protect you from anything you may find there.'

Actually, I was concerned that Toddman's dreadful operations inside the walls of the laboratory might have attracted powerful demonic forces, elementals of the lowest kind which habitually feed off the vibrations of human suffering and pain. These appalling vibrations of human agony can form a magnetic maelstrom of powerful negative energy, and I wanted the absent projection of Romola's mind out of that awful place as soon as possible. But first I had to know what was inside the House of the Four Winds.

'Take a quick look around and return immediately. Don't alarm yourself unnecessarily. If anything materializes – get out at once!'

'I know, Daniel. It must be done.'

Romola's breathing was quickening. 'There is something concealed behind the far wall of the laboratory. It seems to be fronted by a large glass case of surgical instruments. It's a secret door, Daniel. I am passing through it now. I am going down a long, dark sloping passage, cut out of the chalk hillside close behind the house. There are many steps leading down into the earth. I am standing now in a tunnel which is lit by torches in the shape of snakes. They have electrical "flames" burning in their tops. I am going along the tunnel, deep into the heart of the hill – Oh!'

Romola's body stiffened on the leather couch and a chill crept into the tranquil warmth of the library.

'I am standing in a huge cave, one of a system of caves hollowed out of the chalk. I can sense running water nearby. Daniel, these caves are like the ones that Sir Francis Dashwood hollowed out of the hill at High Wycombe to accommodate the orgies of his Hellfire Club. The vault of the roof is high above me. Its top is lost in the darkness. Panels of cold light illuminate the cavern. It is gigantic, like the nave of a great cathedral, but the vibrations are dark – so horribly dark! There are rich hangings on the walls, tapestries – in the style of Hieronymus Bosch – oh, my God, Daniel. . .'

Romola's voice rose in disgust. 'They are so perverted! Erotica of the most horrible kind. They are really foul. Daniel, I don't want to stay in this dreadful place.'

'Come out *now*, Romola. Do you hear me? Now!'

'One moment more. There are other things here that you should know about. They have grotesque masks hanging on the chalk walls with robes underneath them in long plastic bags. The masks are of animals, reptiles, birds of prey, skulls. They are horrible. The robes are black. Some are deep purple. One is scarlet. Oh, Daniel, there is the most awful feeling of *sin* in this place. It is an open gateway to Hell.'

'Come back, darling. Now! Immediately!'

'Wait, Daniel. There is a large basket with a lid. Something is inside it, alive. A black cock and a white hen, and something else. In a dark corner, behind the altar. Above the stone plinth, there is a huge tapestry of the Prince of Darkness. The red eyes seem to be watching me. I must see what is in that dark corner. It is a large glass jar filled with liquid. Inside it is — oh God! It's the body of a *dead baby*. Help me, darling! This place reeks of pain and death.'

Romola screamed and I hurriedly wiped away the conditions of negative force which her aura now contained as her projected astral-body snapped back into her physical body lying on the sofa. The room had become icy.

I worked over her, dispelling the horror and shock from her aura. Then Deborah burst into the room, just as Romola sat up, shivering and crying uncontrollably.

'Daniel, what the hell is going on?' Deborah demanded angrily as I held Romola close.

'You're pretty near the mark. *Hell* is what Romola has just been through.'

'What on earth do you mean?' asked my goddaughter.

'She has been astrally projecting her psyche into Toddman's laboratory. Behind it is some sort of temple dedicated to Lucifer which is used for the Marsden coven's perverted rituals. It seems that Romola has hit the hellish jackpot. It's all right, darling, you've done wonders. We've got the goods on them now,' I said while Romola regained her composure.

'Romola has found their inner sanctum sanctorum,' I explained to Deborah, 'if a place used for the sort of blasphemies that these people indulge in can be so described. I suppose that "Maleficarum" would be more appropriate. Whatever Lev Cowan and Robert

231

do, they'll have to try to penetrate into that cavern and take pictures. I must try to contact them from the Winnebago right away.'

'Why not use the phone here?' asked Deborah.

'It might be tapped by Marsden's lot,' I answered curtly.

She gasped. 'They've got a bloody cheek!'

Fifteen minutes later I was back at the caravan, noting thankfully in passing that Eli Whitgift had returned to his farm. By radio-phone I contacted Lev at the motel near Ashford. The Israeli was taking no chances that either he or Robert would be spotted anywhere near the Marsh till they had returned there well after dark. They were both checking over their plans and equipment in their motel room.

I quickly explained to Robert the results of Romola's remote-viewing over the radio-telephone.

'Such evidence will mean nothing,' Lev commented. His ear had been pressed close to the receiver in Robert's hand. 'Blasphemy and perversion in private are not considered crimes against society.'

'But if you can find evidence of child-mutilation and murder?'

'That's quite different. Well done, Daniel! You've both put a few more nails in the coffins of those bastards.'

I rang off and hurried back to the Manor. Marsden might still have some other scare tactic up his magician's sleeve, but the tense atmosphere I had left when Romola returned to her body had blessedly lightened and, though the pale afternoon sunshine had sunk down to the salmon-pink glow of spring twilight, the library was once again the peaceful, scholarly retreat that we all so enjoyed.

Deborah was standing with her back to the Portland stone fireplace. Her more usual riding-breeches, boots and turtle-necked sweater were now chicly replaced by a cocktail dress that accentuated her slim figure to feminine perfection.

Romola, too, had changed into a dark-blue costume over a turquoise silk blouse, the picture of relaxed elegance. I felt inappropriately dressed in the presence of these two stylish young women. However, neither of them, for the moment, would let me go and change into more formal clothes.

'Romola has promised to give me a demonstration of remote-viewing before Marsden arrives,' said Deborah excitedly.

'Are you sure you're up to it, Romola? That last session shook you pretty badly and we have promised that you will demonstrate again tonight.'

Romola smiled and, as usual, my heart missed a beat. 'No, Daniel, I'm perfectly all right now. I thought Deborah should see how remote-viewing works before this evening's session.'

I had Romola 'under' in a few seconds, putting Deborah's hand in contact with my entranced colleague's forehead. The link was now complete and I asked Deborah to tell Romola where to go.

My goddaughter nodded and quickly gave her instructions. 'My old school, Benenden. Do you know where that is, Romola?'

'Vaguely,' she replied. 'It's somewhere nearby, a few miles away, I think.'

'I'll direct you,' said Deborah, as though she were giving her friend instructions for a shopping expedition. 'Go towards Tenterden.'

'I am there,' said Romola simply.

'Now,' Deborah smiled at the bizarre situation,

'follow that main road towards Burwash.'

'I now know where I am. I can sense Benenden a few miles farther on. I have been there before, a long time ago, but I don't know exactly where the school is.'

Deborah had removed her hand from Romola's forehead.

'Just keep your fingers in contact with her brow, or the rapport will be broken,' I reminded her.

'I'm sorry,' said Deborah. 'I forgot. I was trying to visualize the easiest way to get to the school.'

I laughed. 'You're not giving her directions from a *map*. Just hold the picture of your school in your mind. Shut your eyes if it's easier. Your mind will transmit a mental picture by rapport.'

Deborah did so and immediately Romola caught up the skein of her thoughts. 'I see it,' she said, 'it's quite clear. I'm passing through into the main hall. It's like every girls' school that you read about.'

'That it is,' chuckled Deborah. 'Can you go into the headmistress's room? It's at the far side of the hall.'

'Yes, I'm there.'

'There is a large case of trophies, silver cups, on display. Can you see them?'

'I can. Which one do you want me to pick out for you? The rose bowl?'

Deborah looked at me, wonderingly. 'How did she know I wanted her to do that?'

'Just a guess,' I smiled, knowing it wasn't.

'The one with my name on it, Romola.'

'Wait a minute while I scan them. Yes, there it is, a large silver trophy; it is the rose bowl, with a silver grid on top of it.'

'Correct.'

'It's the trophy for tennis and the date is the summer term 1970.'

'Well done, Romola.' Without thinking, Deborah clapped her hands, breaking the contact. 'That's remarkable.'

Romola's eyes opened and she grinned up at her friend. 'That's not much of a test for me, Deborah,' she said. 'Try again. But this time make it harder.'

Once again the two girls made contact, Edward's daughter lightly touching Romola's forehead as she sat beside her. What happened next is hard to explain in any logical sense.

Immediately Romola went into trance; but this time much deeper than before, while her breathing became slower and more laboured.

I kept a close watch on her because this was quite unexpected. I wanted to see what would happen.

'Don't break the contact this time, Deborah, whatever you do,' I said tensely. 'Romola is going into a very deep trance. I wonder why? What were you thinking about when you touched her forehead?'

'My mother,' whispered Deborah. 'Was I wrong to do that?'

'Of course not,' I said, noticing that the room, in spite of the log fire, had suddenly become much colder. I also smelt ozone, which is, for me, an unmistakable sign of paranormal conditions, but there was no sense of evil.

I watched Romola's face closely as she went deeper into trance, her small breasts rising and falling as her breathing became even slower. Her eyes, below their closed, long-lashed lids, were showing signs of rapid eye movement, indicating the presence of a threshold through which her astral-form would leave her body.

A faint blue glow of static electricity started to shine from Romola's hair. Its lustrous tresses began to move as though in slow-motion with the increasing charge of bio-electricity coursing through her body.

The cold increased, and Romola gave a low moan. I felt that we were on the verge of something miraculous.

Abruptly the sound stopped and her eyes opened wide. I could see that they were unfocused and glowing mistily with a strange inner light. Deborah was shivering and looked appealingly at me.

'It's all right,' I said, comforting her with a steady hand. 'Just sit back and relax. I think you are going to witness something remarkable. Don't be afraid, and trust me.'

'I trust you,' she murmured. 'Is Romola all right?'

'She's fine,' I reassured her. I felt certain of that.

I could see that Romola was trying to speak; as though someone was making the effort to communicate through her and had never before used her vocal chords.

A voice quite unlike Romola's, and which Deborah and I instantly recognized as that of her mother, came quite clearly from Romola's throat.

'Dibs,' it said, in the gentle tones that we both knew and loved. 'Dibs, darling. It's Mummy.'

'Oh, my God!' Deborah was stunned, tears welling from her eyes.

'It's all right,' I said. 'It *is* your mother. I'm sure of it.'

'But how can she be? Mummy's dead.'

'No, Dibs, I'm alive. So alive. I love you very much, my darling girl.'

The voice coming from Romola became stronger. There was no mistaking that voice.

'Is it really you, Mummy?' Deborah's tearful voice was that of a little girl. 'Is that *really* you, darling?'

Her mother's voice laughed joyfully. 'Yes, Dibs! Oh darling Dibs, I've wanted so long to tell you that I am *not* dead. I'm very much alive and your father is here with me. Dibs, Daddy is here, darling. Do you understand? We're both alive — and we are together!'

Poor Deborah was completely overcome. I cuddled her while her slim body heaved with sobs.

The voice issuing from Romola's throat now sounded distressed. 'Don't cry, Dibs. We love you so much. We're here to protect you, darling. Nothing is going to hurt you, my darling girl!' The voice issuing from Romola's throat suddenly became shrill and agitated. 'No, No! I won't leave — I won't.'

Her mother's despairing cries grew fainter as the astral contact faded. I knew that the trance must end immediately and started to brush away the bio-magnetic field which had formed around Romola's head and body. It was like removing invisible cobwebs. Romola sat up, yawning deeply. Then her eyes opened and she saw how distressed Deborah had become.

'What happened, Daniel?' she asked anxiously, her only thought for her friend.

'Deborah's mother came through, only for a few moments, but I'm sure it was her.'

We both hugged Edward's daughter with all the love that we could give her, while her sobs became less and then ceased as she regained control of herself. She looked up at me. 'It was Mummy, wasn't it, Daniel?'

'I'm *sure* it was.'

'This isn't some cruel joke, is it?'

'No, Deborah. Of course it isn't. I know that this is very hard to understand and even harder to accept, but I have seen deep-trance mediumship many times. Of course sometimes it was phoney, or even self-delusion on the part of the medium, but in this case I'd swear that voice was your mother's. I'd have known it anywhere.'

'You loved her very much, didn't you, Daniel?' Deborah surprised me.

'Yes,' I said simply. 'When we were all very young, I was deeply in love with your mother, but she loved your father and she waited for him all through those long war years. Yes, Deborah. Of course I love your mother. She *is*,' I emphasized the word, 'a very lovable soul.'

My goddaughter kissed me. 'Thank you for saying that, Daniel.' Then she turned to Romola. 'And thank you, Romola,' she said, kissing her cheek. 'Thank you for a truly wonderful experience. I know it was real.'

The temperature in that reassuring cosy room had returned to normal and the ozone no longer crackled with electrostatic charges in Romola's hair. What we had all experienced – though, of course, Romola had no conscious memory of it – was something with which science and religion have yet to come to terms. Only those who have been through these experiences can tell whether they are a delusion or not. Deborah and I were both sure that, through Romola, somehow we had heard her mother speak to her.

In the light of the events which had surrounded us so far, that message of love was very well-timed. We *all* badly needed encouragement like that for the hours that lay ahead.

Our guests and adversaries arrived promptly at seven o'clock. Marsden's Rolls-Royce was driven by the peer himself.

'Hammond has the night off,' he explained un-necessarily, as I helped Mrs Charnley out of the elegant car. Her perfume was heady with musk, but not overbearingly so. Frankly, it disturbed me. I was certain that no matter how often she bathed, the subtlety of her own natural bodyscent was the dominant part of that enticing aroma. This woman was the embodiment of sex. The occidental version of the *Kama Sutra*. Her hands alone showed her true age. Their carefully nourished ivory texture had already acquired the prominent veins of a woman past her prime.

However, she was, as usual, perfectly groomed and immaculately gowned, and I noticed when I took her white fox fur jacket from her superb shoulders that Marsden's mistress was wearing an unusually daringly cut dress. Its glowing purple sheen of shantung silk was impudently revealing of her arrogantly lovely breasts, and it soon became obvious to me that this stunning woman must have been briefed to flirt with me as outrageously as possible.

Such a task was neither onerous nor difficult for the sensual Mrs Charnley but, although I kept my cool as well as I could, I soon sensed Romola's disapproval of this one-sided flirtation. Obviously, Marsden was trying out some startling new tactics for the evening's encounter.

To an outside observer, everything would have seemed quite normal and any tension in the air would have been put down to the awkward shyness that usually precedes most dinner parties at which the guests don't know one another very well.

After drinks in the drawing-room, accompanied by the usual pleasantries that are expected at the cocktail hour, we went into dinner in the reassuring comfort of the Manor's elegant Georgian dining-room.

Although Marsden had visited the house a number of times on business, oddly enough neither he nor Rosamund Charnley had dined there before, and it was the first time Dr Toddman had actually been inside

Tolsford Manor.

That dining-room is another of my favourite places. The magnificent panelling, carved by a pupil of Grinling Gibbons, has mellowed from its countless waxings into a wonderful piece of scenic bas-relief. The theme is that of 'Chevy Chase', the mystical hunting scene involving the great nobles of the day in pursuit of a fine stag, while they, in their turn, are being watched by the giant horned figure of Herne the Hunter, the phantom of the chase.

That evening I thought how strangely appropriate that wonderful piece of eighteenth-century wood-carving had become as a background to this unique occasion, when the forces of light and darkness now sat facing one another across the sturdy old Jacobean dining table.

Marsden remarked on the fine quality of the panelling and Rosamund gushed over it in enthusiastic agreement. I saw with great clarity that Marsden had long coveted this manor house with its centuries-old traditions, and I realized that one purpose of his visit was going to be to try to persuade Deborah to part with it.

'Now that your father has passed on, the Manor is going to be a great burden to you with all the complications of death duties,' he might say. 'Why don't you allow me to help you? I have excellent accountants, etc, etc.' I was sure that Marsden would be very persuasive.

Over dinner, the conversation took the oddest of turns.

'You were wondering why I had taken the title of Westenhanger, Professor Fortune,' Marsden said, 'and I intimated, at our last dinner party, that I was interested in the theory of reincarnation. Perhaps tonight you could give us a demonstration of regression into our past lives under deep hypnosis?'

'Perhaps,' I replied.

'Rosamund and I are quite certain that we have lived together before, during the Plantagenet reign, and we both feel that our present happy association was pre-ordained. Would you agree to the possibility of these assumptions?'

Rosamund kept her disturbing eyes fixed unswervingly on my face and I felt Romola's dislike of her growing by the minute.

'I know Dr Gurdjiam, an acknowledged expert on the Cathars,' I said. 'He recorded many experimental regressions, and came up with some extraordinary results which indicated the possibility of reincarnation. On the other hand, crypto-amnesia, that strange ability in human beings to record unconsciously everything that they see or hear, could explain a lot of these apparently paranormal experiences of past lives – as Egyptian pyramid-builders, Chinese sages, Indian wrestlers, American Indian Chiefs and the many other archetypal characters that subjects have described to me in deep hypnotic regression.'

'Quite so,' agreed Marsden, grudgingly, while Rosamund smiled enigmatically in her carefully studied Mona Lisa style. 'However, there are cases which defy a logical Cartesian analysis. Such as the one where Dr Gurdjiam actually heard his subjects speaking the old French of the Middle Ages, of which they couldn't possibly have had any knowledge.'

'That is so,' I ceded the point. 'There is a lot of this sort of puzzling evidence. However, what has always worried me about the theory of reincarnation is that, during the time periods of most of these so-called past-lives, there were, at the most, a thousand million people living on the earth. Today, there are more than 3,500 million souls alive on our globe and I can't see how they could all have fitted into the much smaller number of bodies which were incarnate at the time of the Egyptians, the Caesars, the Medicis, or the Bourbons, or even in Napoleonic times. I'm sure you'll agree that the Bonaparte era seems to be a firm favourite among reincarnationists. I'm not mocking the idea behind it, but I am puzzled by this anomaly.'

'Then you reject the whole concept?' enquired Marsden, his face showing his arrogant opinion of my close-mindedness.

'Not absolutely. The principle behind reincarnation, karma, the long, inescapable path that each human soul has to tread as it tries to sublimate itself into the absolute purity of the essence of God, is an acceptable concept; for me, it is the spiritual equivalent of the material theory of evolution. I was merely stating one of the more obvious objections that scientists have expressed against reincarnation. I am more inclined to accept the idea of both karma and reincarnation being selective and not applicable to every soul on earth at the same time.'

'You are an élitist then?' Marsden's eyes bored into mine.

I replied carefully, 'No. Élitism is a trigger word, indicating Fascist tendencies and as such a pseudo-intellectual concept. Of course, there are always élite groups of people who are brought together by pragmatic necessity, such as brain surgeons, bio-chemists, mathematicians, scientists, fine artists, great musicians, famous writers and the like; but that doesn't necessarily mean that because one has become a part of a small, skilled group of thinkers, philosophers, creators, engineers, craftsmen or what have you, élitism as such is the answer to the world's problems any more than so-called egalitarianism – which usually means equal opportunities for everyone *except* the families of the bureaucracy running the show – is the right *socialist* answer to civilization's needs. Neither extreme social philosophy seems to work.

'Moderation is the essence of common-sense,' I went on, warming to my theme, 'and surely that badly needed world viewpoint is sadly lacking today. Without it, we become anarchic. We can only progress by being less self-centred and more outgoing. I don't believe that élitism is the answer to our problems.'

Marsden gave what he imagined to be a hearty laugh, but it sounded too hollow to be sincere. Rosamund Charnley automatically joined in, her whole alluring personality directed towards me.

'Dear Professor Fortune, Arnold and I *know* that we have been together in a previous life and you must be aware of how strong a woman's intuition can be? I am *sure* of reincarnation!'

This was more than Romola could stand. 'Of course both you and Lord Marsden are entitled to your beliefs. I have also experienced a sense of *déjà-vu* on a number of occasions. In fairness, Daniel – Professor Fortune – was being objective in response to Lord Marsden's enquiry. Reincarnation is such an attractive idea and, of course,' Romola's tone of voice became surprisingly provocative, 'it particularly appeals to over-imaginative people.'

Marsden was genuinely amused by Romola's barbed remark. 'Dr Kobrak has a point there, Rosamund. You have a remarkably well-developed imagination.'

His mistress's violet eyes blazed briefly with a look of contempt for Romola, who returned her hate-filled glance without dropping her eyes.

One up for my beloved little Hungarian!

'Nevertheless,' Marsden summed up the situation in his best chairman-of-the-board manner, 'I am convinced that Rosamund and I have enjoyed a close past relationship, centuries before this one, here at Westenhanger. This is where the "Fair Rosamund", Henry II's beautiful mistress, was kept, safely contained in a tower, from the avenging wrath of Eleanor of Aquitaine. We both feel that here was our home.'

'An enchanting thought,' I remarked, allowing Marsden the satisfaction of the last argument on that matter.

It was strange how hard he seemed to cling to that scenario, as though the thought of a past life, or a coming one, *incarnate* on the Earth, after death, was some sort of Job's comforter for him now that he had so obviously signed the Faustian pact. The concept of life *after* death was not for Arnold Marsden, because of its inferences of remorse and punishment for all his selfish crimes against his fellows. But a karma that slowly progressed towards perfection, in Marsden's concept of personal perfection and his own godlike status, that was something else! It would be far more acceptable to someone for whom self-gratification and self-worship were the ultimate goals of the great work.

Mrs Waverley's excellent dinner progressed from the soup to roast beef with its traditional trimmings, through the delicate syllabub to the cheese and port, which we shared, in modern practice, with the ladies. Our final adjournment was to the library, for coffee. Deborah had suggested that room as an alternative setting to the equally tranquil drawing-room because inside its book-filled octagonal walls we could safely continue our 'Marsden-holding' operation by a lengthy demonstration of hypnotic regression and remote-

244

viewing, and it was now clear that Marsden was equally keen to prolong the dinner party into the small hours.

The coffee and liqueurs were served and I found it impossible to refuse Edward's magnificent pre-1914 brandy as we settled down to hear Romola play. In an impassioned performance of Chopin's Scherzo No. 2 she seemed almost to lose herself in that brilliant cascade of Polish soul-music, entrancing us with her fine technique and delicate interpretation. At the end there was a silence before we broke into spontaneous applause, with the notable exception of Toddman, whose scarred hands, in their white gloves, remained folded in his lap.

Romola was persuaded to give an encore and chose, mischievously, to play the Mephisto Waltz by Franz Liszt. She did so beautifully, and the irony was not lost on Toddman.

At last we settled down to a discussion of Romola's other extraordinary ability as a trance medium and I quickly explained, for our guests' benefit, how remote-viewing worked. I had an idea that Marsden had seen demonstrations of it before, but not at the level that he was about to witness. I was convinced that his abilities as a hypnotist were above those of an amateur but, in view of how quickly I had managed to break the post-hypnotic hold which he had established over Deborah, I felt sure I would be able to best him in hypnosis as a professional. Nevertheless, the life peer was far more than just a gifted dabbler in black-magic and the paranormal arts. He was a powerful magician of the 'left-hand' path and it followed that I must be extremely careful to protect Romola while she was projecting her psyche outside her body. Marsden had brought with him the same aura of menace that I had detected before and it was possible that the dark forces which he automatically attracted might seek to manifest themselves through Romola, as an open channel to her inner-space.

All this may sound like high-flown nonsense, but it is just as real to the experienced parapsychologist as it was to the ancient alchemists and necromancers. Only the definitions have changed, in the contemporary vocabulary of the psychologist. For 'possession' read 'schizophrenia'. For 'overshadowing' substitute 'manic-depressive state', and so on. The secrets of the mind remain as great a mystery as they have been since the first shamans tried to solve them. In fact, we know more about the surface of the moon than we do about our own minds.

I tried to postpone Romola's going into deep trance for as long as possible. She had already been twice into the trance-state within an hour, and I was loath to subject her to further psychic pressure without a decent interval. Besides, all of us in that room were anxious to make our evening last as long as possible.

To anybody who had no working knowledge of the history and governing parameters of the paranormal, our conversation would have seemed like dialogue taken straight out of *Alice in Wonderland*. This discussion was full of words like demonic possession, hexing and spell-binding, succubi and incubi, psychic vampirism, absent-healing, pointing-the-bone and psychokinesis, together with all the other seemingly aberrated vocabulary of paranormal investigation.

It must have sounded like the Mad Hatter's Tea Party, with Marsden as the crazy Hatter, myself as the March Hare, fair-haired Deborah as Alice and the diminutive Romola as an enchanting Dormouse. The difference lay in the presence of the sinister Dr

Toddman, who took no active part in the proceedings.

It was past midnight, which was the time Lev Cowan had picked for the break-in at the Marsden estate, when I finally had no alternative but to allow our guests to see what Romola could do. In the meantime we had discussed, superficially, most of the broad spectrum of the occult and Marsden had, once again, shown that he had a wide basis of book-learning, rather than much actual knowledge and experience in these matters. He expressed regret that Robert was not present, saying he was eager to see my Navajo friend's gift for psychometry in action again, but he accepted without question the explanation that Robert was required at Wessex University. Obviously, one of his minions had kept him informed of Robert's departure by train that morning.

I can still picture the scene in that peaceful library. The lights were lowered to allow Romola to show her unusual abilities to the small group of ill-assorted people facing her as she lay on the long leather sofa, looking somewhat lost in its comfortable depths.

Marsden was seated, leaning forward, in Edward's favourite wing-chair, and Rosamund Charnley looked relaxed while at the same time impatient to see what would transpire. The Swiss doctor's hands lay in his lap, curiously inert. They gave me the impression of albino tarantulas waiting to pounce. Toddman had remained characteristically silent through dinner. He had not once, during the long dialogue between Marsden and myself, been consulted on any point of argument nor had he himself interjected a single remark, either in agreement with, or rejection of, any of the material that we had been discussing. He was considered to be the *eminence grise* by a tacit agreement between us and, as such, we all accepted his

247

anonymity in this strange duel of wits.

Rosamund was to be the first contact and I asked her to place her hand on Romola's forehead.

'Tell her where you want her to view,' I said.

She had already made up her mind. 'My London house in Mayfair. Turn off the southern end of Berkeley Square,' she giggled self-consciously. 'It's a bit like giving directions to a taxi-driver.'

'Nevertheless,' I said, 'you must give Dr Kobrak explicit instructions.'

'Then it is the large, bow-windowed house on the corner. It's a Georgian house with an Adam fanlight over the door, near the end of Charles Street on the right-hand side.'

'I can see it.' Romola's voice was cool and clear.

'Good! Now enter it, please, and describe the room on your left.'

'It is a salon, decorated in the Regency style, with a fine painted ceiling and intricate plasterwork around the top of the central crystal chandelier. Modern gold-striped upholstery covers the original Georgian chaise-longue and armchairs. There are some small occasional tables and, in the corner, a glass-fronted cabinet containing porcelain. Above the mantelpiece of the carved fireplace is a large, gold-framed mirror, carved with rococo cherubs.'

Rosamund's face was a study in perplexity. 'She's incredible! It's exactly like that. Please go upstairs to my bedroom, on the first floor – along the hall and the first door you come to on the left. Tell me what that's like.'

Romola's voice continued, 'The room is square and was once the study and library belonging to a great scholar. Now it is redecorated as a boudoir. The bed is very large and circular. The sheets are black satin and

248

the bedhead is draped with purple silk under a gold crown. There are big mirrors on either side of the great bed. Above the bed there is a mirror set in the ceiling.'

Rosamund hastened to interrupt Romola at that point. 'Tell us *exactly* what there is on the dressing-table,' she demanded.

'A complete antique-silver toilet set of brushes and combs, of very fine workmanship, with repoussé silver reliefs of satyrs and nymphs. The silver mirror is held by a miniature hand, with the wrist forming the handle.'

Her description left Rosamund speechless.

'Come back now, Romola,' I told her, 'but stay in trance.'

Romola sighed and relaxed, breathing deeply.

'Well, Mrs Charnley,' I asked, 'does Dr Kobrak score with that description?'

Rosamund turned to Marsden. 'Arnold, she's amazing! My God, what we could do if – if –' she faltered as she saw his look of disapproval. 'If only we could persuade Dr Kobrak to come to our next party,' she finished lamely.

'Remarkable, truly remarkable! Professor Fortune, your colleague has a great gift. It could be worth a great deal to you *both*.' I felt that, once again, Marsden was hinting at bribery. 'Join me and your financial troubles will be over for life,' his now impassive face seemed to say.

'I'm quite certain that . . .' I paused significantly, 'in the wrong hands such a gift could be used to pry into secrets which would earn the "spy" a fortune. We are only interested in using such gifts for positive applications, such as healing. The aura of any patient becomes a perfect indicator of their condition, or we can use the same scanning-process remotely to help find missing persons or downed aircraft in inaccessible places and for other humanitarian purposes. But I do see what you mean. In other circumstances, such gifts would be invaluable to *unscrupulous* people.'

Now only a surface veneer overlay the stream of probing dialogue that we both used to sound out each other's defences and intentions.

'Perhaps you would like to try your luck, Dr Toddman?' I swung round on our silent guest.

His taut face was expressionless except for the blaze of his intensely dark eyes behind the distorting lenses of his heavy glasses. 'Thank you, no. I do not indulge in such games.'

'Hardly a game, Siggy,' remarked Marsden. 'What Dr Kobrak has just shown us is an amazing demonstration of her powers.'

'But nevertheless you are treating these powers as a game, so I would rather not play.' There was no rudeness in Toddman's statement. Just a firm refusal.

'As you wish, doctor.' I smiled and shrugged. 'That only leaves you, Lord Marsden.'

He nodded curtly and placed his hand on Romola's forehead. As he did so, his eyes wandered over her trim little figure, mentally undressing every enticing part of her. I felt an almost irresistible urge to hit him.

I noticed that she seemed disturbed by the contact of his large, well-manicured, spatulate fingers and hastened to reassure her. 'Romola, Lord Marsden wishes you to remote-view somewhere for him.'

'Very well, Daniel.' Her voice was steady.

'Dr Kobrak,' said Marsden, 'my manor house, Marsden Hall. Do you know where it is?'

'It has been described to me.'

'Has it indeed?' His tone was thoughtful. 'Can you see it?'

'Yes, I am outside the south side of the Hall, near the front doors.'

'Good! Enter it, please, then go straight upstairs to my bedroom. It is the first one, off the main landing. Can you describe what you see?'

'I see a large bed covered in black satin sheets, like the ones in Mrs Charnley's house.'

'Quite so,' purred Marsden smoothly. 'And what else can you see?'

'Large mirrors, a lot of them. They are everywhere, even in the ceiling above the bed. There should be a lot of light, but instead, the room feels dark.'

At that moment, the telephone in the hall rang insistently and I was forced to terminate Romola's trance just when it seemed that Marsden was about to make an unpleasantly penetrating remark. I was sure he now suspected that Romola, under my direction, had already made a complete psychic search of his country home.

She came out of her trance immediately and I felt Marsden inwardly curse.

'I'm sorry,' I said apologetically. 'I should have made sure that the phone was disconnected.'

Deborah had gone to answer the phone as soon as it started ringing, and she now hurriedly returned, looking alarmed.

'They want to speak to you, Lord Marsden. It's most urgent. Apparently there has been an attempted burglary.'

CHAPTER 12

A Succession of Nightmares

Marsden's face was a study. Shock, rage and a dawning realization that he had been deliberately drawn away from his base were all struggling to express themselves on his well-cared-for features as he hurried outside to the phone.

We heard his terse tones in a short exchange of conversation and then he slammed the phone down. His face, when he returned, was blandness itself.

'There's been some trouble at the Hall. Probably that damned poacher again. One of my men. . . *shot him*.' He savoured the words.

I went ice-cold and I heard Deborah gasp.

'How unfortunate,' I said calmly. 'I do hope nobody has been hurt badly.'

Marsden's face was unreadable, but his eyes flashed as he replied, 'The intruder got away, but my man is sure he hit him. Of course, I must leave at once. I'm so sorry, Deborah, Professor Fortune, Dr Kobrak. It was *so* interesting. You have a great gift, young lady.' He looked piercingly at Romola. 'Don't *misuse* it.' His words carried a full measure of menace.

'Of course not, Lord Marsden,' replied Romola coldly.

I held Deborah by the elbow, steadying her, for I could see that she was terrified for Robert's safety. But her voice was steady.

'Good night, Arnold, Rosamund, Dr Toddman. I'm so sorry that the evening had to finish this way. Do let us know what happens. If we can be of any help?' You would have thought that Deborah was enquiring after a sick dog, hurt in a road accident.

This tense charade continued until the Marsden entourage had finally driven out of sight.

'I pray that it's not Robert,' said Deborah weakly, nearly collapsing against my steadying arm.

'Please God, it's not serious, for *whoever* was shot.' Romola's calm words brought us back to sanity.

'I'll try to raise one of them on the radio-telephone,' I said.

'You mean, at the Winnebago? Surely they won't have managed to get back there yet, especially if one of them is wounded,' Romola observed.

'I meant on the bike-radio. Robert picked up a hire-bike in Ashford. He took the radio helmet-set with him.'

'Why did they use a motorbike, Daniel?' asked Deborah.

'It's much better for cross-country work or for a fast getaway. It sounds as if they made their escape that way.'

By this time I had unhooked my own helmet from the back-pannier of my trail-bike and unclipped the microphone and earphones. 'If we connect the jack-plug directly into the radio-receiver speaker in the pannier, we can all hear it. I'll take the whole rig into the hallway.'

I wheeled the bike inside and started calling Robert on the emergency wavelength.

'Para one to Para two: do you read me?' I repeated the call several times.

Our radio link has two channels, so we don't have to wait for each other to cease transmitting before we reply. My transmission would automatically trigger a light and a buzzer on Robert's powerful bike-radio, which of course he had taken along with his helmet.

For a minute nothing happened, probably because

Robert was riding through a 'dead-zone' below the ridge of the downs. Then abruptly, to our intense relief, the small radio crackled into life.

'Para two to Para one. How do you read me?' Robert's voice was calm, as though he were chatting to me on a summer's ride.

'Loud and clear, Robert. Are you all right?'

'A-okay, Prof. Tell Deborah I'm fine. Not a scratch!'

Deborah could hear every word and she gave a sob of relief.

'Is Lev all right?' I asked anxiously.

'He's bleeding pretty badly. But I think he'll make it. Some bastard shot him as he was leaving the laboratory. He managed to make it to the fence while I dealt with the guard. I think I fractured the son of a bitch's skull. I really don't care too much. We've got to get Lev to a hospital.'

'No, Robert. Make for the Winnebago. I've got everything I need to operate there. It will be quicker. Is he still conscious?'

'He's hanging in there, Daniel. I've got a tourniquet on his left arm and he was also hit in the leg. Buckshot! Thank God he was quite a way off when the guard fired. See you at the Winnebago. Roger and out.'

'I must go,' I said. 'I'll leave the radio here for you.' I thought for a moment. 'Romola?'

'Yes, Daniel.'

'Ring Special Branch and try to contact Terence. Tell him I'm sure the whole thing is going to bust wide open. Don't worry, Deborah. But, just in case, can you still use a shotgun?'

For the first time since the latest emergency happened, she smiled. 'I came in second at the Royal Kent Show, clay-pigeon shooting.'

'Good girl! Get out your father's guns and load them

with number six shot; then close up everything and sit in the hall, near the phone. Keep contact with one of us through the *bike-phone*. Just keep the button down and the yellow light on. The batteries will last for hours, certainly till dawn. I'll leave it ready for action. I'll call you as soon as we've got things under control. Don't use your house phone to call me. I'll also contact Special Branch from the Winnebago. I don't mind Marsden finding out that you can call Special Branch, but I don't want him to monitor *all* our calls. I want him to be as worried and uncertain as possible. It will surely make him do something drastic. I wish I knew if I was right about that bloody air-drop; *if* they are going to make it and exactly when and where. Robert or Lev may know more. They had the gun-mike with them.'

I kissed Deborah and then cuddled Romola close. Her warm response made me feel dizzy. 'I love you, darling,' I said simply. 'For God's sake, if you are in any doubt, call the local police!' I drove off in an unaccustomed shower of gravel.

A few minutes later I skidded the Ford savagely round the bend outside the farmhouse and bounced over the track up to the Winnebago.

The lights were on inside and the blinds were drawn. Robert's hired trail-bike was leaning against the side of the caravan. There was blood on the aluminium step. As I pulled up, Robert appeared in the doorway.

'He's okay so far, Daniel. But he's lost a lot of blood.'

'That I haven't got. Please God one of us is compatible.'

Lev was slumped, half-conscious, on the portside bunk. His normally swarthy face was pale with shock. Robert had done a good job and as I eased the tourniquet off Lev's left bicep I could see that the wounds in his forearm had ceased to bleed profusely. The arm was severely lacerated by the blast of pellets, some of which, at the long range at which they had been fired, had also lodged in his left leg, tearing several ragged holes in his thigh.

Lev came round as I was examining him, and grinned groggily. 'Sorry, Daniel,' he whispered. 'I blew it, but we sure got *some* interesting evidence. Robert will tell you about it.'

'Just relax, Lev. I'm going to operate to remove any shot left inside you. You won't feel a thing. Pull out the centre bunk, Robert. I'm giving Lev a shot of morphine.'

While Robert arranged the bunk and two standard lamps so that I would have the most light possible for the operation, I swabbed Lev's arm and gave him the injection. As he relaxed back with a sigh of relief at his freedom from the pain, I quickly scrubbed up in the washbasin. Robert helped me to slip on a pair of surgical gloves. I handed him an old-fashioned gauze-covered strainer and a narrow-nozzled bottle of chloroform. 'It's primitive, but it works. Keep Lev under with a few drops on the gauze over his mouth and nose. It'll make him feel sick later, but I've got no time to do a proper job with a general anaesthetic of pentathol. You keep him woozy and I'll use novocaine for the local anaesthetic on his wounds. I'll need help with the stitching too.'

'OK, Prof, you're the doctor,' Robert said quietly. 'Or rather, the surgeon.'

I worked on Lev for about an hour, during which time I extracted ten pellets from his lacerated forearm and six more small slugs from his left thigh. They had lodged just below the femur. Mercifully neither the radius nor the ulna in his arm, nor the femur in his leg

259

had been touched, but the pellets had gone deeply into the surrounding tissue and musculature, fortunately without hitting a main nerve or, thank God, severing either of the two arteries involved. In a way, it was a lucky night for Lev. Had the gunman been nearer he would have severed his limbs.

Nevertheless, my Israeli friend had lost a lot of blood, and a quick look at his 'dog tags', which he had kept as a relic from his Hagannah days, confirmed that his blood group was a common one and, best of all, matched Robert's, who was as delighted as I was and quickly set up a safari bed and an air mattress beside Lev's bunk so that I could complete the transfusion immediately I finished the surgery. I had already put Lev on a saline and Dextran drip and stitching up the cobweb of lacerations took about twenty more minutes.

His pulse and respiration were good and his blood-pressure was adequate, but it was with a deep sigh of relief that I completed the transfusion hook-up between them and, at last, got some of Robert's rich Navajo/Irish blood into my patient. Obviously the mixture was beneficial, because soon the lines of stress and the pallor of shock were replaced by a much healthier colour. A final check showed me that my patient was responding well and, having completed the bandaging, I sat back on the opposite bunk and turned to Robert. 'Well, what went wrong?'

'Lev got inside the laboratory and was taking pictures and rummaging around. We also picked up something really interesting with the gun-mike. I'll play it for you in a minute. Somehow he must have triggered off an alarm signal in the "lab" and then all hell broke loose. Lev came flying out through the window with a parachutist's forward roll, and was running for the security fence, where I was waiting to give him a leg up-and-over, when the guard suddenly came round the other side of the laboratory and shot him with both barrels – luckily at long range. Lev went down and, as I was hidden, I ran round the back of the bushes and hit the guard as he went past. I think I broke his skull. As he fell, I grabbed the shotgun and blew out the two floodlights which had come on nearby. In the sudden blackout, I scooped up Lev and scrambled over the security fence. I carried him round the corner of the hill, where I had the bike stashed. Then I tied Lev to me on the pillion with my pannier-belt and got the hell out of there before they realized that we had gone.'

I silently thanked God for Robert's strength. 'Well done, Robert. What about this special information that you've got?'

'Wait till you hear this, Daniel!' With his free hand Robert took the small recorder, opened it, ejected the cassette, and popped it into my hi-fi equipment.

A man and a woman were speaking, at first faintly, then more clearly. 'It's our only chance, darling. There's a cool two million in the air-drop tonight. I'll make the pick-up with the bike, as instructed, but the twist is that *you'll* be on the back of my bike and we'll make London with it on our own. I've got a fence there who'll handle it for me. He's an old mate from my mercenary days.' It was Hammond's voice.

'Are you sure it will work, darling? Daddy will kill you if he catches you. He might kill me too.'

There was no mistaking Marsden's daughter, Miranda.

'Don't worry. We'll be out of the country by morning. My pilot friend, Max, will fly us from Lasham airfield. We'll be out of the country in four or five hours and who's going to find us in Holland? I've got good friends there. Your jewels will provide us with our air fare and a grub-stake and we'll make for South America. The fence will pass the drug funds through to me there. It's going to be a piece of cake.'

'I still think you're crazy, but I love you, Peter, and I've got to get away from here.' Her voice was suddenly pleading. 'You'll keep some of the stuff for *me*, won't you darling?'

'Sure.' There was the sound of prolonged kissing and heavy breathing.

'Sensitive gun-mike,' I remarked.

Robert grinned. 'The best is yet to come, Prof.'

'Right!' continued Hammond's voice. 'Check the time. Synchronize our watches. The drop is near Ivychurch. That's twenty minutes from here.

'It's now exactly twelve minutes past midnight. The drop is timed for three o'clock. You be ready and dressed in your full gear, helmet, boots and all, and be outside the empty gate-lodge at the end of the old drive at two o'clock on the dot. Sneak out without being seen, and make your way to the woods at the back of the laboratory. When the coast is clear, *walk* – don't run – down the lane and hide behind the old lodge till I pick you up. Your old man won't be back till about then and he'll think you're asleep in bed. Make up a dummy under your sheets.' There was a significant pause, then . . . 'You and I have got some celebrating to do . . .' Miranda laughed throatily and there was the sound of more kissing and foreplay.

'We've heard enough. We're not audio-voyeurs,' remarked Robert, switching off and then holding still as I disconnected the transfusion drip from both him and Lev. 'They're going to make a big heist, Daniel, and they could get away with it. By the time Marsden finds out, it will be too late.'

'Not if we stop them after they've made the pick-up.

262

Robert, you must intercept them. With your sling you can have them off that bike when they stop to pick up the drugs. But lie still for a few minutes. I don't want you fainting before you start!' I made him some sweet cocoa and insisted that he took it slowly.

'I like your method of attack, Prof. There's a lot of mercenary in you as well as the doctor,' Robert observed grimly and sipped his hot drink.

'Right,' I said. 'I'll wake up Eli and get him to look after Lev. We'll tell him there's been a shooting accident. Edward said I could trust him with my life. I'm sure he'll keep his mouth shut.'

I checked my watch. The time was two a.m. 'The drop will be in an hour. Get to Ivychurch and wait for Hammond and Miranda. Let's see,' I mused. 'He's picking her up at two o'clock at the old lodge, so you've got about twenty minutes to get into position. There's plenty of moonlight. Take the night-glasses with you and keep your radio switched on.'

Robert roared away towards the rendezvous point, which, though vague as to its *exact* position, was definite enough for him to make the interception.

I phoned Eli on the radio-telephone and, after a few rings, his sleepy voice answered grumpily.

When I told him what I wanted, he didn't hesitate and, a few minutes later, he was knocking on the caravan door. I quickly explained the situation, saying that either myself or an ambulance would arrive at first light, and was just about to leave when the door opened again and I was almost blinded by a powerful torch.

'Professor Fortune?' asked a low voice.

'Yes,' I said, edging my hand towards my heavy blackthorn walking stick.

'I'm Nat Levkovitz, a friend of Lev Cowan's.'

'How do I know that?' I asked cautiously, my fingers closing on the stick. There was a laugh from the shadowy figure behind the light. 'Lev's told me about you, Professor. You're an old friend of Dov Bar Lev. You were in the Resistance together, in Normandy. His code name was "Renard".'

I relaxed my grip on the murderous blackthorn. 'Lev's inside. He's badly lacerated but not dangerously wounded. My friend, Eli Whitgift, is going to keep an eye on him till either I come back for him or we get an ambulance. But how did you get here?'

'I was shadowing Lev and Robert as a precaution, but at a distance, with night-binoculars. Lev told me not to interfere, just keep a watching brief. Then I tracked the route of Robert's motorbike, collected my vehicle and followed up. I'd like to take Lev with me now if it's safe to move him.'

I summarized the medical situation. 'Right now he's asleep and when he wakes up he'll be sick. I had to use chloroform as I'd no way of safely administering pentathol. He *can* be moved and doubtless you've got special arrangements for such an emergency.'

The Mossad man nodded curtly as he entered the caravan. 'Special!' he agreed.

I liked what I saw. Lev's associate radiated quiet efficiency. 'But I'd sooner he stayed here for another hour or so,' I said. 'Can you stay with him? Eli can get you anything you need. There's plenty of food and drink here. No alcohol for Lev, you understand, but warm sweet tea would be a good idea later on.'

It took only a moment for this tough, shrewd Mossad agent, a small, well-built, bearded man in his late twenties, to make up his mind. 'It's a deal!' he grinned expansively, revealing perfect teeth. 'Thank you for all you've done. You and your Navajo friend are El-Al – The Tops – with me.'

I could see why Lev had chosen him as his partner.

We shook hands, and after a last quick examination of my patient, I left for the Manor. I had to be there by three a.m. to hear from Robert by radio whether he had succeeded in making the intercept. Deborah greeted me, shotgun in hand and with the other one of her father's pair of twelve-bore Purdeys beside her on the hall table.

'Well, how is he?' she asked anxiously.

'Robert's fine and sends his love. He's out on the Marsh, on a mission.'

Deborah bridled angrily. 'Daniel, if anything happens to him I'll. . .'

'You'll do what, my dear? Shoot me with one of your father's Purdeys? I don't think so. Calm down, lass. Robert is perfectly capable of looking after himself.'

Romola, who had been upstairs, hurried down and rushed into my arms and we clung together while I told her about Lev.

'You're choking me,' I protested, disengaging her arms from around my neck. 'We must listen carefully for a radio contact, because soon it will be three o'clock.'

'What does that mean?' she asked.

'Simply that by three a.m., or thereabouts, the air-drop of drugs will have taken place and Hammond, with Miranda Marsden on the back of his motorbike, will have picked it up in an attempt to hijack it for themselves – but only to be taken prisoner by Robert.'

'Daniel, that's bloody dangerous,' cried Deborah furiously. 'I'm sure that man Hammond will be carrying a gun.'

'Don't worry,' I reassured her. 'I've seen Robert

move at night. Only his shadow makes less noise. He's deadly with that sling. He'll take Hammond off that bike with no trouble.'

She was still unconvinced. Romola, too, was upset, and said so. 'Our job is to tackle the paranormal aspects of this horrible business. You and Robert shouldn't be playing at Cops and Robbers. That's a job for the police.'

'But darling, this sort of opportunity doesn't happen twice, and if we can catch Hammond red-handed, with Miranda Marsden as well, we might be able to get them both under hypnosis. They'll tell us enough to incriminate the whole lot of them. All we have to do is to record them on tape.'

'That's inadmissible evidence in court,' Deborah reminded us.

'Maybe, but it's a good start. Then Special Branch can get a warrant to go in and search Marsden's set-up. God willing, we'll put that appalling doctor away, as well. I owe Lev that.'

The bike-radio lit up. Robert's voice crackled through the speaker. 'Para two to Para one. All hell's broken loose.'

Again I froze, somehow knowing every word of what he was about to say.

'The headlight of Hammond's bike showed up long before they did. I could see it coming down the hill, off the escarpment. They must have been doing over sixty. Behind him, I saw other lights, but I reckoned that the rest of the bike-gang were lying low till the heat was off. Someone else was following them. Maybe a couple of Marsden's security guards.

'At that moment, almost opposite where I was hiding, in the moonlight, I saw something really weird. The whole of the road was covered with. . .'

266

'With giant frogs!' I almost shouted the words into my mike.

'How the hell did you know that, Daniel?'

'The Marsh has suffered from plagues of those ugly brutes ever since someone brought them to the Levels just before the war. What happened next?' But I knew what he would say.

'Hammond hit them at full speed, ploughing into the frogs at well over sixty. The bike shot off the road with those two poor bastards clinging on to it, screaming.' He paused. 'They hit the opposite bank of the dyke with their big machine coming right down on top of them. Mercifully, they must have been killed instantly. The whole bloody mess exploded and the blazing wreckage slid down the side of the dyke and disappeared underneath the water. It was ghastly. One second they were alive and the next, dead, smashed to pieces.'

'I know. I'll tell you why later. The important thing now is to pick up the drugs. Did the plane make the drop, or is this tragedy for nothing?'

'The aircraft turned up about five minutes after the crash. It dropped the package, without a parachute, just as you said. I'll find it, don't worry.'

'How? The directional radio-finder must have gone down in the dyke with Hammond's bike.' But I should have known his answer.

'I'll dowse for it, Daniel, what else? I'll call you again when I find it. Roger and out.'

The radio clicked off. I turned to the girls. 'We *should* stick to the paranormal. Things are getting far too rough.'

A few minutes later the radio crackled back to life. 'I've got the goods!' Robert's tone of voice was relieved. 'Be with you in another ten minutes. Out!'

The fulfilment of my strange nightmare had left me with a mixture of relief and distaste. Sudden death in such appalling circumstances is not a cause for self-congratulation on one's predictive ability. Neither of those two young people was much of a human being, but youth cut short is never a reason for smugness. I was much relieved, however, that Romola and I hadn't been the riders.

When my colleague brought his bike to a gravel-scattering stop outside the Manor, Deborah rushed out and they embraced passionately, oblivious to Romola and myself.

'Any trouble? Did the bikers who were following Hammond show up?' I asked as soon as I decently could.

'No, they must have panicked and scrammed when they heard the crash and saw the fire. No one else came out to investigate. It shows how effective Marsden's terror tactics have been. I dowsed for and found the package without any bother, and I deactivated its radio signal at once.'

I took Robert aside. 'We desperately need Romola to do another remote-viewing,' I told him. 'I've got to know what Marsden is doing at this moment. It's the only edge that we've got on him. By now, whoever was on the following bikes will have reported back that Hammond has crashed, and Marsden is, no doubt, yelling at them at this moment for not finding out the full facts. He may go upstairs to wake Miranda to give her the bad news and find she's gone. It won't take him long to put two and two together and then the sparks will really start to fly. That's the time we want Romola to remote-view Marsden Hall.'

Robert was concerned that the strain would be too great for her but Romola brushed his objections aside. I was equally concerned for her mental health, yet we all knew how important her extraordinary ability would be at this crucial time. Unhappily I could see no alternative.

'You're a hard task-master, Professor Fortune,' said my darling with a gentle smile.

I kissed her for that. Not that I needed any excuse to do so.

CHAPTER 13
The Pacts Are Called In

In the library Robert neatly summed up the situation: 'My guess is that Toddman will make a run for it. After this second break-in tonight I think he'll panic. He certainly won't want the police nosing around his laboratory; that is, if Marsden reports the break-in at all. With the air-drop gone wrong, Marsden will certainly send someone to find the package and they may not have another small direction radio-finder with them to pick up the beacon-signal. But of course they won't find it, whatever means they use because we've got it and the beacon is not functioning. Marsden will be worried. He'll want the drugs in his hands before dawn because of the possibility of their being found by someone else in the coming daylight.'

'Good thinking, Robert,' I commented. 'When the second attempt to pick up the drugs fails, I'm sure they'll panic. Marsden doesn't know for sure that Hammond and Miranda are dead. He may be worried that they have been picked up by the police. Frankly, I don't feel much paternal warmth there. My guess is that he is more worried about himself than concerned about his missing daughter. I think he will try to conceal his own crimes with a big fat fire and blame it on the burglary.

'Marsden Hall is above suspicion, so it is the laboratory and the cavern behind it that will have to go. The lab he can burn easily. I suspect he has already set explosives so that the cavern can be blocked up. Then no one would even suspect that it existed. Romola is the key. We *must* know what he intends to do.'

'It all makes sense.' Robert clapped his hands

together. 'There's sure to be big trouble at Marsden's place. We do need Romola to tell us what she can see and hear there.'

Deborah looked at Romola. 'You can *hear* remotely as well as see?'

Romola smiled. 'Why not? Voices express thoughts, just as people and places convey impressions. I pick up both pictures and sound, clairvoyantly and clair-audiently.'

Once again, Romola stretched out on the leather sofa and I completed the mental circuit by touching her forehead.

As her breathing deepened Robert gave a gasp. 'What is it?' I asked him.

'Her astral! I've just seen her projected psyche leave her body. It was attached to her by the silver cord.'

'What's that?' asked Deborah.

'The psychic life-line that connects the astral-body to the physical body, like the life-line of an astronaut when he leaves the spaceship. Only this one is infinitely "elastic". However, if the astral cord *should* break, death would ensue.'

'How do you see it, Robert?'

'Clairvoyantly. Now it has left the room.'

Romola spoke. 'I'm sorry, I must be overtired. My astral-body was out of my conscious control for a moment. I think it nearly materialized.'

'That would have meant the appearance of a *Doppelgänger*,' I explained. 'That is an actual "double" of a person on our plane of existence.'

'It's all too much for me,' remarked Deborah with a shiver.

After a moment, Romola continued, 'I'm hovering above the estate, about fifty yards from it.'

'Go inside, darling . . .'

274

'I'm entering Marsden Hall. I'm passing through the wall of the salon. Marsden and Rosamund Charnley are there. They are arguing. He is furious. Ouch!'

'What happened?'

'Marsden just hit her across the cheek. Mrs Charnley now has her hand up to her face. She hurries over to the mirror to see what damage he's done She's got a livid mark on her cheek. She's crying. I pick up that Marsden now suspects that Hammond and Miranda were in cahoots. He doesn't know that they are dead. He feels that something is terribly wrong but he can't quite pinpoint it. He is a magician, not a psychic. The house is a very busy place. It looks as if he's moving out some things: filing cabinets, that sort of thing. Some laboratory equipment is being packed into an estate-wagon; it's Toddman's stuff.

'Marsden doesn't want him to leave. He's saying he'll burn the evidence in the laboratory. Both of you are right! He's going to destroy the evidence, but he doesn't want to lose Toddman, because of the elixir. Wait a minute. Toddman is not flying to Switzerland. He's going to Libya to Gaddafi! They've got some sort of reciprocal arrangement with the Libyans.'

Robert was startled. 'Why Libya? What the hell does Colonel Gaddafi have to do with it?'

'Gaddafi is another powerful magician,' I explained, 'deeply into rituals. He probably also seeks eternal youth. It figures that there should be a connection. Perhaps Libya is the source of the drugs. It's possible that the *other* side of the drug traffic is aimed deliberately at subverting the young of this and other countries of the free world. Who knows?'

Romola spoke again. 'The returning bikers told Marsden everything they know. Toddman has panicked. He's determined to clear out. I pick up that

Marsden knows nothing of his Nazi war-criminal background. He must have suspected it but has put it out of his mind. He is now completely dependent on the elixir, or thinks he is. And yes! I pick up that the serum injections have to be fairly frequent. The next one is due on Beltane's Eve. Oh, my God! I see now what he's driving at. The next baby to be murdered will supply the fresh cells for the elixir. May I come back, Daniel?' Her voice rose in pitch.

I felt dreadful about asking her to continue. 'Please, darling, stay there a moment longer. What will they do about the cavern?'

'Daniel, I'm going to frame a mental question. It may get through his panic. Yes, he's picked up the thought. He thinks it's from his own mind.'

'That's incredible,' whispered Deborah.

I silenced her with an urgent squeeze on the arm as Romola continued, 'I can see the cavern pictured in his mind. He is very reluctant to destroy it. It must have taken so much effort to set up.'

'Yes,' I said thoughtfully. 'He can hardly have brought in some swish designer to decorate the revolting place. He must have had those erotic murals and perverted tapestries made somewhere abroad and then assembled them himself with the help of his degenerate coven.'

Romola was beginning to shiver. 'Come out right away,' I whispered. 'You've had more than enough.'

I wiped the 'condition' from her with long passes of my hands, from her head to her feet. She woke and smiled at me with all her tension gone. Her arms reached up and slipped round my neck as I bent over her.

'I hate that place, Daniel. Please don't send me there again.'

'Not if I can help it, my dearest girl.' I kissed her. My mind was made up. I knew what we had to do.

'Robert, you will have to try to stop, or at least delay, Toddman at the airport and I will get back to the Winnebago, contact Terence Naylor and see to Lev. If all that incriminating evidence is destroyed we are back to square one. Can you stop Toddman escaping?' I asked point-blank.

Deborah's voice was tense. She turned to Robert. 'Darling, you can't stop that jet plane with a sling-shot. At least take a shotgun with you.'

'Honey, this is not America. Firing buckshot at people and planes is out of the question. I'll stick to my sling-of-David.'

I had to agree with him. 'He's got a point there, Deborah. You know damned well Robert can't be caught on that airport with a loaded shotgun. He could be deported as an undesirable alien.'

'I think it's dreadful we have to face Marsden's thugs with sling-stones,' Deborah protested.

'That's the way it is. . . Robert, get going, for God's sake! It's our only chance.'

As Robert slipped on his helmet and weatherproof suit, he said, 'I'm going to be all right. One stone through their windscreen or that aircraft's thin pressure-cabin wall will do the trick. I can even sling a shower of gravel into a jet engine. That'll smash the turbines for sure.'

His smiling confidence was irresistible, and Deborah calmed down. Robert picked her up off the ground and gave her a long, resounding kiss. A moment later he was racing away down the drive.

As he roared off, I heard Romola quietly say, 'David and Goliath.'

It sounded strangely prophetic.

'Keep the radio-link going,' I yelled after him and saw him nod.

I knew now what I had to do. I must confront Marsden and play for time, making him a proposition. If I could get through to Terence Naylor from the caravan, and then drive over to Marsden Hall, I would have a fair chance of coming out of it alive. Somehow, Marsden had to be stopped from burning that vital evidence and smashing the cavern to cover any evidence of his perverted rituals. Terence had told me that Hammond was a former mercenary, well versed in handling demolition charges, and a man of Marsden's efficiency would have made sure his chauffeur passed his knowledge on.

Romola tried to insist on coming with me.

'Darling, don't be difficult,' I said firmly. 'You're much more use here, keeping a remote-view of things. If you see that they are going wrong for me, ring the police. I'm going to get Terence moving. Then it's up to me to keep Marsden busy until Naylor can get a search warrant.'

When I got to the Winnebago, it was deserted. Inside, I found a note:

> Couldn't wait. I'm sure Toddman will try to get away by air. I'm taking Lev with me to the airport. The bleeding has stopped. He is conscious and feels much better. Thanks again for everything.
>
> Nat

Two minutes later I was speaking to Terence. I told him quickly what had happened and that I now had the drugs. I explained what I was trying to do.

'That's bloody hairy, Daniel. They're crazy enough to kill you.'

278

'If I can't slow them down, all the evidence will have gone in a big fire. Then we'll only have the drugs, with *no* connection to Marsden. Even when the local police finally locate Hammond's body with the corpse of Marsden's daughter, it still won't prove a thing. Only the hard evidence in that lab and the cavern behind it will mean anything.'

'I see your point. If you can hold him for an hour I can get a regional crime squad taskforce together and raid the place. It's worth a try. Good luck. You're going to need it.'

As Terence rang off, I grabbed my hunting bow and a quiver full of arrows, closed up the Winnebago and set course for Marsden Hall in the Ford Estate. My weapons lay close to hand, on the front seat.

As I drove up the hill towards Lympne I seemed to sense the presence of the long-dead abroad on the Marsh, seething among the rustling waterweeds and swooping low above the deserted flatlands, wrapping the water meadows in their winding sheets . . . grey shrouds of death.

By the time I had passed Westenhanger I had decided on the only course of action left open to me. I would tell Marsden the full story about Toddman. I'd show him that he had been duped. If I could stop him firing the laboratory long enough for Special Branch to arrive, I could smash the whole coven and lift their hex from the Marsh, as Edward would have wanted. My only resources were the sample packet of dope and the fact that Marsden didn't know the fate of Hammond or Miranda. Maybe I could bluff him that they were still alive and in Robert's hands, ready to spill the beans under hypnosis.

I reached the closed, wrought-iron gates of the security fence, swung the Ford off the road and raced alongside the wire mesh until I found a comparatively weak spot. I turned the car and drove off into the open field for about fifty yards, then skidded the Ford round and pressed my foot to the floor, racing flat out over the springy meadow grass towards the link fence.

I must have been doing over fifty when I braced myself against the wheel and hit the fence squarely between two of its supporting uprights. For an instant I thought I was going through the windscreen, or that I would smash my chest against the padded steering-wheel, but the Ford punched its way through the wire links and, with a jarring bounce, I was racing across the west lawn towards the house. A shriek of loose gravel announced my arrival and I was out of the car, running across the drive and stumbling up the steps with only a trace of my usual limp.

Before I could reach up and grab the massive bronze, satyr's-head knocker, the double doors creaked open and I stared into the barrels of an expensive shotgun.

'Come in,' said Marsden, with barely controlled fury. 'You've got some explaining to do, Fortune!'

I felt calm and relaxed and, for a moment, my mind raced back to the time when Jacques Dhery and I had been operating in Normandy just before the Amiens prison raid. I knew then that everything depended on timing, just as it did now. We had waited anxiously for the Mosquito fighter-bombers to make their attack on the prison walls while the icy mist crept over the snowbound fields.

I prayed inwardly, as I had done then, while I followed Marsden into that huge, overdecorated drawing-room.

Rosamund Charnley, looking pale and, for the first time, dishevelled, stood shivering with her back to the fake log fire in the gas-fed grate. She was wearing a scarlet velour robe and her left cheek was red and swollen.

Marsden wasted no time. 'Say whatever you've got to say, Fortune, then get the hell off my property. You're trespassing!'

His last words were so ridiculously inappropriate in the circumstances that I laughed out loud. Marsden's face reddened.

'What's so funny?' he yelled.

I deliberately sat down in an armchair and extended my hand towards him, holding out one of the polythene packets of cocaine for his inspection.

'The air-drop was made on time,' I said quietly, watching Marsden closely for his reaction.

He leant towards the open packet, sniffing the crystalline powder.

'It's cocaine. What does that prove?'

'Nothing by itself, but combined with the evidence that your chauffeur and your absconding daughter are presently giving under hypnosis to Dr Whiterivers, it proves a helluva lot!'

The shotgun came up, shaking, level with my chest. 'I could blow you away for this,' he shouted.

'Calm down, Marsden, or you'll have a stroke. I mean it,' I said, knowing that my life was in pawn.

'For God's sake, Arnold!' Rosamund Charnley's voice quavered as she laid a hand on his arm.

The burly peer shrugged her off impatiently and, with an effort, controlled his temper. 'All right, Fortune, why are you here?'

The deadly moment had passed. I had a breathing space.

'Marsden, your power game is finished! But *we*' – I deliberately emphasized the word – 'are willing to do

281

some wheeling and dealing. You're good at that. So are we.'

The Yorkshireman glowered at me. 'Such as?'

'The names of your associates and the various people you've been blackmailing.'

'That's a bloody ugly word!'

'It's an ugly business. Drugs and children's ruined lives deserve the highest penalties. If I had my way, you would hang by the balls until you were dead.'

I spoke each word deliberately. Marsden reddened again as Rosamund started screaming hysterically.

He swung round on her. 'Shut up, you stupid bitch, or I'll smash your mouth!' For an instant I thought he was going to hit her with the gun butt.

She collapsed sobbing onto the sofa behind her, the mascara running down her cheeks adding to the mess of her once perfectly made-up face.

The big peer again threatened me, the shotgun quivering in his stubby hands. He was studying me closely. 'You wouldn't have come to make a deal unless there was something wrong with your case, Fortune. I know you work with the police and that you used to be with Intelligence. Which lot do you grass for? You college dons are all the same. You're full of theory but no use in practical terms. All right! So you've got some cocaine, and my bastard chauffeur and my stupid bitch of a daughter have blown some mad scheme that *they* were involved with. Not me, them!'

He jabbed at my chest with the gun to emphasize his words. 'You've got nothing on me, or her,' Marsden indicated Rosamund on the sofa. 'It's your word against mine, Fortune. The accusations of an obscure college professor whose academic speciality is as disreputable as computerized astrology, against *my* word as a multi-millionaire peer of the realm. I have

282

very powerful friends in very high places. You've got no idea, in that narrow brain of yours, Fortune, just how powerful those friends of mine are. It's money that talks the loudest in the end.

'There are people from all political parties and in the highest positions in business who will go bail for me if I tell them to. They know that if they don't co-operate I'll bring them all down.'

Suddenly the tension lessened as a new thought struck him. 'Wait a minute! Suppose you are not here on behalf of the authorities? After all, where are they? Why have you come alone? And where are the others of your team?'

He paused. He thought he had the answer. 'What's your game, Fortune?'

Realization flooded in on me. I seized the God-sent opportunity and played my slender hand for all it was worth. The evil-minded always judge others by their own mores and Marsden thought I had come to blackmail him. A fortune for Fortune! The idiotic phrase rang in my brain as Marsden continued on the wrong track.

'You openly refused my generous offers that first time we met at dinner. I see why now. The *others* were there. I underestimated you, you cunning bastard!'

He stopped for an instant, lost for words. Then he smiled, that wolfish grimace that passed with him for a friendly overture. He was sure he'd found a way out.

'All right, Fortune. How much? What will it cost me?'

Inwardly breathing a sigh of relief and heartfelt thanks for my brief reprieve, I strung along with the megalomaniac. Rosamund, sensing the way that things were going, sat up and smiled. She even took out her make-up and tried to repair some of the damage to her tarnished paintwork.

Marsden, to show willing, put the shotgun down in front of him on the coffee table, but still within easy reach. His brain was clearly racing as he made his move. 'Well now, *Professor* Fortune,' he said unctuously, giving me back my title. 'What's it to be? A million? Two million? Pounds or in gold? A numbered Swiss bank account?'

I smiled grimly. 'We'll discuss details later. First I have some valuable information to give you that will upset you even more.'

On the marble mantelpiece an elaborate ormolu clock chimed four times – *four o'clock*! I was nearly home and dry. Dawn was at hand if only I could keep him talking.

'Your revered Dr Toddman is a phoney. Not as a physician. He's a medical and surgical wizard all right but as a man.' I paused for the maximum effect. 'His real name is Kuttner – Werner Kuttner –' Again I deliberately hesitated. 'He is a Nazi war criminal on a worldwide wanted list.'

Marsden looked confused.

I followed up my temporary advantage. 'Your break-in was engineered by Mossad, Israeli Intelligence. Marsden, you *might* get away somehow, with the help of your powerful friends, from a British criminal charge, but as an accomplice of a known Nazi war criminal you will have to appear at an international court of justice. That would finish you, once and for all.'

Marsden was shaken by this information but the manic optimism of his arrogance surfaced and took over. He shouted at me derisively. 'On the word of some Jew boy?' The Fascist in Marsden was out in the open. 'Bloody Mossad!'

284

He swung round towards Rosamund. 'Did you hear that, pet? Toddman's a war criminal.'

'All right, smart arse,' he snarled to me. 'How much? Three million quid and that's final. Take it or leave it.' He grabbed the shotgun.

I made a big mistake. Overcome with disgust at this appalling man and being low on adrenalin at that hour of the morning, I lost my temper. By doing so, I nearly lost my life.

'You can *shove* your three million,' I shouted, all restraint gone. 'You and your degenerate Companions of Chaos are finished. When my colleagues come back with that bastard Kuttner, your grubby little empire will disintegrate into the stinking muck from which it came. Goddamn you and your whole demonic crew!'

Marsden's eyes filled with the baleful light that denoted the dark forces within him. I thought my last moments had come. A fleeting regret passed through my mind at the thought of all the lost happiness with Romola. As Marsden raised the shotgun level with my abdomen I braced myself for the shattering impact of both barrel-loads of buckshot. My senses went into overdrive. I prayed. God, how I prayed!

At that moment, the muffled thunder of Marsden's private jet swelled into the night. As in the distance it opened up its twin jet engines and streaked down the Lydd airport runway on the Marsh below, its powerful, booming roar echoed in the pre-dawn stillness.

Marsden's voice was hoarse. 'So much for your Mossad Yids and Deborah's big, buck Navajo boyfriend. There goes Toddman and whatever evidence you hoped to get on our Great Work. Listen, Fortune, to the collapse of your pitiful plans as my jet flies to Libya. My good friend Gaddafi will welcome the doctor with open arms.' The shotgun shook in his hands. 'You stupid bastard! Did you really believe your feeble efforts would win-out over *me*?'

Suddenly a terrific flash filled the sky. Its distant blaze was reflected in the great mirror above the fireplace and the force of the explosion rattled the windowpanes. For an instant, Marsden's attention was diverted, involuntarily riveted on what he saw through the window. A huge ball of fire was dropping in a long curve towards the sea. Marsden's private jet had disintegrated in mid-air.

In the apocalyptic sunburst of blazing orange light, Marsden's elixir of life had gone for ever. With it went his illusions of immortality. He gave a hoarse yell that was echoed by a scream from Rosamund Charnley. The shotgun wavered. I took my last chance. I dived sideways to the floor, sweeping the nearest bronze lamp across the table's marble surface towards my enemy. I hit the table hard as I fell and I felt an agonizing stab of pain in my good leg.

Marsden caught my lunging dive out of the corner of his eye. He tried to swing the shotgun back. The heavy, rococo lamp swept the gun aside, thumping into his knees, bringing his heavy body down with a crash.

As he fell, yelling curses, he squeezed the triggers and both barrels fired. The gun was twisting in his hands. With a deafening blast, one barrel splintered the big mirror into a thousand flying shards of glass. The second cartridge slammed a cone of lead shot right across Rosamund Charnley's terrified face.

The full force of the disintegrating glass and the flying shot ripped into the upper part of her beautiful body, turning her face and her lovely breasts into a gory mass of shredded tissue. Her agonized shriek faded into a dreadful bubbling cry. I saw all this in one glance as I struggled to my feet, grabbing the heavy

286

leather chair to lever myself upright.

Marsden was lying across the marble-topped coffee table, his shotgun out of reach on the carpet. He was winded and cursing incoherently.

I took no chances. I hurled the second heavy lamp at my groggy prostrate opponent and staggered as fast as I could towards the door. I saw the lamp hit Marsden's head as he tried to sit up. He collapsed with a grunt, semi-conscious.

I reached the door and painfully limped through it into the corridor, making for the front entrance. Both my legs were hurting like hell.

By a miracle the double doors were unlatched. Marsden had neglected to lock and bolt them after I had arrived. That seemed like hours before, but actually only fifteen minutes had passed.

I was out of that accursed house in a moment, stumbling painfully down the broad steps to land in a heap on the gravelled drive. Only then did I realize that I had broken my ankle against the table in that wild dive across the room. Desperately I tried to hop to the car, which was parked on the far side of the drive. Without its usual support from my other, now broken limb, my war-wounded leg also collapsed under me. Down I went, skinning my hands on the sharp gravel.

I heard a muffled explosion. A rumbling sound came from deep inside the earth behind the laboratory.

I groaned with pain and frustration. Marsden must have set off the explosives, demolishing the cavern. There goes the evidence, I thought, as a second explosion blew out the windows of Toddman's laboratory, which immediately burst into flames, lighting up the scene with a bright orange-red glare. All that Marsden needed to do now was to shoot me and push my dead body into the fire. He could tell the

police some cock and bull story about a burglary gone
wrong. Lacking all evidence incriminating either Toddman or himself, and with the scene of their appalling
crimes now hidden under tons of chalk in the collapsed
cavern, the police would have to accept the peer's
explanation. The bastard would go free.

Somehow, I reached the car. At that moment
Marsden appeared in the doorway, a powerful, deer-
stalking rifle in his hands. In the glow of the front
entrance lighting he spotted me half-crawling across
the gravel only inches from safety. My hands grasped
the car door and I glanced back to see the cruel devil
starting to take aim at me. He could hardly miss at
thirty yards. Yet something inside me refused to quit;
and I hung there clutching the car's half-open window.
I could see my weapons just out of reach on the front
seat. Marsden yelled hoarsely and I turned to face my
death, consigning his foetid soul to hell.

But the unfit body of the elderly peer had been taxed
by all his unaccustomed efforts and my lucky hit with
the second bronze lamp had half-stunned him. He was
unsteady and out of breath as he fired his first shot,
and the heavy bullet smashed through the car window
just beside my head.

Praying hard I dragged the door open and hauled
myself inside. I heard a second cartridge click into the
breech. . .

A drumming roar announced another dramatic turn
of events. A powerful headlight beam raced up the
drive towards us. It came from a motorbike, ridden
fast. This diverted Marsden just as he fired his second
shot. The bullet screamed off the windshield, shattering
it into fragments of Plexiglass. Marsden cursed as he
accidentally jammed the rifle bolt. While he wrestled
with it, I made a final effort and dragged myself into

288

the Ford.

A woman screamed. With a shriek of tyres the bike skidded to a halt. A shotgun blasted and Marsden reeled back, trying to swing his rifle towards the bike. Neither of us could see who the rider was behind the glaring headlight. Marsden fired from the hip. The bullet ricocheted off the gravel and screamed away into the darkness. I had to make a diversion. Yelling at the top of my voice, I grabbed my steel bow and a hunting shaft from the quiver. The broken bones in my ankle grated together agonizingly, but somehow I managed to knock the arrow onto the bowstring and swing the bow sideways, drawing and loosing the shaft in one snatched movement. The arrow sped towards Marsden, who was reloading. A second blast of gunshots rang out and the heavy body of the peer jerked under a terrific impact.

For a moment I thought I had transfixed him with the heavy hunting shaft.

Marsden started to crumple, dropping his gun. A final blast of buckshot smashed into him. As he fell, a fountain of blood gushed from his mangled chest. Behind him my arrow had stuck, quivering, in the door.

Into the circle of light rode Deborah on my trail-bike, with Romola clinging to her on the pillion. Romola held the shotgun, but I knew that it was my goddaughter who must have fired those avenging shots. They jumped off the bike, letting it fall, and ran over to me. Both the girls were crying hysterically. Somehow they helped me struggle upright. Supported by them, I staggered across to Marsden's corpse.

One glance at his exploded chest told me that death had been instantaneous. *Too merciful*! I thought.

'I killed him! Oh God, I killed him,' moaned

Deborah, horrified.

'You had to,' soothed Romola. 'He would have killed Daniel, and us as well. You had no choice. None at all.'

'He deserved to die, Deborah,' I added, hugging her tight. 'It's all right, my dear. You saved our lives!'

'You didn't kill him. I did,' croaked a dreadful, bubbling voice, hoarse with choking blood. Rosamund Charnley was crouched, like a dying animal, in the doorway. 'Look what the bastard did to me,' she mumbled, dropping the empty shotgun which had blasted out Marsden's life. The horror-mask of that once-beautiful face was a mass of pulped tissue.

'Fortune, help me!' She gave a last gurgling plea and slid forward unconscious into a bloodstained heap.

As I bent over her to do what little I could, I knew that Rosamund Charnley might recover, but she would never again bewitch men with her devil's beauty.

In a single night, their satanic master had cashed in three of his disciples' Faustian pacts.

ARNOLD MARSDEN

WERNER KUTTNER

Requiescant in Hades

CHAPTER 14

The Name of the Game

Half an hour later Robert and the police arrived. There had been sufficient time between the start of the fire and the arrival of the Hythe Fire Brigade for the laboratory to have been burnt out in the fierce chemically-fed flames. Part of the Hall was destroyed as well, set alight when the laboratory had exploded. Romola and Deborah had returned protesting to the Manor in the Ford, leaving the bike. That way the gunshot damage to the windows of the hire-car and the deep lacerations caused by my charge at the security fence were hidden from too many embarrassing eyes until I could cook up a good enough story to tell the owner when I paid for the damage. I also made the girls take Edward's shotgun with them; there was no point in their getting involved in Marsden's death since Deborah had not fired the fatal shots. Buckshot had killed him, not birdshot, when Rosamund reloaded and shot her lover.

I fixed up my ankle, which was broken across the tibia and fibula, by splinting it from the emergency pack in my medical kit. I didn't take a much-needed painkiller because I wanted my brain to be clear. When Terence arrived with his 'posse', I knew I would have to do some quick thinking.

I compromised by giving myself a local anaesthetic, which made moving about a bit easier. I had also done what little was medically possible for the tragic Rosamund Charnley: staunching the bleeding, dressing and butterfly-taping the worst of the gaping wounds in her face and upper body, covering the whole with gauze and bandages and keeping her agony at bay with morphine. That was the extent of my powers.

My own injured state precluded me from lifting her onto a sofa or bed. The poor creature had to make do with lying under a covering of overcoats to help neutralize the shock. Mercifully, she remained unconscious. Her real agony would start when she woke up to that travesty of a face.

The dead peer's corseted body lay in an ugly heap at the foot of the marble steps. His trunk was impossibly jack-knifed in a welter of blood, shredded lungs and splintered bone. I had covered the remains with a raincoat while I tried to work out a way to explain this hecatomb of blood and death.

By the time the police arrived, I had made my decision and was ready to face this final ordeal. My story was simple and straightforward. I had explained to Special Branch how I intended to try to stop Marsden destroying the evidence of his crimes and his accomplice's ghastly experiments. I should tell them that when my delaying tactics eventually failed, I had been forced to escape, breaking my ankle in the process. So far so good!

As for the Marsden shooting, I told the police that there had been a terrible accident. I said that Mrs Charnley had tripped in the doorway while carrying the loaded shotgun and had dropped it. As it hit the steps, one barrel had gone off, severely wounding her in the face. The second barrel had fired as the gun rolled down the steps, fatally wounding Lord Marsden when the blast hit him in the back and blew out his chest. As the blaze had subsequently set alight part of Marsden Hall, the shot-shattered mirror in the salon should no longer present a problem.

There was no rebuttal of my story and I promised to make my official statement as soon as my ankle had been X-rayed and put into a proper cast.

Robert came with me to Ashford hospital in one of the two ambulances which had arrived with the police and, on the way, as we were alone in the back, filled me in with the details of what had happened to Toddman and to Marsden's private jet.

'As soon as I left you and the girls, I made for Lydd airport. Then I realized what a klutz I had been! The bike sputtered and died. I was clean out of gas and still over two miles from the airfield.

'I ran – probably the best two-mile run of my life. I kept up a good pace towards New Romney and I cut across fields for the last mile.

'At the approach to the airport, I heard the sound of the twin jets starting. My final dash was along the narrow approach road and through the security checkpoint, which was unmanned. Marsden's jet was moving out from the private sector of the airfield and was taxiing towards the far end of the north-south runway. It reached the turn-off from the taxi track just as I rounded the end of the hangar.

'As I ran, I unwound my leather sling and took the first heavy stone from my pocket. I must have been seventy yards from the aircraft when the jet engines started to rev up to full power. I knew it was then or never. I ran flat out.

'At fifty yards I stopped running and slung the first rock. In the moonlight I saw the flash of the stone and heard the thump as it holed the Duralumin fuselage. The jet started to move onto the runway and, immediately, swung round to line up with the white line painted down the centre. I ran behind it. At twenty yards I stopped again and slung a second stone, which crashed through one of the cabin windows shattering it completely.

'That seemed to stimulate the pilot into taking off without first standing on his brakes and running up his jets. He just slammed his throttles open, slowly gathering speed down the runway. I got off one more stone before the plane was out of range and I think I hit him again, but the roar of the jets drowned out everything else. I was cursing my luck in not being able to stop him when I realized that his pressure-cabin system was useless because of the smashed window. The pilot would have to keep low and land in France for repairs, which might mean that you, Daniel, could get him through Interpol. But here comes the weird part! Before the pilot got Marsden's jet airborne, a car moved out from the staff parking area and raced through the open gate in the security fence. It ran on a parallel course to the runway, going balls-out!

'The jet reached the "overshoot" at the end of the tarmac and the pilot lifted her off at full power, retracting his wheels and flaps as he did so. The plane climbed quickly, heading out over the sea.

'The car skidded to a halt and the sunshine roof slid open. Someone stood up in the opening, holding what looked like a short stovepipe angled back over his shoulder. As the Marsden jet turned parallel with the shore, the man followed its movements, swinging the stove-pipe thing through a short arc. He seemed to be looking along a gunsight as he tracked the plane.

'Then from the back of the pipe a gush of flame roared out over the roof of the car. A rocket-propelled missile soared up into the sky towards the banking plane. It was uncanny. The missile followed every bloody move that the pilot made.'

'A heat-seeking infra-red missile,' I commented.

'Ten seconds later, the rocket hit the rear-mounted jets. There was an almighty bang and the whole sky lit

296

up. The aircraft just vanished in a huge fireball.'

'I saw it,' I murmured. 'It distracted Marsden's attention and saved my life.'

'Jesus, Daniel, it was as though an avenging angel had wiped out that cruel bastard. I felt sorry for the pilot!'

'Perhaps it was divine intervention.'

'With the help of Mossad. It was their car. They came back down the field towards me as the blazing wreckage cartwheeled into the sea. It was Lev Cowan and an assistant. Lev, incredibly, had been driving while his friend fired the missile. He's amazing. That Israeli is as tough as rawhide. They gave me a lift back to my bike before the hullaballoo started at the airport. No one saw it happen and no one saw us leave. There was nobody in air traffic control at that hour so we got away unnoticed. Lev's friend stopped the car and helped me to siphon petrol into my bike. We bade each other an emotional farewell. Lev Cowan sends his love!

'I went straight back to the Manor and found the girls gone. A note said that they'd taken your bike because the Range-Rover had a flat tyre and there was no time to change it. Romola had picked up clairvoyantly that you were in real trouble.'

'That explains their dramatic entrance,' I remarked.

'Deborah and Romola really are something else! Daniel, you must have had quite a night.'

Indeed I had!

At Ashford hospital the registrar set my ankle in a new-fangled German plastic cast. It didn't hurt too much. Robert returned to the Manor and, later that morning, Terence Naylor went over to see that they were all right. Robert told Terence what had happened at the airport, without implicating the Israeli or his assistant. I suspected that somehow Lev had already made his unofficial report to Special Branch.

'We'll leave the plane crash to the Air Accident Branch,' Terence said with a straight face. 'They'll explain it, probably by pilot error! By the way, Marsden's pilot was on our list as a possible dope smuggler. Don't feel too upset about him.'

My Special Branch friend then drove over with Romola to see that I was receiving every care and attention. Terence assured me that there would be a discreet handling of the whole affair.

'It seems rough that ordinary – or rather,' he grinned, 'extra-ordinary citizens like you and your friends have to assist us to do our dirty work, but as you know, Daniel, we have no choice in these matters. The concept of citizen's arrest has always been there to help out the overstrained, undermanned police and security forces of the Crown. We suspect that Marsden and his corrupt crowd have also been trafficking in high technology with the KGB and in arms and explosives for the IRA provos as part of deals with the Libyans in return for drugs, gold and God knows what else. What has happened has cleared up a lot of this stinking mess.'

After Terence left, my other friends turned up in Deborah's Range-Rover, and we drove back along Ham Street where it runs the length of the escarpment. At Lympne we stopped and looked out over the Marsh.

The morning mist still hung there, at midday, like a veil, obscuring Dungeness and hiding the power-station from view. The network of water meadows and yellow, rectangular fields where the rape crop bloomed looked like a giant patchwork quilt. The lines of the 'seams' followed the pattern of dykes and sluices until they disappeared into the curtain of sea fog covering the great seawall.

Below us, the marsh birds rose from their nests among the reeds and circled high above the canal. Everywhere, the Levels were dotted with tiny woollen specks of grazing sheep and their attendant lambs. The sense of peace was so strong, I could almost smell it!

It was the scene which I had known and loved since boyhood. Blessedly, its seductive tranquillity and feeling of timelessness had returned. Suddenly I sensed Edward very close.

He seemed to say: 'This is the true realm of the Lords of the Levels. Our spirits are here, watching over the Marsh.'

Requiescat in Pace

EDWARD HENRY JAMES
LAST BARONET TOLSFORD

AFTERWORD

In one way, Marsden had been right. The whole stinking mess *was* hushed up. The truth about the life peer and his despicable career was consigned to the destruct files. A deafening silence fell. However, there were repercussions which resulted from our efforts.

Several people in very important positions retired early, and ironically were given either knighthoods or life peerages. A large merchant bank in the City went bankrupt and the chairman committed suicide. The Marsden Group was taken over.

The peer's shattered body was buried in the family vault in Yorkshire and six weeks later Rosamund Charnley drove her Rolls-Royce off Beachy Head.

On the Stock Market the *Financial Times* Share Index dropped almost a hundred points, and the pound sterling lost a few more cents against the dollar. But nobody, except the people directly involved, and a select few in government and big business circles, knew the truth. Nobody, apart from ourselves and our friends, seemed to care.

I learned something important.

> The name of the game is:
> Don't make waves!

However, I intend to continue to do so. Next time, I will have my wife with me. I married Romola, with Robert as my best man. Deborah was Romola's bridesmaid and caught the bridal bouquet. I hope that means something.

When the summer term commenced at Wessex University, one of my younger students asked me, 'All this paranormal stuff, Professor, is it really of any use to the world?'

That was one reason for writing this book.

Professor J.D. Fortune, BM, PhD
Wessex University, 1985